AN EVENING ALONE

"We would know." He cleared his throat. "And that's a thing you can't unknow."

When his eyes met hers, the flush on her face grew even stronger. When her gentle fingers brushed against his cheek, he ceased to breathe. Then she said with a tart smile, "I only mean to sleep. Just keep each other warm."

He had never been a man of many words, but now he could barely eke out a breathless syllable. Her touch burned his skin, and muscles all over his body contracted. Had he caught a fever from the rains? She moved in close to him, and he was struck by the sense of rightness and pleasure. It should feel awkward, shouldn't it? Unnatural. This woman, of all women. It should feel wrong to slide his hands around her waist. Her finely muscled arms should feel like an affront. Touching his lips to hers should feel like burning in the fiery pit of hell.

And yet . . .

That inexplicable, irrational sensation overtook him, just like the night at the coaching inn. Her closeness unraveled his brain. Something in him reveled in her softness. Her mouth, her skin, her full hips. A thrill shot through him when she wrapped her arms around his shoulders and pulled him closer. He traced the line of buttons down her blouse with his finger and grew hot when she shivered against him. His good sense had fled, and he could not make himself seek it.

One thought invaded his mind: *More.*

Books by Amara Royce

NEVER TOO LATE

ALWAYS A STRANGER

ONCE BELOVED

Published by Kensington Publishing Corporation

Once Beloved

AMARA ROYCE

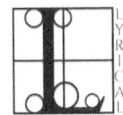

LYRICAL PRESS
Kensington Publishing Corp.
www.kensingtonbooks.com

LYRICAL PRESS BOOKS are published by

Kensington Publishing Corp.
119 West 40th Street
New York, NY 10018

All Kensington titles, imprints, and distributed lines are available at special quantity discounts for bulk purchases for sales promotion, premiums, fund-raising, educational, or institutional use.

Special book excerpts or customized printings can also be created to fit specific needs. For details, write or phone the office of the Kensington Sales Manager: Kensington Publishing Corp., 119 West 40th Street, New York, NY 10018. Attn. Sales Department. Phone: 1-800-221-2647.

First Electronic Edition: November 2015
eISBN-13: 978-1-60183-321-1
eISBN-10: 1-60183-321-0

First Print Edition: November 2015
ISBN-13: 978-1-60183-322-8
ISBN-10: 1-60183-322-9

Printed in the United States of America

To all who take second (or third or fourth, etc.)
chances, in the hope that you ultimately find what
makes your life complete.

ACKNOWLEDGMENTS

Many thanks go to my understanding and supportive agent, Jessica Alvarez of BookEnds, LLC, and to my kind and wonderful editor, John Scognamiglio, and everyone at Kensington Publishing/Lyrical Press.

Thanks also go to the many book-loving friends I've made on- and offline, including fellow authors, thoughtful reviewers, and avid readers. Each connection pushes me to be a better writer, as well as a better reader.

In particular, I am grateful to Liz McCausland, who gave me valuable feedback on my drafts, providing keen insight into my characters and their growth. Thank you, Liz, for helping light my path when I stumbled and struggled.

And thanks to the Twitter friends who shared their sheep stories with me, especially Emily Jane Hubbard and Miss Bates.

To Cora and Mary and Paul and Stan and Chris A and all my family and friends who have been nothing but supportive of my writing endeavors: You make me feel I can accomplish anything.

Finally and most importantly, to my husband and my son, I can't believe you keep putting up with me and my many foibles. You inspire me, and I love and thank you with all my heart.

Chapter 1

Helena paced through the small sitting room while her boys raced through the halls. Mrs. Clarke and Mrs. Duchamp were due upon the hour, and then they would all be on their way. Her stomach clenched at the thought of exiting through that safe, solid door. A brief and familiar trip to the market was one thing; this outing to the Great Exhibition was quite another. Still, she couldn't renege now; Mark and Tommy would be so disappointed. She closed her eyes and pictured a stone fortress. She built its walls in her mind, one large stone at a time, girding her for the upcoming assault on her senses. A crash from the vicinity of the back parlor disrupted her thoughts.

"Boys!" she said to herself as she made her way toward them. "What was that?" She asked it without expecting an answer. They were trying to entertain and divert each other as they waited. Could she blame them? "Do not tire yourselves before we get there!"

Mark appeared in the hallway, his brown eyes tinged with guilt. "I'm sorry, Mum. We did no harm. Tommy tripped and knocked over a chair. He's fine." Tommy walked warily into the hallway, his hair mussed and his knees scuffed. It was a familiar condition for him. "I'll see that he behaves himself," Mark added.

"I know you are both trying your best," she replied gently, as she gave each boy a quick hug, startled anew that Mark's height was now level with her own. If he was this tall at fourteen, he'd tower over her as an adult. "Just do not tire yourselves before we get there."

His expression brightening, Mark led his younger brother to look out the front windows. Their heads glowed like halos. Such good boys they were, so deserving of a day of fun. Realizing she didn't tell them this as often as she should, she went over and did just that. She didn't miss the glint of pride in Mark's eyes at that, although he still seemed to brace himself, as if he knew that their trip could be canceled any moment now. She laid her hand on little Tommy's bright head, feeling the warmth from his exertions, and noticed one of his shoes had come undone. Both children were growing so quickly they would need new shoes before the summer ended. Too quickly. She could hardly believe Bartholomew was already grown and out at sea. It would be a year soon. How had that happened? Her handsome boys growing too quickly into men, men she hoped her husband would have been proud of.

Tommy tried to fix his shoe, but his young fingers struggled. As she bent to help him, she said firmly, "We shall have a lovely day, shall we not?"

Tommy bobbed his head vigorously, and Mark's narrow shoulders relaxed a bit.

"What are you two looking forward to seeing today?"

"Mum, it shall be grand!" Tommy said. "Mark read me all the news about it. It's a huge palace! And it's filled with all sorts of amazements. Do you think I'll get to see a train?"

"Not a complete train, no, dear. But perhaps you can see parts of one." She smiled at his unrestrained enthusiasm, the kind only a five-year-old could muster, an exuberance she hadn't felt herself in years, not since Isaiah's passing. He would have enjoyed this as much as their sons. She tucked those thoughts away, knowing all too well how they'd derail her efforts to make this a good day.

Tommy dug into his pocket. "Here's all my savings so we can get in." He held out his hand, proudly displaying his precious coins.

Her heart swelled at the sight. "Oh, my dear boy, how sweet of you! That is yours to keep. I have more than enough for us."

He grinned as he put his money away and then hugged her tight.

"They're here!" Mark exclaimed, as he jumped up to open the front door. "Mrs. Clarke! It's a pleasure to see you! How fares your family? I hope the Clarke children are well." He gave Marissa an amusingly formal bow before turning to a bewildered Honoria. "Mrs. Duchamp! How pleased I am to see you as well! I hope your bookshop is thriving." Helena was equal parts amused, startled, and dismayed by her son's precociously sociable greeting. He was always polite, but this was a bit more formal than usual. Her friends' faces indicated they were equally surprised. He was trying far too hard to display his best behavior.

In characteristic take-charge fashion, Marissa swept into the house, giving each boy a dramatic buss on the cheek before announcing, "I've no doubt you boys are nearly jumping out of your skin to be on our way. Why don't you go outside with Mrs. Duchamp and hail us a cab while your mother and I make sure all is in readiness?"

Tommy bounded toward the door until Honoria held out her hand toward him. He dutifully took it and walked out calmly with just a residual spring in his step. Mark paused by the hall mirror and adjusted his hat before following them.

Before Helena could so much as open her mouth to thank Marissa for helping to chaperone the boys, her friend grasped her shoulders firmly and looked her full in the face. "You're fretting. Cease that nonsense immediately. You planned carefully. Today should have light attendance. We shall arrive at the opening hour. Honoria and I are here for whatever you need. All will be well. The best, the most innovative, the most exemplary of British industry is on display, along with all manner of international finery. Your sons shall be enraptured. You may even find that you enjoy yourself!" Marissa winked at her and gave a securing tug on her bonnet ribbons, as if she were a girl again.

Helena recalled the seemingly endless catalog of things the boys wished to see there and nodded. She hugged her dear friend tight and echoed, "All will be well." She pasted a smile on her face, despite the weight of dread in her chest. After closing up the house, she focused on the boys' happy faces as they climbed into the hired coach and the heaviness in her lifted. They would enjoy this tour of the Great Exhibition, no matter what she had to do to get through it.

It wasn't until the cab approached the entrance to the famed Crystal Palace that Helena felt the familiar but unwelcome tingling along her scalp and neck. The sight of the crowds waiting to enter set her heart beating faster. Flanking her, the boys buzzed with excitement. Mrs. Duchamp listened attentively to little Tommy's chatter; her quiet, studious nature balanced so well with his relentless inquiries, those endless "whys" and "hows" to which the very young are so prone. Meanwhile Mrs. Clarke maintained a lively discussion about the unusual architecture with Mark, who had been reading every article he could find about the building and its designer, Mr. Joseph Paxton. With everyone else in the cab preoccupied, she looked away from the crowds and out on the expanse of Hyde Park. Even with the crowded skyline beyond, the grassy areas were enough to calm her nerves a bit. Without Honoria and Marissa, though, she would not have been able to cross the opulent threshold of this massive glass and iron cage.

Mark must have noticed something on her face because he sat straighter, touched her arm, and said, "Mama, are you all right?" So sensitive to the tenor of others, that child. So eager to please and to smooth over rough spots for everyone else. Since his older brother left, he'd become even more sensitive, taken on even more responsibility. If she didn't make too many mistakes, he would be as fine a man as his father was.

Before she could answer, dear Mrs. Clarke said, "Of course, she's all right, dear. Your mother is just enjoying the lovely day. Isn't that right, Helena?"

She nodded and tried to smile. She could do this. Her boys asked for so little and had already lost so much. Her husband would have made this such an adventure for them, as enthusiastic about all the wonders and trinkets as they were. She could endure a morning stroll—just a simple morning stroll—for their sakes. It might even be enjoyable. Everyone else seemed to think so. As soon as the carriage came to a halt, both boys popped up from their seats with mad grins. She could endure a few hours here for them.

By the time they entered, the waiting visitors had spread out to various exhibits, giving her some blessed room to breathe. The sky helped too. What a marvelous sight . . . being able to see the world from inside this towering greenhouse. As long as she focused on the metal and glass above and around them, she felt secure. Her heart lifted as Tommy grabbed her hand and pulled her toward a large and elaborate elephant statue. All went swimmingly until they entered the technology wing.

She'd underestimated the popularity of the exhibits that would be of greatest interest to her boys: the engines. They were fascinated by the massive fire-engine pump and got as close as they could to watch the new electro-magnetic engine running. As the crowd grew, she lost sight of her children, and her throat seized. She tried to call out to them, but she couldn't even hear her own voice amid the din of the ever-increasing crowd. On some level, she recognized that tightening of her chest, the rising panic jangling in her ears, as the crush of bodies swelled around her, everyone jockeying for the best view. *Don't be silly*, she thought. *You're far too old to be done in by such irra-*

tionalities. It's just people. She told herself this every time, tried to quell her physical reactions by sheer force of will. It wasn't helping this time. It never helped. She struggled for breath. How had all the inhabitants of London conspired to flood the alcove for this demonstration?

The boys are fine. Marissa and Honoria will watch over them. Simply make your way to another room, she reasoned with herself. Already she could see Honoria inching closer to where she'd last seen the boys. Her skin prickled as perspiration broke out along her back and throat. *Get out. Go now.*

Marissa was close to her; she grabbed for her friend's hand and barely caught it. When her friend turned to face her, she couldn't find enough air to speak. Her trusty companion immediately went into action, trying to shoulder through the swelling crowd. The press and overbearing smell of the throng choked her as she clung to Marissa's hand with a sharp sense of desperation. She was caught in a sea of strangers, all jostling and crashing against her.

Now Mark stood close by Tommy on the far side of the display as Mrs. Duchamp hovered behind them. The boys were too focused on the machinery to notice her distress, thank goodness. The sight of them eased her distress a fraction.

Then a surge of humanity shoved her against a pillar, and she almost lost her grip on Marissa's hand. An invisible vise constricted her throat, and her field of vision shrank. *God in heaven, please get me out of here.* Another ripple in the crowd made her stumble and lose contact with Marissa. Panic. Tiny bright lights flashed before her eyes, and a strange but familiar tang flooded her mouth. She tried to speak, tried to cry out for help, but nothing would come out. Dizzy, she couldn't feel her arms or her legs. She tried to push through a couple to her right, but they simply frowned at her and said something she couldn't hear over the clamor in her head. Her chest seized. Colored lights flooded her view just before the world went black. Her last thought was *Heavenly Father, the boys shouldn't have to see me like this.*

Chapter 2

"Make way," Daniel bellowed as he waded across the alcove. He had the advantage of bulk. In most situations, people moved out of the way when he approached. Why should London not follow the same pattern? "There's a lass injured. Make way."

In retrospect, he had no idea why that matronly woman had caught his attention. She could have been anyone, just another nameless, nondescript woman. And yet, she wasn't. She had an air of fragility, a vulnerability that he could sense from yards away. He'd noticed her perhaps three-quarters of an hour before, standing with her companions, glancing periodically at the children who were undoubtedly her offspring. This mother and her boys all had the same dark hair, the same thin faces, the same high cheekbones and sharp noses. At first, she'd seemed somehow familiar, but he could not place her. What was most peculiar about her was that, unlike everyone else, she paid no attention to the actual exhibits. People came to the Great Exhibition either to see the myriad wonders or to see—and be seen—by the populace. At least that was what he'd observed thus far during his trip. This woman appeared to have no interest any of that. In fact, she appeared to be suffering, enfolding like a moonflower at dawn, intimidated by the vibrantly intrusive sun. If that were the case, why come at all? As a massive group invaded the alcove, her agitation increased conspicuously as she was separated from the rest of her party. When she clawed at her throat with a panicked expression, an alarm sounded in his head, urging him to close the distance between them. Could no one else see her distress? When the woman's head lolled back like a rag doll and she suddenly dropped from view, Daniel knew he had to move quickly.

A sharp feminine voice cried out, "Back away, all of you! You'll crush her!" When he was within a few feet of where he'd last seen the woman, the crowd parted enough for him to see one of her companions pushing people away from her lifeless body, slumped on the ground with dusty shoe marks on her skirt. He gathered the woman into his arms, careful to cushion her head. Her dead weight disturbed him, but her breath blew warm and regular against his jaw.

"Please, I say again, make way." He used the voice he reserved for calling to farmhands across the Lanfield grazing hills. "This woman needs medical assistance." When he used that voice, he expected to be obeyed. It worked about as well here as it did with the farmhands, the sea of people parting immediately as they murmured and gawked. He made his way out of the alcove toward a secluded bench, where he cradled her in his arms. Later, when he knew more about the woman in his arms, he would feel uneasy about holding her so intimately, so insistently. Something about her warmth and her softness called to his protective nature. But in this moment, the low whimper that escaped her simply made him clench her to his chest more tightly.

"Your assistance, sir, is appreciated," said that same feminine voice, a bit more softly and gently, "but perhaps you might give her some room to breathe."

He looked up to see one of the woman's companions looming over him, frowning, but with her eyes focused on the woman he held.

"Beg pardon?" he said, as his arms tensed.

"No need to beg pardon, sir. Simply unhand my friend so that I may attend to her properly. You might also make yourself useful by fetching a physician."

He opened his mouth to object, but this singularly bold woman had already moved to untie the ribbons on her unconscious friend's bonnet. Some pins clattered to the bench and to the ground from the removal, and dark brown waves of hair, nearly ebony but glowing with red and gold and silver in spots where stray beams of light fell, went askew. He'd only caught a glimpse of the dark locks framing her face, but free of the bonnet, the soft strands that brushed his supporting arm may as well have been on fire, so visceral was his body's reaction to them.

"Helena," the woman said, as she fanned her friend with the bonnet. "Helena, can you hear me? You must wake. Your sons are worried."

That startled him, the mention of the boys he'd seen her watching.

Her sons, of course. They now stood a small distance away, watching intently. Even if they hadn't looked so similar, anyone could tell by their seriousness that she was their mother. The younger boy looked as if he wanted nothing more than to run to his mother and cling to her, but the older boy took his hand and whispered something unintelligible in his brother's ear, something pacifying that straightened the young one's spine with resolve. Their controlled concern made him suspect they'd witnessed her collapsing before. Only then did the woman's words sink fully into his consciousness; he was embracing a total stranger, a respectable woman, in front of her children, no less. He ought to establish a proper distance, lest her people, including the husband she must have, be outraged by his familiarity.

"Is this your mother, young man?" he said to the older child, who nodded solemnly. "She's breathing easy but should be watched. Your coat'd make a fine cushion for her head. Be a good lad and bring it here."

The boy rushed over as he tried to shrug out of his coat without releasing his brother's hand. It would have been comical seeing them bluster along, if their expressions weren't so somber. Something nagged at him as he looked at them, that strange and fleeting sense of familiarity. As gently as he could, he laid the woman on the bench with her son's coat pillowing her head and moved a respectable pace away. He should go see if he could find a physician, as the other woman had suggested, but he found himself reluctant to leave her side, reluctant to lose sight of her.

She was lighter than she looked. When he carried her, he felt her soft, fleshy curves against his arms and chest, reminding him of a painting he'd once seen by some famous painter. Yet she felt light in his embrace. But then, ladies probably wouldn't appreciate knowing that they felt lighter than the average ram or on par with a ewe ready for breeding.

"Thank you, sir. This is most kind of you," her companion said, her attention focused on her friend. She rapped the woman's hand and said firmly, "Helena, you must wake up." But she didn't appear to be alarmed.

"Has this happened to your friend before?"

"Unfortunately, yes. She sometimes has these spells, especially when surrounded by large groups of people. Fortunately, they don't last long. She should wake on her own momentarily."

That explained the unconscious woman's odd demeanor earlier. Still, why would she choose to come here voluntarily with such a condition?

"She could have been severely injured if you hadn't caught her," the woman continued. "Is there some way I can repay you for your assistance."

"No man worth his salt would ignore a woman in distress. Nor would he accept repayment for his aid."

"I wish all men thought as you do." He thought he heard her sigh and she straightened. Her flowered hat tilted rather precariously from all the activity. "I am Mrs. Frederick Clarke, and my husband and I would be delighted if you would join us for dinner."

"Pleasure to meet you, Mrs. Clarke. Daniel Lanfield. I'm in London only for a short time. Your hospitality is—"

The woman he now knew was named Helena gasped as she revived.

"I must get out of here!" she exclaimed as she tried to rise, only to be restrained by Mrs. Clarke, who admonished, "Mrs. Martin, you shall do no such thing. You've just had an episode, so you will now sit quietly until we are certain you have suffered no ill effects."

"Marissa! I can't breathe! Let me go!" She pushed Mrs. Clarke away, her expression filled with unseeing panic.

"Ma'am, you've had a spell," Daniel said quietly. When she focused her glazed eyes on him, he continued, still unsure whether she truly heard, "You were breathing just fine during your episode." He knelt near her head, conscious of maintaining enough space to keep her from feeling trapped. "It appears you may be a bit overwrought. Mind you, your fine lads are just over there, quite worried for your health."

A play of emotions ranged over her face as she listened, and then confusion and indignation shifted to clarity and concern when she turned to look at her sons. Slowly, she sat up and composed herself. He was struck then by her fine features, which conveyed a gentle demeanor and undeniable motherly affection. He wondered at the husband who must watch over her, wondered what type of man he was, wondered whether he roused his wife's fear or tamed it, and wondered why he would allow her to visit this place without his care.

That nagging sense of familiarity struck him again. He knew this woman somehow. Yet, strangely, his instinct told him he should leave.

Immediately. With his first appointment for the day scheduled after noon, Daniel had sufficient time, he hoped, to enjoy what he'd come to London for. Of course, for the sake of furthering Lanfield business, he'd spent the past few weeks taking every meeting he could wrangle in order to propose supplying major London manufacturers with their family's materials. And, of course, he was much more adept at such business dealings than his elder brother, Gordon. But this was what he'd been looking forward to, the opportunity to examine all these clever machines up close, the opportunity to explore these modern engineering marvels, ones he should have been designing himself.

Warmth. Firm, secure warmth beneath her. A murmur seemed to grow louder, though, a discomfiting mélange of people, so many people. If she could just focus on the warmth surrounding her, she could ignore the mob. Then the warmth left, replaced by a cool, hard slab. A familiar voice cut through the chatter, Marissa's usual commanding tone. She adored her friend, but really Marissa could be so overbearing. For the first time in years, she'd felt comfort and relief, at least until the cold slab beneath her. If Marissa would quiet down, perhaps she could find that warmth again. But, no, of course, Marissa would not be deterred. And then a different voice entered her consciousness, a deep and resonating voice that warmed her from the inside. And that voice spoke of her sons.

Helena opened her eyes and sat up. It took her a few moments to comprehend the situation. Above, beams of light passing through clouds were crisscrossed by the iron grid of the roof. But something dark eclipsed half of the cloud-framing roof—a man's hat. A silhouette loomed above her, large and broad, and the faint but comforting scent of fresh wool that somehow made its way through the myriad odors that always seemed to accompany large gatherings of people.

Merciful heavens, what has become of me?

She tried to stand, and a sharp pain reverberated through her skull as she heard her head crack against his. She reached up to rub her temple as strong hands grasped her shoulders. A string of curses flitted through her brain, sounding remarkably like what she heard the deep voice beside her muttering.

"Helena, dear, you must stay still and rest!" Marissa cried out. Right. Marissa was by her side so this couldn't be as bad as it seemed. Of all people, Marissa would not have left her alone with a total stranger, a stranger who even now felt too close.

"What happened?" she asked, as she inched away from the man crouching nearby. Now that she could see his face, she thought she could detect pity in his expression. She cursed inwardly at her weakness as she realized what must have occurred.

"Sweetheart, you had a bit of a fainting spell," Marissa explained. "With the press of the crowds, we were quite lucky that this gentleman rescued you from being trampled."

Trampled. The mere word filled her vision with the memory of Isaiah's broken and bloodied form, and along with it the impotent fear and rage as she knelt by him. She swallowed hard as a sharp pang hit her chest at the thought of him, a stab no less trenchant for the passage of time. Gone two years, he loomed large and close in her mind, the loss of him no less devastating. She'd soldiered on, of course, for their children, all of them lost and wounded, bereft of the sun around which their family had revolved. Over those years, this clawing panic when among masses of strangers had grown and dug deeper into her mind. She knew her reactions were irrational, but the fear became stronger, enveloped her faster at each succeeding occasion.

She'd thought being here would be different. Or at least, she'd wanted to believe her Needlework for the Needy partners when they'd said it was time, she would be fine, and the Exhibition wouldn't be as crowded now that it was winding down.

But something about the crowd sparked that ageless fear all over again. And now, Mark and Tommy looked so distressed. She'd ruined it.

"Come here, boys," she said, as she sat up and reached her hands out to them. She cupped Mark's cheek. "No harm done. I suppose all this was just too much excitement for me." She glanced at Marissa and inclined her head in question. Relieved by her friend's smiling nod, she continued, "You two should go on exploring. Just don't stray too far from Mrs. Clarke and Mrs. Duchamp. I shall rest here for the time being. Then perhaps we can stop for ices on our way home."

She tried to sound strong, calm, unperturbed, and the boys seemed to take her at her word, both of them pressing Marissa and Honoria to return to the machinery exhibits.

Honoria went with them easily, but Marissa hesitated and said, "I would feel better if you received medical attention, dear."

"You are sweet, but I assure you I am fine, especially in this quiet corner. The boys deserve to have their outing."

Still, Marissa wouldn't leave. With a little shake of her head, she said, "Silly me. Introductions are in order! Mr. Lanfield, we really cannot thank you enough for your kindness. Helena, please allow me to introduce your rescuer, Mr. Lanfield, I believe?" He nodded and Marissa continued, "Sir, I am pleased to introduce you to one of my dearest friends, Mrs. Martin. I cannot thank you enough for coming to our aid. You handled her distress quite well. This world could use more thoughtful and capable men like you."

As her friend spoke, Helena froze, a chill spreading downward from the crown of her head to engulf her. *Daniel Lanfield.* It couldn't be. There must be plenty of Lanfields in England. After so many years and so many miles, what were the odds that one of the Marksby Lanfields would visit London—would be here at this place and this time? Inconceivable. They were devoted to the village and to their family's business and held a disdain for anything metropolitan. Still, with dread sinking into her skin, she turned to look fully at the man beside her.

He looked nothing like the boys—young men—she remembered, but much change was bound to happen over a score of years. No, she was wrong. He did look like the boy who was supposed to be her brother-in-law. His brown eyes could be Daniel's eyes. The shape of his face was perhaps broader from time and age but still that same strong square that marked the Lanfield men. His broad shoulders and his bearing reminded her of the elder Mr. Lanfield. The fall of curling hair beneath his cap, that was what had always distinguished him from his brother Gordon, who'd kept his straight hair closely cropped. This could be Gordon's brother. *Please, heavens, let it not be him.*

"Someone should stay with you to make sure you don't suffer a relapse," he said, his accent nostalgically familiar and his faint smile achingly conscientious. She couldn't deny it any longer. While his older brother had been rather distant and stern, Daniel had always been the kind one, the attentive one, the one to reach out to help others. The polite concern and deference in his eyes now said he didn't recognize her. Best to keep it that way.

"No, no, sir. You should feel free to go about your business. You too, Mrs. Clarke—I'm sure the boys need more attending than I do. Now that I am free of those chaotic masses, I will be quite well." She had to make him leave before he figured out who she was. Averting her eyes, she said pointedly, "I do not do well in the presence of large groups of people. I would be much better off by myself."

Marissa nodded and said a hasty good-bye to Mr. Lanfield, exchanging cards with him and insisting he dine at the Clarke household as an expression of gratitude.

"Far be it from me to cause you discomfort, Mrs. Martin," he said after Marissa left them. "I'd not feel right, though, leaving you unattended. 'Tis no trouble to spend a few moments in your company while you indulge your sons. This visit to London has been filled with activity—meetings, dinners, interviews. Today's been my first chance to breathe all week."

"You are not from London?" She shouldn't ask, shouldn't encourage conversation, but she craved information about her childhood home. It had been so long.

"Does it not show? I'm but a country bumpkin from a small village to the north, near the city of Bradford. Surely, I must stand out like a pig amid a herd of sheep."

"Not at all," she replied honestly. His speech and mannerisms were as cordial and appropriate as any of her husband's business associates had been. He didn't have the smoothness of a metropolitan industrialist, but his forthright demeanor held its own appeal. And that voice, the stretch and twist of the vowels . . . it stirred a deeply buried longing for the home she'd given up when she ran off with Isaiah, breaking her engagement with Gordon. If this truly was his brother, Daniel, she prayed he wouldn't realize her identity. "But I really think I would benefit from some quiet. I hope you understand."

"Aye, of course. 'Twas a pleasure to meet you, Mrs. Martin. I wish you well." He stared at her a fraction too long for her comfort. She nodded and was relieved when he finally turned and walked away, his gait slow and hesitant, as if he was reluctant to go.

She put her bonnet back on and had just finished tying the ribbons when she felt a strange awareness and looked up. He hadn't gone far, it turned out, and he looked at her with a puzzled expression. Then, to her chagrin, he began walking back in her direction. She calculated what she could do, where she could go, before he returned, but there was no way to escape without being obvious.

"Mrs. Martin," he said, coming to stand before her again. "Forgive me if this seems intrusive, but I can't help feeling that perhaps we have met before. May I know your husband's name and, if I may be so bold, his occupation?"

Now she had a choice to make: tell him the truth and risk his recollection, or lie and risk him later finding out the truth from Marissa, assuming he accepted her dinner invitation. Despite that one long-ago promise she'd broken, she strove to maintain her integrity in all things, and this could be no different.

"My husband was Captain Isaiah Martin," she said formally, a tendril of pride wreathing through her. Even now, she sometimes couldn't believe he'd chosen her to be his wife those many years ago. And she couldn't believe how fortunate she'd been to choose him as well. "When he retired from the military due to injury, he worked in various capacities for what is now the LNWR."

Daniel Lanfield blinked twice, gave the curtest of nods as his expression turned ominous, and then turned on his heel and walked away without another word.

So apparently he hadn't forgotten her.

His reaction was better than she'd expected.

Chapter 3

"It has now been three days since you've set foot outside this house," Marissa said impatiently as she barged through the door. "That simply won't do."

"A bright and happy hello to you too, my dear," Helena replied, accustomed as she was to her friend's extremely direct manner.

"Yes, yes," Marissa said, giving her a quick buss on the cheek. "Now really, Helena, the children said you haven't gone out at all since the incident at the Exhibition. You know I am strongly in favor of children learning to do their part in the household, but isn't it a bit much to have the boys going to the market? Why, didn't I just see Tommy trailing behind his older brother and carrying a basket twice his size?"

"They're fine, Marissa," she said shortly. Marissa sometimes reminded her of a dog with a bone. She wasn't obligated to leave her home every day. Why should she? "I have much to do here. In fact, I finished writing the article I promised Honoria for the next pamphlet. It's upstairs. You can go start reading it while I make us tea."

With her friend thus occupied, she took her time preparing and loading items onto a tray to bring up to the study. The sugar was almost empty, which had prompted her to send the boys out this morning. But there was enough to offer a guest, thank goodness. She just had to keep Marissa's attention on the plight of the factory girls she'd written about. Their close-knit Needlework for the Needy Society had spent so much time interviewing anyone who was willing to speak with them. It was difficult, though, to find those brave enough or desperate enough.

"Here we are, Marissa. You should try these raspberry tarts my neighbor baked. They're heavenly."

"You should save them for the boys. I remember when mine were their ages. Like locusts, they would sweep through the pantry and cupboards, leaving nary a crumb," Marissa said, her eyes focused on the article. "This is excellent, Helena. You captured that young woman's suffering so vividly."

"It was the least I could do. You and the others take so much more risk producing and distributing those pamphlets and sheets." An image of Honoria's bookshop—defiled and in shambles—rose in her mind. Someone had figured out that they produced and distributed their writings out of Honoria's shop, and its destruction had been a warning that they had gotten too close to a truth someone wanted hidden. Instead of discouraging them, the vandalism had galvanized the women not just to restore the shop but to take stronger action on behalf of those too weak and powerless to defend themselves. This new pamphlet would be sent anonymously to all the members of Parliament.

"You can give this to Honoria yourself at dinner this evening. I've invited Mr. Lanfield so we can honor him properly."

Helena's hand shook, spilling the tea she was pouring. "What do you mean, dinner this evening?" Helena asked, horrified at the thought of seeing Mr. Daniel Lanfield again. How he'd looked at her, as if she were a demon who'd escaped Hades and threatened to steal his soul. Between one breath and the next, his entire being had transformed from kind gentlemanly concern to horrified disgust. She'd have laughed at the memory of his absurd transformation, except . . . even now, she felt that tiny shard twisting in her heart. In all these years, she never regretted anything about her life with Isaiah, and yet Mr. Lanfield's tacit condemnation left her with a lingering pinprick of shame. How could she endure any more time spent in that man's company?

"Well, dear, clearly you have no other plans. And Mr. Lanfield was so helpful and attentive. A total stranger, he took charge immediately, your safety his only concern. He seemed like such a nice person that I insisted he dine with us and the other Needlework ladies so we could show our appreciation. The evening will give you the opportunity to thank him properly."

"What do you mean by that, Marissa? Am I to pay him for services rendered?" She could hear the sharpness of her tone and cringed, but the very thought of thanking a man who loathed her, of being beholden to such a man, chilled her.

"Don't be silly, Helena! What has gotten into you?" Marissa stared at her. "Honoria was quite pleased to hear it."

"What about Elizabeth?"

"You know your sister much better than I. She said she couldn't attend but seemed a little perturbed. I would have thought you'd like a chance to speak with your rescuer under less trying circumstances."

Less trying circumstances. God must be laughing. When she didn't answer immediately, Marissa cocked her head and continued to stare, as if she were a puzzle to be solved. She had to say something, but what? The only thing worse than suffering through dinner with him at Marissa's home would be bearding that lion in his own den, which she would never do since she'd determined long ago never to set foot on Lanfield property again. But how could she bow out of the dinner without raising Marissa's suspicions? The very last thing she wanted to do was raise old ghosts, especially in front of her friends. Only her sister knew what had happened before she'd been swept into matrimonial bliss by her Captain Martin. The others knew she'd been estranged from her parents, but they didn't know why, didn't know the details or how extensive their repudiation had been. They didn't know how completely she'd been shunned. If Elizabeth hadn't followed her to London a few years later, all of her family ties would have been severed.

He knew. This man knew what she'd left behind, the disappointments and the doors subsequently closed to her.

"I admit that was an odd overreaction, but, Marissa, I feel that terrible foreboding again that I get when around strangers." She wasn't lying. Her stomach twisting, her palms moist, she felt ill at the thought of seeing him again. She simply wasn't presenting the whole picture. When Mark stopped in the doorway to hand her the day's post, she turned her attention to the stack of notes and moved away from Marissa noncommittally.

A letter addressed in handwriting both familiar and yet not quite right drew her whole attention. Gran. Her grandmother's vibrant, dramatically rounded script—how often had she watched Gran write letters and lists and notes? But, as she quickly opened the letter and began reading, it was clear that the hand wavered. Mr. Lanfield dropped from her list of concerns as a chill ran across her skin. The paper in her hand shook; only then did she realize her hands were trembling.

"What is it, Helena?"

"My gran. I've a letter from her." Fate could not be this cruel.

"Does she still live in Marksby? When was the last time you heard from her?"

She shook her head without speaking. Since leaving Marksby, she'd never received anything from her grandmother or from her parents. The first few years, their repudiation had devastated her. She'd missed the feasts at harvest time, full of laughter and old stories, even stories so trite and staid the entire assembly would take turns spinning out bits of it. When Bartholomew was born, she'd so keenly wished her mother were there. But no one had responded to her letters. She'd lost hope by the time Mark arrived.

"Too long ago to recall," she replied. It took her several tries to comprehend Gran's unsteady writing through watery eyes. When she finally deciphered the letter, she was surprised to find that she was sitting on a settee as Marissa loomed over her.

"You look terrible, Helena. What is the news from your grandmother?"

"She . . . she is ill. . . . She wishes me to return to Marksby to see her. 'To say a true farewell' to her, she says. She has summoned both me and Elizabeth. Our families too, if we can manage it."

"A true farewell? She thinks this is her end?" Marissa spoke gently, calmly, in a way that should have been soothing, but the placating tone only agitated her more.

Helena nodded as tears filled her eyes again. "She says she's dying. She is too weak to leave the house and is sure the end is near." Suddenly, she felt lost, felt every second of the past twenty years weighing on her. "Part of me suspected she would outlive us all."

"And?"

She looked up at her friend, confused by the question, unable to reply.

"And think, Helena! Do you mean to go?" Marissa had that impatient look.

"I . . . it's been so many years. . . . It would be more than a day's travel . . . but she is my gran." A lifetime of memories flooded through her, Gran's gentle but commanding voice echoing in her ears. Her chest hurt at the thought of never seeing Gran again, and yet that prickling of her skin had already begun. She hadn't left London, hadn't traveled more than an hour's distance, since Isaiah's death. And she'd have to take a coach or train. Her clothing felt too tight as she began to perspire. "I don't know. I would give anything to be by her side, anything for her not to be alone at the end . . . but I don't know if I could manage it."

"How could you expect to manage that when you can't even leave your home to go to the market?"

She lifted her chin. Marissa might be one of her dearest friends, but Helena wouldn't be cowed, not over something so important. "I will manage. I must."

"Do you think Elizabeth could go? What about all the children?"

"We shall see. It will all work out. It has to." Steeling herself against Marissa's skeptical gaze, she admitted, "When my mother passed into eternal life, I should have insisted that I return for her services, should have fought harder to reunite with my father. Instead, in my cowardice, I stayed away. It is one of my greatest regrets, as is missing *his* funeral. Gran has asked for us. I will not fail her. This may be my last chance." Her voice cracked on the last word, and she burst into tears. Sweating and nauseated, she set her mind on her dear grandmother's wish. There must be a way.

Having completed his last appointment, putting the final nail in this coffin of a business trip, Daniel took a sweeping look around the smoking room. He'd heard impressive things about the Gresham Club, and he was not disappointed. These were men with a vision of the future. It was small consolation compared to the utter lack of enthusiasm regarding his proposal for Lanfield wools and materials. The merchants and traders he'd met with during his trip to the city resisted taking on such a small-scale supplier. More than one pushed him for exclusivity. *Not a chance.* That was one point on which he and Gordon had agreed. His brother hadn't been in favor of seeking these connections at all. The stubborn fool couldn't see that their entire foundation was crumbling, their industry dying. At best, the head of Tavish had not given him an outright no; an alliance with the manufacturer could be the lifeblood they needed. Yet it could just as well prove disastrous, depending on too many variables. Would it be better to risk the ever-present threat of illness wiping out a flock or the stormy effects of a partner company's whims and tribulations? Better they establish a strong web of multiple contacts than place all their eggs in one seemingly strong but uncertain basket. For that matter, Farley and Sons was still considering exporting Lanfield goods to the Americas. Still, it would be foolish to put all his stock in such lukewarm responses. Perhaps he could still salvage this trip on his last day; all it would take was one solid prospect. He took another swig of the excellent port, focusing on the richness of it coursing through his system, and settled into the plush armchair. Who had he yet to approach?

"Mr. Lanfield, I was pleased to see you on the club register today," said an unfamiliar voice.

Another prospect? He perked up, adjusted his damned cravat, and stood to meet the newcomer. When the attendant made the requisite introductions, it was easy to see why this man, Mr. Frederick Clarke, was the perfect balance for his self-assertive wife. He tensed. Mrs. Clarke had invited him to dine with them, and he'd sent his regrets claiming illness. It was, in a way, true. He had been sickened when he'd recognized Mrs. Martin. The very thought that he'd carried her in his arms sparked a roiling burn in his wame. He had been right to reject their invitation, but you never knew who might take offense.

"Pardon me, sir. I didn't mean to startle you," Mr. Clarke said. "Mrs. Clarke was quite disappointed that you could not come to dinner last evening, after all. She's been concerned about your health ever since. It seemed like fate when I saw you were here. May I confirm that you are in good health and good spirits?" Mr. Clarke pulled a chair close and sank into it comfortably. His manner seemed easy and undemanding.

"Yes, thank you," he replied, relaxing back into his seat. What else could he say? *No, not at all. Good spirits are nowhere to be found. I am failing utterly.* "It was a passing ailment. You may assure your considerate wife that I am well today."

"Considerate is quite a nice way of putting it," Mr. Clarke responded jovially "She's perpetually meddlesome, but she has the heart of a lion and the soul of a saint. I find my life is more comfortable and orderly when I do whatever she tells me to do. When she puts her mind to something, it is inevitably the right course, and one would do well not to deviate from it."

"Well, as I said, I am quite fine so there is no need for her concern."

He could still picture Helena Thorton—Mrs. Martin now, he should remember—before he walked away from her that day at the Crystal Palace. A vulnerable, helpless woman whose first thoughts upon waking were her children. Knowing who she was brought a bitter taste to his mouth. She'd aged, of course, but not enough to satisfy him. She ought to look like one of *Macbeth*'s gnarled witches, her outside matching her base and ugly spirit. No one with a soul could live with bringing about the ruin of her village. He'd never in his life do a woman harm, but he could wish he hadn't noticed her distress, to begin with. As if this trip weren't enough of a dismal failure, meeting that viper again made London a new level of hell.

Another attendant arrived at the table to refill their drinks, and he frowned at the direction his thoughts had taken. His collar felt too tight, but he couldn't loosen it here. How could he still hold such sharp, boiling anger over a woman who was ultimately a stranger now? What did it matter that she looked normal, that she looked sedate and well-fed and secure? Water under the bridge. London might be a thousand times larger than the tiny hamlet of Marksby, but it stood to reason that everyone would visit the Great Exhibition. Mere coincidence that, amid the throngs of thousands, she would appear before him. He wasn't such a monster that he would resent aiding a person in need, even one so undeserving as that woman. Was he?

Mr. Clarke swirled the liquid in his glass and nonchalantly said, "Now she has in mind that your heroic rescue of our friend, Mrs. Martin, needs grand and proper recognition. It would be best for you to concede with good grace and simply allow her to make a fuss over you. Dinner this evening or tomorrow, whatever suits you. And I must admit it would be a relief to have some masculine reinforcements when Mrs. Clarke has her sewing circle in attendance."

So this was how the affable man got on with his bold, outspoken woman—he acceded to her wishes whenever possible. Daniel could easily picture the cycle—she demands, he acquiesces, she advances, he retreats. Daniel knew that cycle all too well, knew too accurately what it was like to try to please an increasingly unsatisfied spouse. Another swig of port. If his mind continued to follow this path, the day would truly be ruined.

"That would include Mrs. Martin, I take it?" he asked. Under no circumstances would he break bread with that woman. Surely, she would be just as averse to the idea. The image of her insensible and so very fragile loomed behind his eyelids, sparking a contradictory impulse to see her again and make sure she was safe. He tossed back the remainder of his glass. His mind wouldn't stop racing, diving down these unexpected and unwelcome paths. One moment he wished he'd never laid eyes on her, and the next he longed, however fleetingly, to see that she was intact. *It must be the strain of this trip. Get yourself together, man.*

"Undoubtedly," Mr. Clarke said. "Mrs. Martin is most keen to convey her appreciation as well. She cares deeply for her friends and watches over them all like a mama bear. But I suppose you don't know about their little coterie." The man stood abruptly, as if just remembering an important appointment. "I say, would you care for a stroll? I don't suppose you've done much sightseeing. During one of the many recent episodes when Mrs. Clarke has sung your heroic praises, she has mentioned that you are visiting Town on business. I would be happy to introduce you to some of my colleagues who I expect to be out and about at this time of day."

He breathed an inward sigh of relief and agreed. He found the man's demeanor puzzling, but this chance meeting could be a profitable turning point after all. A sorely needed spot of hope. Once they'd exited the building, he fell into step with Mr. Clarke easily, and they ambled toward Hyde Park. After talking perfunctorily about how Marksby weather differed from London's, Mr. Clarke circled back to the topic of the little group of which his wife and Mrs. Martin were members—self-importantly called Needlework for the Needy—as if they'd never been interrupted.

"She's known those women for a dog's age, all fine and upstanding. I don't know who you would have met. Obviously, there's Mrs. Martin. You might have also seen their partner in crime, Mrs. Duchamp. She's quite a bluestocking, that one. Widowed. Owns her own bookshop. Quite enterprising."

He could appreciate business acumen, but he wondered at Mr. Clarke's admiring tone. Independent women . . . bluestockings . . . his wife had admired such women too. Mrs. Martin had apparently found like-minded women to reinforce her self-absorption. All the more reason to avoid her.

"The other member of their merry quartet is Mrs. Martin's sister," Mr. Clarke continued, "but I believe she's had her hands full these last few weeks. Some minor illness struck the family, and you know how it is."

"Mrs. Martin has a sister?" he asked absently. What did he care about the Thorton sisters? He should just make clear that he knew the women from their youth. If they considered the sisters their friends, they deserved to know the truth about the heartless, selfish nature of these women. But then again, he was no sniping gossip and would, with any luck, be a stranger to these people again in a day or so. If the Clarkes didn't know any better, it wasn't his job to enlighten them.

"Yes, although they look nothing alike upon casual observance. I suppose the only resemblance is their eyes. I believe they're from your area, if I recall correctly." Mr. Clarke's gaze focused on the intersection ahead, and his voice sounded innocuous enough.

As they passed a fountain in which some street urchins played, Daniel made a noncommittal noise in response. Ah, yes, the Thorton sisters. One light sister, one dark. One bright, one gloomy. Both deemed fine bonny lasses. In the end, they'd both been faithless and self-serving, abandoning their home and family for this cesspool that was London.

A bell on a passing omnibus was clanging loudly, shaking him free of his thoughts. Again, such bitterness. What was wrong with him?

Mr. Clarke continued rambling, not appearing to care for any response, "Those ladies are quite something when they work themselves into a lather. Individually, they might not catch one's eye. Not even my own firebrand, Marissa—though she was quite the stunner in her day—but when they join forces, man, they are a sight to behold. All that shrill, passionate indignation."

"It's common for women to form such attachments," he responded, just to be able to say something. "My . . . wife had just such a group of friends, as close as sisters. They met every week for tea and gossip."

"Are you married, sir? I should have thought to ask. Why, then you do know how they get!" Mr. Martin had steered them toward a quiet corner of the park, one with an impressive statue.

"My wife is gone, sir," he responded. He'd learned to use short, vague phrases about her absence. If wasn't his fault if people took him to mean his wife was dead. She might as well be.

"My condolences. With all due respect to your dearly departed Mrs. Lanfield, the Needlework ladies are more than a flock of gossips. They rather see themselves as crusaders. In fact, they can be quite a nuisance to those they see exploiting the weak and innocent."

"That sounds rather dangerous, them meddling in other people's affairs. How do they know who is doing the exploiting?" Now the pieces of Mr. Clarke's descriptions combined into a whole picture. He'd heard of such people, men and women, claiming concern for the social good. Likely, these women grasped onto whatever social cause was fashionable from one week to the next. But sometimes such do-gooders underestimated the forces against which they raised their flag. "Do you not worry about your wife's safety? What about the other women's husbands? Do they not take responsibility for their wives' well-being?"

"Given that Mrs. Duchamp and Mrs. Martin are widows, I would say they take responsibility for their own lives. Mr. Addison and I, well, we have faith in our wives." The man shrugged. Actually shrugged. Had the man no backbone at all? "Have I been alarmed at some of Mrs. Clarke's antics? More than once. But she was a nurse before I married her. She can handle herself. I trust her judgment, and she and the other women are very cautious and mindful of each other. Oh, only look at how we've rambled," Mr. Clarke said, as he stopped in front of an unassuming townhouse. "This is my castle! Oh, and look at the time! We've arrived just in time for tea. Mrs. Clarke would have my head if you didn't join us."

He felt the jaws of the invisible trap snap shut. Mr. Clarke was obviously a domesticated puppet. Nothing to do but move forward. He would be polite and leave as soon as propriety allowed. He gritted his teeth. If Helena Thorton—Mrs. Martin, he must recall—appeared, he would have to feign sudden illness. Well, truly he probably wouldn't have to feign anything. The thought of socializing with her did make his stomach turn.

Chapter 4

Simple furnishings, Daniel noticed as they crossed the threshold. People who had fancy chairs and knickknacks irked him, made too much of themselves and their trinkets. These Clarkes were solid folks, by the looks of their home. With any luck, those Needlework women Mr. Clarke described would not join them, especially not the Thorton sisters. He followed Mr. Clarke's lead, while vowing to himself that he would make his escape at the first opportunity, only to stop short as his host halted in the entryway. He caught a glimpse of Mrs. Clarke. The woman he'd met at the Exhibition didn't match the one he saw now, though. Before, she'd been calm and decisive. Now, with her startlingly red hair escaping its bun as she bounded up the stairs and her shrill, curt greeting to her husband without so much as a pause in her step, she seemed to border on hysteria.

"Marissa, what has got you in such a state?" her husband called out.

She paused, reminding Daniel of a fawn hearing the crack of a twig or the report of a shot. Her distracted expression as she stared at them in the doorway resolved into clarity.

"Oh, my dear, thank goodness you're home," she said hurriedly, poised halfway up the staircase. "I've just been to see Helena, and she's in a state! She and Lizzie just received an urgent post from their grandmother. She's gravely ill and wants them. Lizzie cannot go with Mr. Addison away! Meanwhile, Lena is already packing. She won't listen to reason. She needs immediate funds. I told her I would lend our trunk. Oh, and you simply must hear of her brilliant plans. She's determined to make a mad dash for the train, get herself to York, and then improvise from there. Can you imagine? Helena improvise? Alone? She's been so fragile these past few years. God only knows where she might end up or who might take advantage of her!"

At the mention of the sisters' grandmother, Daniel tensed. He hadn't seen the elderly Mrs. Thorton in the village in the weeks before he came to London, but surely he would have heard something if she were seriously ill. The Grand-dame, as the Lanfields had fondly come to call her, had always been a kind woman; it would be a great loss when she passed. Recalling how attentive and generous she'd been when his father died, he found himself speaking without conscious intent.

"Excuse me, Mrs. Clarke, but what's the matter with their grandmother?" he asked.

Only then did the harried woman appear to notice him. Her eyes narrowed, and her entire demeanor changed, as abruptly as the closing of storm shutters.

"Oh, my heavens, Mr. Lanfield. I didn't see you there." She smoothed her unruly hair and came down the steps much more sedately than she'd gone up them. "It is quite kind of you to ask after Mrs. Martin's relations, but it wouldn't be my place to discuss her family affairs."

He admired her blunt refusal, shielding her friend from an apparent stranger like a ewe keeping herself between strangers and her newborn lambs. If these people didn't know Helena Thorton's past, they deserved to. If they knew of her betrayal already, they couldn't possibly know the depth of it. He had to tread carefully, though.

"Mrs. Clarke, I'm well acquainted with the Thorton family. Only after our encounter at the Crystal Palace did I see who your friend was, though. We lived in the same village as children. Her grandmother is well-respected, and there was no talk of the Grand-dame being ill when I left Marksby. I'm worried, especially if her health's become dire in the short time I've been away."

"You knew Mrs. Martin and Mrs. Addison? What an unusual coincidence." Coolness crept into her voice, as she stopped at the bottom of the stairs, still as a statue. Perhaps this woman knew more about the Thorton sisters' past than he'd thought. "Were your families close?"

"Our lands are adjacent to theirs so, aye, I knew them as well as country neighbors generally do."

"So you might know a bit about her history and her departure?" Her voice dropped a few more degrees, and her husband eyed him curiously.

"I know enough. What's wrong with Mrs. Thorton? She's been remarkably hale and spry, given her age."

Mrs. Clarke's eyes narrowed, but she replied, "Their grandmother has apparently taken a serious turn. Two weeks ago, she came down with what appeared to be minor sniffles, but it quickly escalated. The note said that she has taken to her bed and has grown quite weak. Given the family's silence these twenty years, it must be severe if she's sent for her granddaughters." The woman's tone turned sharp at the end. So blind to the truth.

"When I return home," he said calmly, "I'll send word back to Mrs. Martin and her sister regarding their grandmother's condition."

"Oh, but Helena—that is, Mrs. Martin—has gotten it into her head that she must go to see her grandmother."

"She mustn't," he said flatly. Impossible. Foolish, reckless woman! He kept his questions about her sanity unspoken. She'd have to be self-destructive to go back. Not to mention the havoc her arrival would wreak on the village. She couldn't be so senseless.

"Can you believe it?" Mrs. Clarke shook her head. "She hasn't traveled any distance from London since her husband's death. Why, she's barely traveled more than a few city streets in the past two years. The Exhibition was the farthest . . ." When Mrs. Clarke trailed off, it took him a moment to decipher her silence. Apparently, Mr. Martin had been gone, what, at least a year. Yet this woman's expression spoke of more than her friend's grieving. Her husband whispered something in her ear, and she turned away. The memory of Mrs. Martin's unconscious form, slumped against him on the wooden bench, raised a niggling alarm in his head. There was more to Mr. Martin's death than anyone was saying. He stomped on the delicate sprout of sympathy he felt trying to take root.

"Does Mrs. Martin have a history of fainting?" he asked the Clarkes. "Would she even be capable of such a journey?"

"She insists that she is!" Mrs. Clarke turned to her husband and added, "She refuses to listen to reason. We have all tried to dissuade her, to no avail. It is most frustrating."

Mr. Clarke took her by the hand and leaned over her, whispering again. They maintained a decorous distance, but the familiarity, the intimacy, of their demeanor made Daniel intensely interested in the wallpaper.

"You ladies are a formidable lot," her husband said fondly. "I'm sure she will come to her senses before long. She won't leave her children."

"Something isn't right," Mrs. Clarke insisted. "Helena is irrationally obsessed with the idea of returning. Her arguments have been so emotional and vociferous. She's already begun packing. I promised to lend her some items; I came to fetch them in hopes that my delay would give her time enough to reconsider. I fear she won't be dissuaded."

Daniel rolled the matter around in his head. The return of Mrs. Martin spelled disaster. The village would be in an uproar, and old wounds that had never healed would be torn open afresh. With that woman's health already uncertain, no good would come of such a trip for anyone.

"I can convince her," he said firmly. "I'll frighten her if I must, but I'll get her to stay."

"You, sir? You'll forgive my doubt, but why would you succeed when those closest to her have not?" Mrs. Clarke said, her eyes narrowing with suspicion.

He hadn't intended to reveal the details of their past acquaintance, but it seemed there would be no other way.

"Mrs. Clarke, I don't know how much your friend has told you about her past in Marksby and the circumstances under which she left the village and her family."

"Like you, I know enough," the woman responded through clenched teeth, "but do go on." Her husband looked at her questioningly, perhaps because of her sharp tone, but she shook her head and gripped his hand in both of hers. Whatever their silent exchange meant, her husband held his tongue.

"Your Mrs. Martin was once engaged to marry my elder brother, Gordon," Daniel admitted, striving to tamp down the bitterness of the words, "and their match would've combined our families' lands. It so happened that the intended land consolidation was of interest to a railway company, which promised great prosperity for everyone in the village. Captain Martin was one of the railway representatives who came to complete the deal. Within two months of his arrival, he eloped with then-Miss Thorton and the railway decided Marksby wasn't an ideal location after all."

Mrs. Clarke blanched, her face shifting as she combined the information with what she already knew. "She said there was a scandal and that her parents refused to acknowledge her thenceforth."

"Oh, that's quite true, ma'am. 'Twas a grave scandal. Destroyed the prospects of the entire village and residents throughout the parish. Her parents were devastated by her betrayal. Never recovered. No one in Marksby truly did."

Mr. Clarke interjected quietly, "Land deals fall apart for many reasons. That is the mercurial nature of such transactions. How certain were the principals in the transaction that their elopement ruined everything?"

He bristled at the question, at its genteel attempt to undercut the righteous anger of his community, but he respected the man's sense of loyalty to the Martins, misplaced and misinformed as that loyalty might be. He may have been a young man at the time, but even then he'd understood enough about the circumstances. "There were obvious signs. And the close timing was undeniable. 'Twas as if those railway people were marauders, sweeping in to pillage and plunder before the company rushed on to its next target. Many families finally had to move to Manchester or Liverpool to find work and scrape by."

"So you're saying everyone there blamed Helena for all this?" Mrs. Clarke sounded skeptical, as only a person unfamiliar with village life could.

"*Blames*, Mrs. Clarke. There's no past tense about it. They *still* do hold her responsible—which is why she cannot return. Let me be perfectly clear. She'd not be safe there."

"I think she means to brazen her way through," Mrs. Clarke replied.

"Pardon me for saying, but being brazen was what caused her disgrace, to begin with."

"You'll have no pardon from me. That is uncalled for, sir, and, whatever she did in her youth, she is a fine and moral woman now."

"My words may be blunt, ma'am, but they're no less true. And not nearly strong enough, considering the public feeling against her. Take me to her, and I'll convince her myself that she mustn't go."

The vague whisper of an idea caught his attention. If she was so damned insistent on returning to face her own ruin, it might be gratifying to witness. After all the suffering she'd caused, why shouldn't she suffer too. Why shouldn't she see for herself what she'd wrought?

* * *

The older boy he'd seen with Mrs. Martin at the Great Exhibition opened the door for them and immediately hugged Mrs. Clarke before pulling back suddenly, as if aghast at his behavior. The child attempted a look of dignity as he inclined his head toward the front room and shook his head.

"It's good of you to come, Mrs. Clarke," the young man said, his voice wavering. "Mama is not acting like herself. She still speaks of going away, but I fear she would come to harm. She won't agree to take me with her! Please help us!"

The boy's tension drew Daniel's sympathy. To have her as a mother . . . she'd been a selfish git twenty years ago, and it seemed little had changed. Helena Thorton would follow whatever whims struck her, and damn the consequences. If her own children couldn't sway her, 'appen the threat of village scorn and enmity might.

Mrs. Clarke nodded and said, "I'll speak with her, Mark, and I found Mr. Lanfield, who may also be able to assist us. You can go upstairs and play with your brother. I trust you to keep him occupied while we talk things over with your mother."

The boy gave her a grateful smile and gave Daniel a polite nod. "Pleased to see you again, sir. Please don't think ill of my mother. I fear these rare instances do not show her at her best, but she is really a fine English woman." Mark fled up the stairs with a quick glance toward the parlor. Such an odd child—so polite and controlled, teetering on the verge of manhood.

Mrs. Clarke led the way down the hall, but held her hand up for him to wait at the threshold of the sitting room. What little he could see of the room still showed signs of mourning—black crepe taken down but not put away.

"We could have Gran brought here, Helena," said a female voice that sounded vaguely familiarity in its light, nasal tone. This had to be the other Thorton sister, Miss Elizabeth. "She could stay with one of us, and we could share nursing duties."

"How can we ask her to make such an arduous journey in her condition?" He recognized Mrs. Martin's voice, now tense and shrill.

The Grand-dame would never agree anyway. Daniel knew that much. She was a fixture in the village, determined to live and die there, even in spite of her granddaughters' faults.

"It's such a long journey, Helena, and I'm sure much has changed," the other Thorton sister said. "It is unwise to put yourself in this situation. Think of your safety."

He wondered at how Mrs. Martin's sister avoided referring to the animosity throughout Marksby. The younger Thorton had remained in Marksby for a year after her sister's elopement. She must have seen and heard herself just how much Helena Thorton was despised and condemned. Daniel could attest to that too. Helena Thorton had jilted Gordon, after all, a man who'd done her no wrong, a man who had been the most eligible single man in the village, one with the most prospects for success. Daniel had been enraged on his brother's behalf. And that was before the economic consequences of her elopement had been realized.

"You could accompany me, Elizabeth," Mrs. Martin responded.

"Gran is as dear to me as she is to you, but you know I can't go," her sister said, sounding on the verge of tears. "The baby needs me. With Mr. Addison away, there is no one—"

"Of course not, Lizzie," Mrs. Clarke interjected as she made her presence known. "Lena, you shouldn't go either, especially given your recent health."

"Marissa! When did you arrive?" He couldn't see Mrs. Martin's expression, but he could detect annoyance in the woman's tone. "I am perfectly fine, Marissa. We have discussed this ad nauseum, and I have made my intentions plain. I cannot ignore Gran's entreaty, not after all this time. Do you not understand? For so long, I have despaired of ever being welcomed back into the Thorton home. I need to do this."

"If you won't listen to any of us, perhaps you will listen to someone who knows your village far better. Mr. Lanfield, if you please."

The dramatic introduction made him feel a bit ridiculous as he strode into the room, and the matching looks of surprise on the faces of the erstwhile neighbor girls only added to the absurdity. Mrs. Martin stood at a finely carved sideboard on which rested an open valise. Her hair was uncovered and glowed a brilliant chestnut in the afternoon light. Fully conscious and apparently at ease in her own home, she was easier to recognize now. She had the same delicate, expressive features that he knew from childhood. Every emotion showed on her face. And now her concern and anxiety, presumably over her grandmother, were overlaid by sheer embarrassment. The younger Thorton sister was rising from an upholstered chair, looking startled and on the verge of bolting. Her blond hair had darkened mildly, adding to the impression of her as a doe in flight. Her protectiveness hadn't changed, though. She walked over to Mrs. Martin and whispered in her ear. Then she turned and said in a tight voice, "Good afternoon, Mr. Lanfield. I hear I have you to thank for coming to Mrs. Martin's assistance during the family's outing recently. That was kind of you."

"'Twas no trouble, Miss Elizabeth." Now what devil prompted him to needle her?

She turned bright red, as Mrs. Clarke interceded. "Oh, dear, that's right. You would have known her as a miss. It has been a long time for you all. She's Mrs. Addison now, has been for some fifteen years now. How her husband would laugh to hear her called a miss these days."

State the case and get out. Make it plain. Helena Thorton cannot return to Marksby.

"Good afternoon, ladies. Please excuse my intrusion," he said mildly as he removed his cap. "I was in conversation with Mr. Clarke when we encountered his wife. She mentioned your grandmother's poor health and Mrs. Martin's ill-considered plan to visit her childhood village."

Mrs. Martin's eyes narrowed at his words, and her cheeks flushed a bright pink. She took a single, deliberate step forward, her hands clasped in front of her, and said coldly, "You have caught us unawares, Mr. Lanfield. I have not yet begun entertaining callers since my husband's death. Uncouth as it may sound, we are poorly equipped to offer you hospitality just now."

An obvious dismissal. What a polite and civilized way to make him feel unwelcome.

"Helena, dear, do be cordial," Mrs. Clarke admonished before he could respond. Mrs. Martin turned on her, the hardness of her expression conveying far more anger than her words had. Mrs. Clarke continued, "I invited Mr. Lanfield here because you must hear what he has to say about conditions in your village. This is important."

"What can he possibly say that overrules my grandmother's deathbed request?"

"You don't know that she's on her deathbed. Anyway, only let the man speak. Why don't I go put on some tea? I brought some biscuits for the children, but there should be more than enough for all of us."

Mrs. Martin pursed her lips but nodded curtly. "Elizabeth, you remember Mr. Lanfield, do you not?"

"Your servant, Mrs. Addison." He tried his best to keep the disdain from his voice. She bobbed the slightest curtsy without speaking. He steeled himself against the sisters' matching expressions, eyes narrowed, chins lifted, shoulders squared. That these two women, the Thorton sisters of all people, stood poised as if to do battle with him, well, the whole situation was absurd. As if they were the victims and he the transgressor. Ha!

"I've no wish to waste your precious time, ladies." He tried, really, to keep the disdain from his voice. It wasn't easy. "When Mrs. Clarke made clear that you intend to return to Marksby, Mrs. Martin, and wouldn't be dissuaded, I felt it my duty to enlighten you."

"Your *duty*? To enlighten *me*? How charming," Mrs. Martin replied, folding her hands over her chest. If her tone were a pitchfork, he'd be naught but a sieve in just those few stabbing words. The look on her face brought to mind her younger self. More than once, he'd seen that look when someone told her *You can't* or *You mustn't*. But he would say his piece, whether she liked it or no. What the woman chose to do with the knowledge was her business.

"My choice of words aside, ma'am, you need to know that you are not welcome in Marksby. It would be unwise to return. Your sister knows perhaps even better than I what a disaster it'd be for you to show your face there."

Miss Eliza—Mrs. Addison—gasped. This couldn't be a surprise to her, could it? She blanched and moved close to her sister. When Mrs. Martin looked at her, she whispered, "I'm sorry."

"Is what he says true, sister? You never said I was utterly unwelcome, only that Mother and Father had turned away from me."

Mrs. Addison shook her head, her mouth agape, her eyes downcast, but she repeated, "I'm sorry, Helena. It was bad enough that our parents disowned you. There was no reason for me to pour salt in that wound. You had no intentions of returning to the village anyway. It can't still be as bad as it was. It simply can't." Then the younger Thorton sister looked at him pleadingly.

The tension in the room sharpened as Mrs. Martin turned to him and said slowly, "Perhaps you could elaborate, sir."

"You mightn't be aware, but your elopement did a great deal of damage to the village."

"I was sorry to hurt your brother so. It was terrible of me, but it was a personal matter."

"My brother's feelings are not at issue here. The personal affront, bad as it was, became just one part of a much more severe catastrophe. You must've known that your marriage to Gordon would have combined the Lanfield and Thorton lands." When she nodded warily, he continued, "What you mayn't have known was that our fathers were on the verge of an agreement with the very railway company your Captain Martin represented. That's why he and his associates were there, you know. The deal would've transformed Marksby. It would've put our little village on the map."

Mrs. Martin shook her head, her features screwed into a frown. "No, that can't be right."

Mrs. Clarke and Mrs. Addison rushed to her side, twin columns of calico to bolster her. Neither woman looked surprised by the news or by Mrs. Martin's reaction. A bitter laugh rose in his throat, but he stifled it.

"Aye, Miss Helena," he said, addressing her deliberately, "what you did couldn't be right. Your whimsical, headstrong decision ruined Marksby's greatest prospects."

"No, no, no," she said, shaking her head more vehemently. "Elizabeth, is this true?"

Her sister looked suitably askance as she replied, "Father was furious. You know, he was never one to talk of business matters at home, but I overheard many heated discussions between him and the elder Mr. Lanfield and some of the other village elders. The railway was mentioned, but I couldn't discern the details."

"Elizabeth, why?" Mrs. Martin asked plaintively. "Why did you never tell me any of this?"

"It would have served no purpose, Lena. Truly. You were happy here in London. When I arrived, Bartholomew was a babe. You had no intentions of returning. Why trouble you?"

The stunned woman stumbled from the loose embrace of her friend and her sister and slumped into an upholstered chair. He felt a sharp flare of pity for her but quickly snuffed it out. Ignorance of the consequences didn't absolve the sin.

"Our fathers fleetingly considered pairing Miss Elizabeth with my brother immediately after your departure, Mrs. Martin," he said, flatly. There! That pained confusion on their faces was the least penance these two could provide. "But the damage had already been wrought." He couldn't—and wouldn't—keep the bitterness out of his voice. "The company decided Marksby was an unsuitable location after all and moved on. Even with the continued possibility of merging our lands, the village was found lacking. That was the sweeping result of your little *personal matter*."

He could practically see Mrs. Martin turning the news over in her mind, making sense of it, as she grew paler and paler. She looked back and forth between her sister and her friend; whether for confirmation or for absolution, he couldn't tell. It didn't matter. The devastation wrought by her decision couldn't be rectified; there was no pardon to be had. She simply couldn't return.

Chapter 5

How could this be? How could she have been kept in the dark for all this time? No, the idea that one girl's choice of husband could harm the entire village was preposterous! Mr. Lanfield had reason to despise her, but Helena would not be dissuaded from honoring Gran's request. Her heart swelled as she recalled the words written in Gran's abnormally wavering script. *Come quickly.* So she would. She'd hoped for so many years that her parents would send that invitation, but they hadn't. Now she had the opportunity she'd longed for, to return to her childhood home and see what was left of her family there.

"I have just the solution, ladies!" Marissa exclaimed in her characteristically abrupt and domineering manner. "You should accompany Mr. Lanfield home to Marksby! It's perfect, as if the Fates conspired for you—" Really! Marissa's ability to take charge of a situation was essential when the Needlework ladies saw an opportunity for social improvement, but this was one of the worst *solutions* she could ever suggest.

"Mr. Lanfield?" Lizzie interrupted with a horrified tone that matched the emotion rising in her throat. "Oh, Marissa, you have no idea how awful that plan would be! Lena simply shouldn't go."

The man grimaced too. He was no more in favor of that ridiculous idea than any of them were.

"I thought, Mrs. Clarke, that the point of my presence here was to dissuade your friend from her disastrous plan." He gritted his teeth, almost laughably, and said, "As a gentleman, I could hardly refuse to assist a lady in need, but I can't emphasize too strongly how very poorly your friend's return to Marksby would be received. It would be disastrous."

Could hardly refuse. Hmm. As if any force in this world would persuade her to accept assistance from a man whose every word, deed, and look conveyed his hatred and disdain. Unbidden, she felt the fleeting sensation of being cradled in firm warmth, the first sense of security she'd felt in years. Fine, perhaps not every deed. But he hadn't known who she was in that moment. Nothing since then suggested he would offer her the slightest glimmer of warmth, or care one whit for her security. She would make her way to Marksby according to her own devices.

"My dear Marissa," she began tightly, refusing to address Mr. Lanfield, who had not, in point of fact, offered assistance. This was Marissa's harebrained idea. "Dear, it must be obvious that I cannot impose so much upon Mr. Lanfield. We've just met the man. Our long-ago acquaintance does not justify imposing upon him so greatly."

"But, my dear stubborn Helena, if you insist upon returning to Marksby, you will need a knowledgeable guide. Mr. Clarke said only yesterday that Mr. Lanfield was highly regarded at the club, and, for goodness's sake, we first met him coming to your aid. Moreover, he is going to your precise destination. It could not be more perfect."

"I cannot go with him. It would be unseemly." When Marissa still appeared unmoved, she grasped for more reasons. "Just think, it would be wholly inappropriate for the two of us to travel together. We are not related and . . ." Her breath caught as she saw Mr. Lanfield recoil. She hadn't intended to remind him that they were once intended to be related through marriage. She pressed forward, saying, "And, Mr. Lanfield's wife would strongly object, I'm sure."

Marissa shot back, "His wife has passed on, God rest her soul. You are both widowed. You are both traveling to the same hometown."

"Vanessa could go with you," Elizabeth interjected.

She shot her normally sane sister an *Et tu, Brute?* look and felt a brief sympathy with Mr. Lanfield over his loss. What a sad commonality they shared, one she wouldn't wish upon anyone.

"You know, Lena, how concerned her father and I have been about how her eye strays," her traitorous sister continued. It was true that they all worried about Vanessa's wild streak. She suspected some boy or other had caught her niece's fancy, and she hoped the girl would make wise decisions. So it made a kind of sense when Elizabeth continued, "This would be a brilliant way to free her from some . . . questionable influences and even show her a bit of life outside of London."

"She would be a great help," she admitted, "but she'll hate you for sending her with me."

"She's a good girl at heart, and she'll do what's right in the name of family." Elizabeth sounded like all had been decided.

"But she and I shall use public transport. We shall not be beholden to the Lanfields. It would be too much."

Marissa, damn her eyes, wouldn't listen to reason. "Lena, dear, be sensible. Traveling with Mr. Lanfield would give you protection on the roads and would take you more directly. It would also likely be far less expensive than trains and cabs."

Mr. Lanfield hadn't spoken in quite some time. She'd almost forgotten his presence, but now he responded sharply. "No man of dignity would accept money in such a situation. But—ah—I'm afraid that my humble cart would serve as poor, uncomfortable transport."

His forbidding demeanor spoke volumes. He'd been scathingly honest about the consequences of her elopement on the village, and she could only begin to imagine how everyone had fared in the intervening years. He didn't want her company any more than she wanted his. A dual opposition could overcome Marissa's stubbornness.

"You see?" she said to her friend. "Vanessa would be miserable, vocally so, riding in a cart all the way to Marksby. We can't do that to the poor girl. You wouldn't want to make such a trip with her under those conditions, and you know it."

"I certainly wouldn't, and she's my own child!" Elizabeth added. Helena felt the tide turning. She would go to Marksby. That decision was no longer in doubt. But she would go on her own terms.

Marissa looked at her carefully and then said with uncharacteristic gentleness, "But, Helena, what if you have your spells?"

She had no answer.

"Vanessa would know what to do," Elizabeth said for her, but her sister's tone was not convincing.

For the first time since his arrival in her home, in the home she'd shared with her husband, the home where she was raising her fine sons, she met Mr. Lanfield's gaze fully. She was certain of one thing. "Mr. Lanfield has explained to us that my return to Marksby would be a mistake. He would not wish to take us there, any more than I would for him to."

* * *

He looked at Mrs. Martin for a long moment, almost rudely long, long enough for her to redden satisfactorily. Such rudeness was nothing compared to the outright animosity she'd encounter in the village. Even now, this foul woman showed no honest remorse for how severely she'd hurt the village that had once called her their own. Here she stood staring at him challengingly. She should see for herself what she'd wrought. How sweet would it be to deliver her, to have her face her acts of betrayal and their consequences? Did the prodigal daughter, once so eager to wallow in city life, have an accurate sense of what would await if she returned to the village?

Only when Mrs. Martin turned away did he realize that her voluble friend Mrs. Clarke was still trying to convince her. ". . . so you wouldn't have to deal with—well, you'd be much safer and you could go without making a hodgepodge of travel arrangements along the way." Like a wily sheepdog, this Mrs. Clarke was. Then she turned on him and said, "Are you sure you could take her, Mr. Lanfield? It wouldn't affect your business?"

This is your opportunity to bow out gracefully. Take it. But he owed it to the Grand-dame. If she sent for her granddaughters, after all that had passed, he should do whatever he could to see her wish fulfilled. And if Mrs. Martin deemed the situation dire enough to show her face in Marksby, well, he had to be a witness to that. It might prove to be entertaining, much like the lions and gladiators of the ancient Coliseum. "Not at all. My appointments have been fulfilled. I would have remained in Town to explore other opportunities, but I have nothing pressing."

Mrs. Helena Martin—he couldn't even think of her name without sneering—opened and shut her mouth repeatedly like a caught fish. She had no inkling what awaited her. He would do his duty as an honest man, but she would have to suffer the effects of her desertion as Marksby saw fit.

"May I have a word with the young gentlemen, your sons?" he asked abruptly. He gestured to the Martin boys, who now were huddled in the doorway, clearly eavesdropping and bursting to speak.

Mrs. Martin nodded, hastily wiping her face. Was that wetness upon her cheeks? This was what she wanted—to return to the village and see her grandmother. Even if he and the rest of the room dictated the means, she was still getting her way in the end. When she left the room, he said, "Would you boys like to see my horse?"

"Oh, yes, sir!" Tommy said. Mark only nodded, suspicion in his eyes.

"Talos is a good beast, a strong and hearty one," he said as they walked outside. "You worry for your mother. You heard that she's going on a trip. You'll miss her, I know. Yet the best way to help her now is to make her journey as easy as you can."

Mark finally spoke. "The last time our parents went away, our father came back on a stretcher and died without opening his eyes. We never even got to say good-bye to him properly. I should be the one to watch over my mother, to protect her."

That gave him a moment's pause. He hadn't heard the particulars about Mr. Martin's death. It shocked him to hear the boy speak so emotionally and vividly about its impact. He was a precocious one.

"I swear to you that I'll keep her safe," he said solemnly. "I shall speak with your mother and her friends about the nature of your mother's spells. Once I've an idea of what symptoms to watch for and what situations to avoid, she'll manage better."

Tommy nodded dutifully, but Mark, that smart boy, remained unconvinced. "We don't know you. How can we trust you?"

Mrs. Martin might deserve to be condemned for her choices, but he wouldn't violate his own family's honor just because she had.

"You're right. I can only ask you to have faith in my word. Your mother needs help, and your great-grandmother has been very, very kind to me over the years. I'm going home to Marksby. And I owe it to your great-grandmother to keep her kin safe. If your mother chooses this path, can you support her? Can you ease her way just that much?"

"Are you a man of honor, Mr. Lanfield?" Mark asked solemnly, with a seriousness that belied his years.

A quick one, this boy. Getting straight to the heart of the matter. Daniel searched his motivations for a way to answer truthfully.

"I'd say I am, yes, Mr. Martin. I shan't do your mother harm."

"I entrust my mother to your keeping. If she comes to harm, I shall hold you accountable." The weight of his words carried the menace of an adult. He would be a formidable man someday.

* * *

Realizing the sound it would make and the punishment she would bring upon herself, Vanessa caught the bedroom door she'd been about to slam. As if her parents didn't already think her immature. But really! Banished to the wilds of northern England! With skittish Aunt Helena! It was a wonder her parents didn't turn into papists so they could tuck her away in a nunnery! And what hypocrisy! She knew full well why her parents wanted her to go. But Mama had been only a few years older than Vanessa when she and Papa married. They couldn't continue treating her like a child.

She slipped the kerchief Billy had given her out of her pocket and stroked one of the roses embroidered on it. Hidden by the tall hedge maze at the park, he'd given it to her as a promise of his affection. The roughness of the cloth reminded her of his shirt, warm against her cheek as she clung to him.

She could refuse to go. They couldn't force her. If they insisted, she'd hide away at Billy's. He hadn't shown her his home yet or taken her to meet his family, but he worked so many long hours. She was certain he'd be happy to have her with him.

Aunt Helena even said she'd be fine traveling alone.

But then . . . Auntie was a bit frail. And those spells of hers. A vision of Auntie collapsing in a graceless heap hovered in her memory. Some street brawl had erupted at the market, and suddenly down went Aunt Helena. She was so confused and alarmed the first time she'd seen her aunt faint straight away. Not prettily either, the way some of the girls pretended to do when a handsome fellow tipped his hat at her. Vanessa knew what to do now, but those first few incidents had been chaotic and frightening, especially when Mark and Tommy were there to see their mother unconscious. No doubt Auntie needed a traveling companion, but why did it have to be her? Why? And why would Auntie take such a risk, to begin with? Yes, their grandmother was ill, but neither Mama nor Auntie had seen her in decades.

She threw herself upon the bed and began tracing the flowers on the kerchief. How terribly dramatic she was being. Petulant, that was the word. No, this train of thinking definitely wouldn't convince her parents she was mature enough to marry her beloved. But there must be a way.

She bolted upright. If she had to accompany Aunt Helena (and her mother had made it perfectly clear that she did have to), this could be the perfect opportunity to prove herself! She could demonstrate how absolutely capable she was, how mature she was. Then, when she revealed to her parents the truth of her relationship with Billy, they would recognize her as an adult and support her plans wholeheartedly. She tucked Billy's kerchief back into the top of her chemise. She could survive a month away from him if it meant they would be together permanently. She would be on her best behavior.

Chapter 6

The first leg of the journey passed without incident, to Helena's relief. She'd resolved to say as little as possible, and Mr. Lanfield likewise didn't seem inclined to talk with his passengers. She'd been surprised when he'd offered her and Vanessa assistance to climb into the back of the cart, not because of his offer, which was only gentlemanly, but because she didn't feel that spike of anxiety or awkwardness at his touch. She knew he was as reluctant about her company as she was about his, but he must have hidden his feelings. Vanessa's continuous narrative of the views they passed filled the time, almost to annoyance, but it was easy to indulge the girl's verbose curiosity. She'd expected her niece to rail against being sent on this trip, but instead she'd been the very picture of amenability. The changing landscape as they moved farther from London really was remarkable. Ultimately, Marksby would be quite a revelation for one who'd only known crowded city streets. Or at least the Marksby she remembered would be.

"Just look at the endless green fields, Auntie! And this vast sky, it's the color of a robin's egg! Even in Hyde Park, the view isn't this vibrant. I thought my mother exaggerated when she described the fog over the city as a horse blanket God threw over it in haste. And those pastoral poems Mrs. Duchamp insists on reading to us, I thought they were flights of fancy."

Helena smiled nervously, expecting Mr. Lanfield to make some caustic remark about her niece's naïveté, but he didn't appear to hear them from the driver's seat. So much the better. She'd much prefer silence to whatever censure hovered on his tongue. Marissa had served as their go-between for the remaining travel plans. She still couldn't believe he'd offered, no matter how grudgingly, to take them with him. She knew enough to realize that the Lanfield family would have been happy to see her burning in hell all those decades ago. When he'd spoken to her in her own house, the anger in his expression had been abundantly clear. Perhaps he was ignoring them purposefully now, but why put them both in this uncomfortable circumstance?

At the first stop, she decided she must ask him. But, damn, there would go her own resolution to avoid speaking with him. When he'd arrived to collect her and Vanessa, Lizzie had fussed over her daughter and had gnashed her teeth about not being able to go see Gran; Marissa had helped a tight-lipped Mr. Lanfield load their things into the cart. Finally, Marissa had all but pushed Helena into the back of the cart as well. She saw now how well everyone had orchestrated her compliance. And she'd followed along like the meek, mild little lamb she'd become. Well, even a lamb could bite when it needed to.

While the horse was being fed and watered, she got down from the cart. She caught Mr. Lanfield's eye and inclined her head toward a more secluded area by a grove of trees. Gratified when he followed, she asked, "Why are you helping me? I could have—my niece and I—could have easily used public vehicles. The trains might even get us there more quickly."

"And here I thought Londoners were known for their relentless propriety. Why bother to start with a genial comment about the weather or the roads? Nor even a hasty thanks."

She winced at his words. He had the look of someone who had seen that his expectations were well founded, and she felt a stab of irritation. He didn't know her, not now, and he had no cause to place judgment on her.

"I do apologize, Mr. Lanfield," she said, trying not to clench her teeth. "Of course, I give you many thanks for allowing us to ride with you on your return to Marksby. You are too kind." She had to pause to fight against choking on that last statement. She could say the words, but she couldn't muster the energy to mean them. She really couldn't. The boy she'd known as Daniel had been kind; this man was the Daniel who'd shouted curses at her when he'd caught her and Isaiah making their escape. "You said yourself that it would be a mistake for me to return. Why then are you delivering me there yourself?"

"Because you're maddeningly determined to go. And, of all the absurd plans you've considered for getting there, this one will ensure you arrive safe and sound."

"Safe and sound? And ready for the villagers to eviscerate me?"

He shrugged with what she could only interpret as smugness. Ugh! Infuriating man!

"Even more reason for me to ask, then. Why are you helping me? This arrangement must be as distasteful to you as it is to me. Why suffer it when there are other methods of travel my niece and I may use instead?"

"'Appen I wish to be able to witness the worldly prodigal daughter's return to Marksby. 'Appen I find the payment of my traveling expenses appealing, since it's my destination anyway. Or maybe I believe myself to be a man of honor who holds great respect for your grandmother. And maybe I wouldn't be able to consider myself my mother's son if I turned my back on a resident of Marksby in need— a woman, to boot—even a scapegrace like you."

"You hate me so much, even now." He didn't deny it, and she had to suppress a shiver as the depth of his feeling struck her.

"Why would you return after all this time?" he shot back.

"Gran. Only in truly dire circumstances would she correspond with me. The last time she contacted my sister was to inform us of our father's death. I've sent her letters, but I don't know if she's ever read any of them."

"Mrs. Martin, why'd you turn your back on your family? Why'd you never return before now? Your niece has a right to the truth of her beloved aunt's character."

"Tread with caution. You cannot know what went on between me and my parents. Do you think I did not try to mend the rift? For more than a year, I sent my parents letters every week trying to explain, begging them to understand. When my first son was born, my heart ached to share the news with them. I sent word but never heard a response. Most of my letters were returned to me, refused by my parents. My husband began to suspect that my father took perverse pleasure from making us pay the postage both ways. If your claim is that I am an inconstant strumpet . . ." She heard a feminine gasp behind her and whirled around to see Vanessa standing a few feet away. The girl's curiosity never ceased. Well, what better time for a lesson. "Vanessa, bear this in mind. When others wish to shame you with their snide whispers and innuendos, face them head-on. When they would cower in veiled language, call them out for it. Do not let them label you." She braced herself and faced Mr. Lanfield again. "Now . . . if your claim, sir, is that I am an inconstant and immoral strumpet, I must point out that you do not know me. You know of an incident that happened twenty years ago, and you continue to judge me as though time stood still from the day I left Marksby."

"Not at all, Mrs. Martin. I consider it my moral duty not to judge."

She looked into his eyes, unable to find an adequate response.

"Thank you," she said simply.

"'Tis naught." He turned back to the horse. "I'd best go check Talos's shoes. We've a long way to go yet."

"Wait!" She caught his arm and froze. His arm, thick with muscle, tensed at her touch. The sensation, combined with the flare of something bright in his eyes before he shrouded it, made her mouth dry. She hadn't touched a man in years, at least not one outside of her circle. Her friends' husbands didn't count; they might as well be her brothers. But this electric moment, her sudden awareness not only of his firm flesh but of his blue, blue eyes and his earthy scent, left her utterly speechless.

"What is it?" he said impatiently as he pulled away from her.

"'Tis naught," she said, echoing him as she composed herself. "I'll make sure Vanessa is ready to go."

When they came to a stop in front of the coaching inn, Helena breathed a huge sigh of relief. The day's travel had been more taxing than she'd expected. She'd forgotten how tiring it could be just to sit in a jostling cart or carriage. She was glad of the young stable boy who came up to the back of the cart to assist them, but he focused his attention on their bags.

"Leave off, lad," Mr. Lanfield called out, as he came into view. "We've no need of help."

She gave the boy an apologetic look before he ran off.

"The boy was just being helpful," she said quietly. "There was no need to be so brusque with him."

"How you ever could have thought you and your niece would have traveled by rail . . ." He shook his head skeptically and then reached for their baggage. She was too tired to bother prompting him to finish what promised to be a disparaging thought.

When they entered the inn, her mouth watered at the aroma of roasting pheasant. A welcome respite, indeed, and one she had to admit they might not have encountered by train. As she and Vanessa were led to their room, she had to acknowledge that this was vastly different from train travel. They'd rarely encountered people, and then only in passing. Even here, the inn was unusually quiet and un-crowded. The very thought of a full train car made her feel a bit queasy, the sensation fading as she stepped into their modest but ser-viceable room. Quiet. Alone. Secure. This was what she needed, and she wouldn't have been able to get any of this through public trans-portation. She wondered momentarily if that was what Lanfield had been about to say—that she wouldn't have been able to make this trip on her own. Presumptuous man! She wasn't so soft that she couldn't do without creature comforts, and she wasn't so inept that she couldn't handle mundane travel arrangements.

She and Vanessa met him in the dining room, and they found a table in a quiet corner, removed from the few other guests. In her inimitable way, Vanessa kept conversation going almost single-handedly during their meal. And Daniel maintained his laconic demeanor. But Vanessa must have run out of topics when she lit upon the Needlework for the Needy Society. Helena groaned inwardly and braced herself.

"Aunt Helena and the other Needlework ladies have been working to stop an angel-maker in the city."

She looked sternly at her niece, trying to think of the best way to divert her. "There is no need to discuss such gruesomeness. I'm sure Mr. Lanfield has no interest in the unpleasantness of city life."

"I've birthed countless lambs and calves," Daniel said. "I can han-dle gruesomeness. Who, pray tell, are the Needlework ladies and what on earth is an angel-maker? Why would something that sounds so cherubic be gruesome?"

Vanessa looked near to bursting with pleasure at the opportunity to expound. "Oh, the Needlework for the Needy Society is wonder-ful! My mother, Auntie Helena, and their friends—" Thankfully, the girl finally caught her glaring and stopped abruptly. But it was too late.

"Aye, Mr. Clarke did say something about his wife's friends mak-ing a formidable little group. Something about knitting for justice."

Vanessa responded quickly, "Oh, they are impressive, and they do much more than knitting."

"Vanessa, dear, really, do not bore Mr. Lanfield with women's trivialities."

"Mrs. Martin, 'appen you could tell me more about these evil angel-makers?"

Well. Surely, she could talk about them without revealing the machinations of the Needlework ladies. "There are a growing number of unscrupulous independent nurseries that will take infants and children into their care for payment."

"An orphanage?"

"Nothing so organized. Many appear to operate out of private homes, under deplorable conditions. We've heard stories from factory women, usually about someone they knew leaving their children in the care of a baby nurse. The floors were apparently lined with crates for the babies and children. Not proper beds, mind you. And surrounded by filth. One woman came to us after her babe died in someone's care, and we have since learned of other, similar cases. However, the operation seems to have moved."

"Surely accidents happen. Bairns do take ill and die."

"Surely," she responded dryly. "But there is a vast ocean of difference between accidents and neglect. What's particularly loathsome in these cases is that the whole purpose of these angel-makers is the money. No care is given to the children, and yet their parents must work or risk being thrown into the workhouse."

"You seem personally affronted."

"The deaths of these innocent children are deplorable. Unconscionable. I could so easily have been in their shoes. Those mothers with so little, having to trust their precious children to the care of a stranger week after week—it's heartbreaking."

"You would never have abandoned your children so, Auntie," Vanessa said vehemently.

"Your faith in me is admirable, my sweet, but just think—had your uncle proved to be insincere, he could have abandoned me in the squalor of London or along the highway. Even married as we were, had his company proved a failure, we would have had little choice but for me to work as well." She looked at Mr. Lanfield unflinchingly. He cocked his head as if a question hovered in his mind, yet he didn't speak. It was unlikely he could think any worse of her so there was little harm in revealing the full circumstances of her elopement. "If my husband had been a very different type of man, not a gentleman but a seducer, I could easily have been one of these women, at the mercy of an angel-maker. There's no need to look so scandalized, Mr. Lanfield. I am certain people suspected, especially after my abrupt departure."

"Whether they did or no, to speak so bluntly in front of your niece is scandalous. You've no concern for her morals?"

Vanessa's chin went up. Never a good sign. "Better for me to know the truth and be prepared for the perfidy men may commit than to fall prey to one out of sheer ignorance!"

Putting her hand on her niece's shoulder, Helena offered a calmer response. "Rest assured, sir, that I have made clear the moral ramifications of my choices, as well as the pitfalls and consequences many young ladies face when they trust the pretty words of a lover."

She thought it exceedingly wise that Mr. Lanfield declined to comment.

"It's become a serious problem and not just in London. As with so many injustices, it targets the needy, the destitute, those in such dire straits they have few other options, if any. From what we've found, the parents generally believe they're placing their babies in safe keeping. We need more regulation and more frequent inspections. We need more severe punishments." She stopped abruptly, realizing her voice had grown shrill and strident. It was so difficult to remain composed when facing such inhumanity.

"You care deeply about these people." He said it as a statement, not a question, but she responded anyway.

"Of course," she said simply.

"Funny how you can show such fierce attention to the injuries of strangers and so little to the people you yourself have injured."

Heat immediately suffused her face. Awful man. She didn't have to suffer his unpleasantness. There was a sign at the innkeeper's desk showing public coach times. She resolved to ignore Mr. Lanfield for the remainder of the meal. He'd proven that politeness was lost on him, and she had none left to spare. Instead, her mind whirled with plans.

Chapter 7

Helena waited until her niece fell asleep, the girl's soft but regular exhalations and sweetly slackened features reminding her so much of her sister, Lizzie. Yet another way Vanessa was obviously her mother's daughter. As Helena lay in the moonlight waiting, her ire over Mr. Lanfield's presumptuous condemnations expanded, each bitter word from him whirling into an expanding vortex of anger and resentment. What audacity. What ridiculous provincialism. Apparently not just his but the whole bloody town's, if she could believe his account. But she and Vanessa would be free of him very soon.

When she finally slipped off the bed and went to put on her robe, her hands shook so much that she had difficulty with the closures and gave up after the top two. She barely managed enough composure to scratch discreetly on Lanfield's door, suppressing a callow instinct to pound on it and jar him awake. This would be the last time she spoke with him voluntarily, and, by God, she would set him to rights. In the morning, she and Vanessa would take the first coach and leave him behind.

He opened the door a crack, squinting at her. The dark room behind him suggested she must have woken him. So did the sliver of bare chest she could see through the opening. That gave her pause.

"What?" he asked, his voice hoarse and gruff.

"I need to speak with you."

"Now? Nay, we've all had a tiring day. Anything you wish to say would benefit from waiting until we've slept and our heads are clear."

"Your patronizing tone notwithstanding, it is imperative that I speak with you now. Tomorrow will be too late."

His brow wrinkled as he stared at her. She held his gaze, lifting her chin and wrapping her arms tightly around her torso. He would hear what she had to say, even if she had to stand here all night. After several long, tense, silent moments, he huffed and said, "Suit yourself. I can see you've a bee in your bonnet. Far be it from me to stand in your way if you're determined to be stung."

The wryness of his voice curled her shaking hands into fists, but he opened the door wide and went across the room, so she entered. She waited until he'd lit a lamp before closing the door firmly behind her. At the click of the door latch, he paused in the act of shaking out his shirt and raised a brow at her.

She answered the question he didn't voice. "There is no need to air our grievances in the hallway where strangers might happen upon us. I wouldn't want your gallant public façade to be dented and tarnished." She cleared her throat, suddenly very, very aware of the small room and Lanfield's bare arms and torso. He seemed somehow larger, broader in this state of undress. She gestured to his shirt as her cheeks suddenly burned. She meant to lambaste him, but the sight of his vulnerable throat, of the hollow there at the base, of his heartbeat pulsing in that spot—well, her body had other ideas. Unfamiliar, wayward ideas, and she froze as she tried to decipher them.

"Well?" he said, gruffly.

She closed her eyes for a moment and tamped down these renegade sensations.

"Helena, are you unwell?"

How dare he use her given name? That snapped her from her muddled, wayward thoughts. "Mr. Lanfield," she said as coolly and formally as she could. "We need to talk. Please, do go on. You should be fully clothed so we might have the semblance of a civil conversation."

Although he donned his shirt, he didn't fasten the collar. Raising her gaze to meet his, she felt heat spread from her cheeks to her ears as she realized he'd seen her staring and he'd deciphered what it meant. "What you said about my desertion of Marksby was entirely distorted. I would go so far as to say your account was delusional."

"Would you, now? How could you possibly know the effects of your actions on the village when you weren't there to witness them?"

"You cannot convince me that one young woman's elopement could destroy the future of an entire village. Communities do not hinge on one insignificant person. The loss of a central figure, like the mayor or the blacksmith, perhaps, but I know full well that the sun doesn't rise and set by my force of will."

"Again, suit yourself," he said, with a dismissive flick of his hand. "Don't believe me. You'll see for yourself soon enough. The village never recovered. It continues to struggle onward, but you'll find it much changed. Not for the better."

"That is your perception." She held up her hand when he opened his mouth to interrupt. "It may well be true," she conceded, "but you must acknowledge what a ridiculous scenario it would be. A village full of high-minded, knowledgeable, industrious people brought low by one young woman? Unable to recover its glory or reestablish a new path to prosperity over a score of years? Surely, the effects of one insignificant girl's personal decision would not have such deep, long-standing repercussions." She felt herself beginning to babble, but she couldn't stop as her mind raced along myriad paths of consequences, each possibility more horrifying. "Surely, I couldn't . . . be prosecuted for . . ."

"British courts can't compare with the collective memory of town elders," he cut in. Even in the dim lamplight, she could see his stormy expression.

"Look, I deeply appreciate your willingness to transport me and my niece, especially in light of your obvious distaste. There is no need for us to continue in such an unpleasant fashion."

"What are you suggesting?"

"You must recognize the difficulties of continuing this journey together. I have talked with the innkeeper about my options and found that it would be just as fast for me and much less of an inconvenience for you if Vanessa and I take a coach to the nearest train station and continue from there. Therefore, I have already arranged other transportation. Vanessa and I are no longer your concern."

She hadn't thought it possible for his demeanor to grow more irate, but it did. His eyebrows shot together, his eyes grew stormy, and his jaw tightened so much it was a wonder she didn't hear his teeth crack in his skull.

"Already arranged! Nearest station! Such a fond hoit!" Immediately after his outburst, he took a few steps back, perhaps just as startled as she was by his vociferous reaction.

His insistence alarmed her as much as his intensity. How could he possibly care about her traveling plans? If anything, he should be relieved. Her chest felt tight. She struggled to take in more air as she stared at him. He crossed his arms over his chest and turned to face the window. For some strange reason, the sight of his shoulders, broad and tense, shook her.

"Sorry, Mrs. Martin, for speaking so." She barely heard him, but at least he'd restrained himself. When she didn't respond, he met her eye and continued, "Hope I didn't frighten you. There's no denying this is an uncomfortable alliance for us both, but I gave my word to your lads, to your sister, and to your friends, the Clarkes, that I would see you and your niece safely to your grandmother's house, and that's what I shall do."

"So your word to them matters more than my wishes. I assure you I will tell them I chose differently. And my niece and I shall be fine without you."

"I gave *my* word. Your wishes hold little sway with me, just as everyone else's wishes hold no sway with you, then as now. You're under my protection, and I'm responsible, should either of you come to harm."

"I am not your responsibility. And my existence isn't a means to practice your moral superiority. I've come to thank you for your assistance thus far and to inform you that I have arranged other transportation for me and my niece."

She winced as he let fly a string of curses, including some things she couldn't interpret, which was probably for the best. His breathing came in fierce puffs.

"Sir, we have barely been reacquainted," she said, refusing to be cowed by his bull-like behavior. "Contrary to your obvious misconceptions, I am not a weak, helpless female in need of male protection." In the dim light of the lamp, his figure seemed imposing, even from that distance. She went to pull her robe more tightly around her body but realized she might appear nervous or even frightened. Showing such weakness would belie her argument. She forced her arms to her sides and straightened her spine.

He cocked his head, and his gaze swept down her body with a smirk. Damn. He'd noticed her discomfort. He took a step closer. What a long stride he had.

"Mrs. Martin, when we first met in London, you swooned and were nearly trampled. I understand it's not the first time."

"As long as I plan carefully and control my environment, I can easily avoid such spells."

He took another step, nearly crowding her against the door.

"You're fooling yourself. Have you been on a train for more than a day?" he asked.

"No," she admitted, "but I have taken shorter train trips without incident." She didn't mention that she'd taken them with her husband, nor that the last train trip had been three years ago.

"Have you been to Manchester in recent years? Are you familiar with its streets and transports?"

Another damned step. She pressed her back against the door, the knob digging into her hip.

"No, my husband never took me," she stammered, but squared her shoulders. "But I am sure any rational adult could work out the logistics. I am far from that naïve girl who ran away from Marksby, and I am capable of taking care of myself."

He leaned in, so close her chest brushed against his when she breathed. She stopped doing so.

"I wish it were so. But you've shown no such evidence thus far. Even if you weren't prone to fainting under stress, you'd be easy prey for pickpockets, bandits, and swindlers. If I'd taken a minute longer in chasing off the stable boy out there, your bags would've disappeared with that thief you thought was so kind. You've no sense at all of how vulnerable you are."

Vulnerable was exactly how she felt with his immense body crowding in upon her. His shadowy figure all she could see, she felt surrounded. Her cheeks burned, and she took shallow breaths to avoid brushing against him. He was trying to make her faint again, trying to prove how weak she was. She gritted her teeth but refused to be cowed.

"I assure you I would manage, sir."

"What would happen to your sons if you were harmed? If you were fatally injured?"

"Stop!" How could he know? He voiced her deepest fear, her worst memories, and that keen insight of his shook her deeply. She lashed out to deflect him. "You would cast yourself as the Good Samaritan, selflessly assisting a helpless woman, but I am not your charity case. Taking that man for a servant of the inn was a mistake I shall not make again. And your moral high-handedness is quite rich as you condemn me for my supposed transgressions. This is not your decision to make, short of you kidnapping me and my niece. I came to do you the courtesy of informing you that, while we appreciate your assistance thus far, our plans have changed. I have now done so and bid you good night!"

"For the sake of your sons, I'll see you safely to Marksby," he said, as if she hadn't spoken.

"I will not be forced. Certainly not by someone who despises me."

"I don't despise you," he said firmly, but he had the grace to look away. "I did once. You caused my family a great deal of pain and humiliation. But that was long ago. Now I . . ."

She was far from convinced, but it was a relief when his voice trailed off. She didn't want to know how he might end that sentence. Then she realized she couldn't leave until he stepped away from her, away from the door. Before she could speak, he laid his hands on the door above her shoulders. She should have felt trapped by this dark silhouette imprisoning her, and for a fleeting moment, she wondered at the missing sense of panic, but then he leveled his face with hers, noses almost touching. Rational thought dissipated. Were his lips as harsh as his tone or as soft as his breath, mingling with hers?

"As you've said, I don't know the woman you have become. You don't know the man I've become either." His tone held a note of roughness. Her entire body tingled, and she feared he could sense it. Then he tilted back ever so slightly, his eyes visible only as glittering points catching the candlelight. "'Appen you mistake your own guilt for what you call my moral high-handedness. Unlike you, I don't break my promises. I don't abandon women under my care. Accept it with good grace."

Abruptly, he backed away from the door and said, his voice as calm as if their heated conversation hadn't just occurred, "And now I bid you good night as well."

Of all the—! It was useless to continue arguing with this stubborn, presumptuous ox of a man. She'd given him fair notice, and she would take Vanessa on the coach in the morning.

Weak rays of dawn filtered into Helena's consciousness, and she heard the muffled scratching and thumping and creaking of the inn coming to life. The coach! Goodness, she needed to get Vanessa up and ready. It took a Herculean effort to get the girl up and out. One might think her niece deliberately dragged her feet, mumbling all the while about being packed in with strangers, to avoid traveling by mail coach. Where the child got her high instep was a mystery.

By the time she could rush Vanessa down the stairs and out to the yard, the coach had arrived and some passengers were disembarking. A small distance away, Daniel stood with Talos hitched to the cart. He tipped his hat at her in greeting, and she gave a perfunctory curtsy before gripping her bags more firmly and continuing toward the coach.

"Auntie, must we really ride in that?" Vanessa kept her voice low, but her petulant tone was unmistakable.

"I'm sure it's finer than it looks."

"But it's already so full. There's no room for us."

Helena suppressed a shudder as she realized Vanessa's observation was all too true. The coach was full to bursting, inside and out, even after three passengers exited. They'd practically have to sit on the laps of others.

"Nonsense, dear. See, we may take the seats vacated by those who just disembarked. Anyway, it will only be until Birmingham. We shall take the train from there, which shortens our travel time significantly." She tried to sound unperturbed, but her mouth flooded with bitter saliva. *They all look like decent, hardworking people, Helena. Don't be silly.* She realized with chagrin that their belongings would have to be stored with the other luggage, separating them from their valuables. Could she trust that their things would be safe? Meanwhile, she felt Daniel watching her. When she looked toward him, though, he was talking casually with one of the stable hands and stroking Talos's muzzle. He hadn't given more than acknowledgment and made no move to intercept her or Vanessa. He appeared ready to leave and yet he lingered.

"I've a schedule to keep," the coachman said brusquely. "Are you ladies coming?"

"I don't like the looks of this, Auntie," Vanessa whispered, wringing her hands. "I feel an inexplicable dread about this. Please, let's not. Mr. Lanfield is right over there. I'm sure he wouldn't mind if we continue on with him."

As dramatic as her niece could be, she'd never seen the girl in such a state of increasing agitation. It added to her own misgivings. Reluctant to hand over their bags, she asked the coachman, "Are you sure there are seats for us?"

"Can't guarantee there's space for you to sit together." He looked at the vehicle, his eyes narrowing as he assessed the space. "There's one seat available inside, one seat in front, and one for standing in back."

"Oh, dear. That won't do. My niece and I should not be separated. When is the next coach? What is the likelihood more seats will be available?"

"Couldn't say, ma'am. Can't see into the future. Wouldn't be here if I could. Now, are you and the young miss coming or not?"

"I—we—If you could just give me a moment more—" she hedged. She felt no more amenable to this situation than her niece, but she had to prove she could do this. She must be able to ride a public coach without incident. After all, she'd survived an evening in an inn full of strangers. This was the next hurdle, and she would not be undone by it. Her own unease must have infected her niece, and they would both return to normal once they were on their way.

"Don't see what another minute would serve," the man replied, his tone clipped and overbearing. "These passengers have paid good money to get where they're going. If you want to join them, now's the time."

"Good morning, Mr. Lanfield!" Vanessa called out.

Biting back a curse, Helena chastised, "It is improper to shout in public, dear, and quite improper to do so in order to draw attention from a man not in your—"

"Good morning to you, Miss Addison. Mrs. Martin, how nice to see you this morning." Mr. Lanfield's voice sounded much closer than she'd expected. He was beside them in only a few lengthy strides, his looming presence reminding her vividly of their conversation in his room last night. Vanessa needed to learn to hold her tongue. "There a problem?"

She shook her head, but Vanessa quickly responded, "There is no room for us on the coach."

"Now, see here, girlie. That's not what I said. There's room enough." The coachman looked annoyed now and, presumably seeing two fares slipping from his grip, yelled to driver, "Have one of the gentlemen inside give up his seat to these ladies." The driver scowled but slid open the window behind him and murmured unintelligibly. Voices from the inside of the coach sounded resistant. People began to gather in the courtyard.

"My humble cart remains at your service, ladies." Daniel's voice sounded sincere, even guileless, and yet something in his expression made Helena sure he was laughing at her and deeply enjoying her discomfort.

She and Vanessa replied simultaneously.

"No, no, Mr. Lanfield. We couldn't possibly—"

"Oh, Mr. Lanfield, we'd be obliged—"

Helena shot Vanessa her best Medusa face. *Headstrong girl.* "Vanessa, please. I am responsible for both of us. Mr. Lanfield, as I said before, your kindness is appreciated, but we really must move on." She went to hand the coachman her bag.

"You'll have to secure your own luggage, ma'am," the coachman interjected. "There's space for it in back."

Vanessa blocked her way and grasped her arm, pulling her away from the others. In a fierce yet low voice, her niece said, "Auntie! What has come over you? You are always so prudent. But this is not wise. You're being so unreasonable." Her niece sounded startlingly distressed. She stopped. Vanessa's face was pale, and her chin shook. "Please, Aunt Helena. I beg of you." Her voice dropped to a whisper. "We know Mr. Lanfield is kind and won't cause us harm. He's certainly had plenty of opportunity. I don't—the coach—I fear for our safety."

It would be heartless of her to ignore her niece's plea, to dismiss Vanessa's intuition. She gave her niece's hand a squeeze and nodded.

"It appears my niece feels rather unwell and is unable to ride in a coach today. I am deeply sorry for any inconvenience we have caused you and your passengers."

The coachman scowled at her and immediately turned, shouting "Driver, make ready." She caught wisps of mumbled curses and unflattering descriptions of pampered, selfish women. So be it. She couldn't please everyone. In recent years, it seemed she couldn't please anyone at all. Why should today be any different?

When she turned to face Daniel again, he was conversing with Vanessa, whose demeanor had brightened considerably. Now she couldn't help but suspect her young niece had balked about the coach for reasons other than safety. She'd have to watch carefully. Surely, Mr. Lanfield could be trusted to behave honorably, but Vanessa's wayward emotions had prompted her mother to send her on this trip. Surely it was only her niece's well-being that made her tense at the sight of them laughing together. She consciously unclenched her jaw, readjusted her grip on her bags, and pasted a smile on her face. "It seems we are to continue imposing on your good will, kind sir. Climb aboard, Vanessa. By all means, let us be on our way."

Daniel handed Vanessa into the cart and then turned back and offered to assist Helena. "I told you," he said in a low voice, "I keep my promises."

She should have felt affronted by his high-handedness—and she did—but there was another undercurrent of feeling as well. The tension in her shoulders eased a fraction. It had been so long since someone else was in charge. While she couldn't stomach a total loss of autonomy, there was something comforting about not having to make every single decision, not having to weigh all the consequences all the time. Isaiah hadn't been overbearing, but with him gone, everything was on her head. The house, the boys, the money, every responsibility large and small was heaped on her. She'd felt guiltily relieved when Bartholomew had joined the Navy; as much as she worried for his safety, his fate was no longer solely in her hands. Her sister and the rest of the Needlework for the Needy ladies certainly assisted her in more ways than she could count, but they had their own families, their own burdens.

Ignoring his hand, she clambered onto the cart. "We shall see."

Chapter 8

The second day of travel passed tensely, and Vanessa could see that her aunt was furious with Mr. Lanfield. Yet she couldn't understand why, nor why Aunt Helena had been so unreasonably insistent that they take the coach. What sense would that have made? It had been filled to bursting, and some of the passengers had appeared . . . questionable. And it had been filthy. Riding in the cart was a dusty mess, to be sure, but really. That coach was entirely unappealing. On the other hand, Mr. Lanfield's cart was at least roomy and comfortable, and he was a perfectly nice man with an almost fatherly manner. She felt sure they could trust him to watch over them, which she could not have said of the coachmen. He was the kind of man she could picture Billy becoming in a few short years. Billy was nearly as tall and as broad, but his body hadn't the same confidence that Mr. Lanfield's conveyed. But she could see Billy growing into that man as he climbed through the ranks at Dyson's. He wouldn't be a clerk forever, and she would be proud to stand by his side, as a good woman should.

"Hold tight," Mr. Lanfield called over his shoulder. A moment later, the whole cart bounced and shook as they rumbled over what must have been enormous ruts in the road. The straw bales might not be the height of comfort and luxury, but they were enough to cushion the blow. The coach's wooden benches would surely have been less forgiving.

Several uneventful minutes later, she couldn't help but notice that Auntie Helena still clung to the side of the cart rather desperately. Her aunt's face was pale and blotchy, and she stared into the distance with a strange, empty look.

"Mr. Lanfield! Please stop! Something is wrong!" she shouted. Auntie didn't react at all. Her eyes were open, unblinking, and her breathing was rapid and shallow. She followed her aunt's gaze but saw only the same road, the same landscape, she'd seen for miles. What in heaven's name was the matter? Her skin prickled with anxiety. What should she do?

Mr. Lanfield glanced back from his seat and immediately eased the cart to the side of the road. He would know how to help her aunt!

"What's happening?" he asked, turning in his seat.

"I don't know! Before we hit that rough patch of road, she was fine. Now she seems to be in some sort of trance." She cringed at the alarm in her own voice. *Don't be a child, Ness.* But this wasn't like Auntie's previous spells in which she slipped into unconsciousness. Now she looked horribly awake but seemed to be experiencing something unconnected to her actual time and place. Something was happening in her mind to cause that terrified—and terrifying—expression. "What can this be? What do we do?"

Quickly, he secured the cart and climbed into the back. He knelt before her aunt, his brow furrowed.

"This one of her spells?" He clapped his hands directly in front of Auntie's face, but there was no change.

"No! It's never been like this before! I have no idea what this is." Her head felt full to bursting with the stress. She hated feeling so helpless, so incompetent. She dug into her satchel for the bottle of salts her mother had given her for emergencies. "Here. Perhaps this may work anyway."

He took out the stopper and waved it under Auntie's nose. Vanessa held her nose to block out the pungent smell, but it still took several moments before her aunt reacted.

"Don't let them!" Auntie's whole body tensed even more. Her eyes opened even wider, but whatever she saw wasn't in the here and now. The terror in her voice was chilling. "Isaiah, don't leave me! They're not our concern! Please, I beg you, drive on!"

"Wake up, Helena," Mr. Lanfield said forcefully. "Where are you? Come back. You're safe, Lena. Now come back to us." His voice rumbled like thunder. He shouldn't talk so familiarly to her aunt! He shouldn't look at her so—an ear-piercing whistle from him made her wince and made Auntie jump. Perhaps she couldn't fault him for his approach, if it worked. Aunt Helena blinked a few times and then stood shakily, nearly knocking the bottle from Mr. Lanfield's hand. Her aunt's eyes darted around, and she looked confused and wary.

She looked like a stranger. Mr. Lanfield rose too but was careful not to touch her. He made soothing noises until she sat back down, appearing deflated and so very sad. Vanessa wrapped her arms around her aunt's shoulders, and the tremors running through this woman who was a second mother to her alarmed her even more. A sick feeling spread through her stomach. This was so much worse than the previous spells.

"What happened to your husband, Mrs. Martin?" he asked softly. Vanessa rested her head on Auntie's shoulder, hoping to hear her response but, at the same time, dreading the answer.

Aunt Helena shook her head. "It was a long time ago."

"Not so long in your mind, I'd bet."

"Auntie," she said cautiously, not wishing to send the delicate woman into a relapse. "Uncle Isaiah wasn't truly in an accident, was he?" No one in the family ever talked about it, but she remembered when he had been brought home. A freak accident, her mother had said. He'd never woken. She could picture Auntie trying to spoon broth into his mouth, could see him fading quickly in just a few days. She could still hear the muffled weeping when her aunt had shut the door on everyone near the end. *A terrible tragedy no one could have foreseen*, her mother had repeated in the months that followed. Uncle's death had devastated everyone. It was no wonder Aunt Helena hid away in her house, shrouded by grief.

But this reaction, Auntie's trance-like state and abject terror—this was something else entirely.

The trembling eased, and she felt her aunt straightening, pulling away, and then their positions somehow switched, with her aunt's arm around her, supporting her.

"Dearie, your uncle is gone, and nothing can bring him back," Aunt Helena said. The flatness of her tone was at least a marginal improvement over fear. "The particulars are in the past."

"If I may say, Mrs. Martin, the past can be a stubborn beast, rearing and bucking long after you thought it domesticated." He seemed about to say more, but shut his mouth when Auntie looked directly at him. There was something inscrutable in that look. She was surprised Mr. Lanfield could speak so vividly, so succinctly poetical. He'd been so cold to her aunt, but little glimpses of compassion like this one reassured her. Now if only Aunt Helena would soften a bit, perhaps this journey would be less of an ordeal.

"You've given me more than enough warning, sir, about how Marksby clings to my past transgressions," Auntie snapped at him, "and I am well aware of how persistently the past forces itself into the present . . . and the future."

This agitation couldn't possibly be good for her aunt, whose face had gone from chalky white to an uncomfortable redness.

"Shall we get down and walk a bit, Auntie, if you've a mind to? A turn in the air could do you good."

"That sounds like a fine idea." Her aunt patted her shoulder and stood, more solidly this time, then climbed down from the cart with efficient, confident movements. Pray God there would be no more of these episodes. If they'd taken the train as Auntie intended, she would have been at a loss about what to do, and they wouldn't have had Mr. Lanfield to rely on. After a brief stroll, they all agreed that Aunt Helena had returned to normal and didn't appear to be at risk of relapsing. At least not immediately. Still, it took many miles before Vanessa felt the tension leave her body, and a nagging voice told her things would only get worse.

Chapter 9

From a distance, the village looked exactly as she remembered it. The houses, the storefronts, the chapel, all as sedate and tidy as she'd pictured in her mind. It wasn't until they entered the main thoroughfare that she saw all the small indications of age and decline.

"Is that the Farington house? What happened to them?" The fine white exterior so vivid in her memory was now stained with spattered mud, overgrown with weeds that had taken root in cracks along the base of the house. A few of the windowpanes had been knocked out.

"After their eldest son died in India, they moved to Manchester."

"Jack is dead?" He had been just a boy when she'd left, probably no older than Tommy. He'd grown up and joined the military and was already gone. A chill ran through her, and she said a brief, silent prayer for her own Bartholomew's safety. She shook her head in disbelief and barely managed to catch the rest of Daniel's explanation.

". . . so the Faringtons followed their remaining sons to Manchester in hopes of starting fresh."

Starting fresh. The way he said it sounded hollow, false, almost as if he were trying to soften the news. They passed more houses and shops that appeared abandoned and neglected. The fields beyond the village, in contrast, looked as though time stood still. Aside from some new structures and fences, the familiar hills and dales brought her surprisingly great solace. Lazily grazing sheep dotted the landscape, and a warm breeze gusted through the tall grass in the distance, making it undulate in waves. Keen, sweet nostalgia swept through her in a rush at the picturesque sight. How often had she stood, watching herds graze, watching the land breathe? How often had she run through those fields as a child? The warmth of memory drained abruptly. The

Lanfield and Thorton properties were to have become one, just as their families had intended her and Gordy to be. She had to find a way to make amends.

Mr. Lanfield slowed the cart as it turned off the main road and followed a track that lodged her heart in her throat. She focused on the path behind them, fearing what changes time had wrought in this place she once called home. As the cart pulled to a stop, the luggage shifted in the back.

Vanessa had already hopped down from the cart. "Auntie, surely you don't mean to unpack here in the lane. This looks like such a charming old place. I cannot wait to go exploring."

"Just you wait, my girl. It shall be a whole new world for you. We're not in London anymore." As she turned to her niece abruptly, a zing of panic caught her by surprise. She couldn't bring herself to look at the house now that they were stopped before it. From a distance, it had been exactly the home she remembered. She swallowed a sudden bitterness in her mouth. Of course her home wouldn't be the same. But what changes had time wrought? "It is too soon to talk of exploring when we've only just arrived. Your great-grandmother may need a great deal of care. We must first see what we can do to ease the burdens of the household. Once we know what's what, then we'll start making plans."

That was the suitably responsible course of action. It just happened to align quite nicely with the leaden ball of dread coalescing in her belly. Feeling suddenly heated and suffocating, she undid her bonnet and took a deep, fortifying breath. Then she looked up.

Blinking quickly against the telltale stinging of her eyes, she climbed down from the cart and stood before the great house. Her mind raced to take in everything at once: the sturdy brick, the hedges that her father would never have allowed to grow so random and riotous, the broken fencing around the barn. Her eyelids stung as all these concrete reminders spoke of one truth: her father was well and truly gone. Mother too. Long ago, she'd resigned herself to never seeing them again, and she'd mourned their deaths when the news came to her. But the Thorton house's state of decay and neglect made the loss real. Without her parents here to care for it, all they had worked to build and nurture was crumbling.

"Do you wish me to bring your things in for you?" Daniel asked.

It was a kindness she wouldn't have expected at the beginning of their trip. Staring at the house with a lump in her throat, she appreciated the gesture more than she could say.

"No, Mr. Lanfield. You've been more than kind to allow us to travel with you. We can manage this last little distance," she replied, attempting to smile.

He didn't press. Instead, he looked at her strangely and nodded. Perhaps he understood. She needed to take this step without assistance. Once she and Vanessa bade him farewell, she suggested her niece wait at the bottom of the stairs with their things while she went up to the door and knocked firmly.

She nearly burst into tears when Mrs. Weathers opened the door, her hands gnarled from years of domestic labor and gray hair escaping her cap. Oh, the dear sweet woman and her husband had served Gran for as long as she could recall. The scent of yeast and flour that wafted from the old woman shot Helena back to when she was a girl running around the kitchen, trying to sneak a bit of bread or cake for her sister or for the neighbor children. She suspected now that Mrs. Weathers had let her get away with it, at least some of the time. Judging by Mrs. Weathers's shocked expression, Helena's letter responding to Gran had never arrived.

"Saints preserve us, it's you," the housekeeper said breathlessly.

She bobbed her head, feeling as if she were fourteen again. "It is a pleasure to see you, Mrs. Weathers. I hope you have been well." When the woman nodded, she turned to Vanessa and continued, "Please allow me to introduce my niece, Vanessa. She's one of Elizabeth's girls."

Mrs. Weathers shifted her focus, and her expression immediately cleared. Elizabeth had always been her favorite. "Why, of course! The very image! Miss Vanessa, I'm happy to see you. Hard to believe your ma could have a daughter who's now almost grown herself. Come in, lasses! It's good you've come."

After brushing crumbs off a faded, threadbare apron, the housekeeper moved closer, as if to embrace her, but then pulled back with a frown. The woman's obvious pleasure at her arrival dissipated like vapor. They'd both been caught up in the moment. Crossing this threshold for the first time in a score of years, she'd felt at home again. But she'd forgotten Mr. Lanfield's warnings. "Your grandmother is in quite a state," Mrs. Weathers added, brusquely. "I'll take you to her straight away. The rest can wait."

She nodded and gestured to Vanessa, who stepped into the breach with her usual aplomb. Bright and cheerful, Ness chattered away as Mrs. Weathers led them upstairs to the room that had once belonged to her parents. As they came up to the closed door, she realized that she was holding her breath. Her whole body was tense, bracing as if her parents stood beyond that door, waiting to confront her for her abandonment. But they weren't. They couldn't be. With that realization came another. Oh, how sharply her heart longed for even their censure, if it meant she could see them again.

The housekeeper rubbed her hands on her apron and reached for the doorknob, then said, "You should be prepared. She might not be very alert today."

"Much has changed, it's true, Mrs. Weathers. But I can only hope that she recognizes me at least a little."

"Don't get your hopes up. 'Tisn't you. I knew you right away. Some days are particularly bad for her. You cannot tell her state just by looking at her, though. And her breathing doesn't sound so good today."

Another slip of time jolted her as the room assaulted her senses. The curtains were the same, the afternoon light making them glow. This room was so familiar, echoing with laughter and warmth. And yet it wasn't, not anymore. The bedding was faded, and dust had accumulated in the crevices of the wardrobe and the shadowy corner beyond it. Even the smallest dust mote wouldn't have dared defy Ma. Then the smell hit her. The scent of a sickroom, dank and tainted.

But it was the sight of the tiny, motionless woman tucked in the bed that made her heart seize. Gran had always been thin, but now she appeared gaunt and lifeless. She was never one to sit for a moment; to see the dear woman languishing pricked Helena's heart with a thousand arrows. Gran's hair had already been gray, but now it was patchy and fragile. Her grandmother looked so small under the covers, and it took every ounce of strength she had to keep from bursting into tears yet again.

"Grand-dame," Mrs. Weathers whispered in her ear, "you've some bonny visitors. One of your lost lasses has come home."

Gran coughed thickly as she opened her eyes. She struggled to raise herself to a seated position while Mrs. Weathers adjusted the pillows behind her. Helena tried to assist, but the housekeeper waved her away with a cursory, "I've got her." She stepped back to stay out of the way, and when her eyes met her grandmother's, she could see the dear woman's eyes glistening. A single tear slipped as Gran said, "My Lena girl." Awe and disbelief shone on her face. If Helena let slip a tear or two as well, it was no wonder. To see this precious woman who'd been such a great and vibrant light in her youth was something she'd never thought would happen again.

"How are you, Gran?" she asked, when she could find her voice. She approached the bed hesitantly.

"Ah, these days I am thus and so. Naught to say about my health," Gran replied faintly. Awake, she looked slightly less frail and shrunken, but her skin was still pale. And, of course, Helena couldn't forget what Gran had written in her letter.

"We received your note. You wrote to say you were at death's door, and Lizzie and I should hurry home, ananthers we should miss you. Your words, Gran. Matters were urgent, aye?"

Gran frowned and shook her head at the floor, her confusion evident. Helena couldn't keep her distance any longer. So many years had passed. She knelt by the bed and covered her grandmother's hand with her own, trying not to notice how the skin hung off her delicate bones. "Was it you who wrote to us?"

She saw the tears welling in her grandmother's eyes, even as her own vision began to blur again. A delicate hand touched her cheek. "Honestly, I don't recall, my sweet Lena. I must've, for here you are." Gran's wan voice stretched as she struggled for breath. "You always were such a bonny lass. Is this your daughter, then?" she said, peering at Vanessa.

"No, Gran, this is Elizabeth's eldest daughter, Vanessa. She's here in her mother's stead."

"Lizzie couldn't get here herself?" Gran's face fell, but a spark flared in her eye. "What's that girl about? Your parents raised you girls better than that. Family comes first."

"But, Mrs. Thorton," Vanessa interrupted, moving to the edge of the bed, "my mother is home with my young sisters and cousins. She would be here if she could, I assure you, but she sent me because it was the only way."

Gran stared at her for a few long, tense moments. "You look like your mother, child, pretty and docile. But I sense you have a wild streak in you. Lena, you need to keep a close watch on this one."

Vanessa blushed deep red, the color Helena recognized as a warning sign. The poor girl was deeply embarrassed and on the verge of lashing out.

"Don't mind her," she whispered in her niece's ear. "Let's get our things unpacked and then see about making ourselves useful." To Gran, she said in a normal tone, "We'll let you rest now, Gran. We'll see you closer to suppertime."

"You go on, but I would like Miss Vanessa's company for a bit longer."

Even after all these years, she could hear the command in Gran's unsteady voice. And even now, she could not dare think of disobeying. She nodded but pulled Vanessa aside to say, "Don't let her upset you. It's been a long time, and she seems a bit confused. Be kind. I'll come get you in a quarter hour."

"She can't be that confused if she's already found my wild streak." To her credit, Vanessa didn't pout or flounce. In fact, she added, with a wide smile, "Mother said much the same thing to me when she convinced me to come with you. I'm sure we'll get along famously."

Not for the first time, Helena was impressed by her niece's newfound aplomb. She gave the girl a pat on the cheek and went to find Mrs. Weathers.

In the room that had once belonged to Helena and her sister, the housekeeper clucked apologies for the condition of the bedrooms and moved to uncover the furniture. Helena wondered if Mrs. Weathers had already decided they weren't worth the hospitality. Her slow motions were not those of the brisk, hardy woman Helena knew from childhood. Then she caught the old woman grimacing as she stretched up to pull the covering off the wardrobe. *For shame, Helena. Whether or not she resents you, you cannot let her do all this for you.*

"My niece and I shall see to the rooms, ma'am. There's no need to trouble yourself on our account. We mean to help, not to be an added burden to anyone."

The housekeeper's relief was undeniable as she straightened her spine and rubbed the back of her neck.

"It's been quite some time since these rooms have been used. I'm not as young as I once was, Miss Helena."

"None of us are, Mrs. Weathers. Please don't let me keep you from your other duties." She added, quietly, "It's Mrs. Martin. I haven't been Miss Helena for a long while."

The housekeeper made a noncommittal noise and then met her gaze. "How long do you plan to stay, Mrs. Martin?"

"I don't yet know. I wish to speak with Gran's physician about her illness." As she helped uncover the furniture, she continued, "And about the possibility of relocating her to London, where Elizabeth and I can both see to her care." Only when the other woman gasped did Helena realize what she'd said. She should have been more circumspect, waited until she saw the situation more fully. But the strain of travel had loosened her tongue.

Mrs. Weathers looked shocked, and even perhaps offended, at the idea. "She won't go, you know."

"She might not have a choice, depending on what's best for her health."

"For those of us who know the meaning of home and family, leaving isn't a choice."

Well, now she knew where the old housekeeper stood.

Helena sighed and said, "I would hazard a guess that my niece and I shall be here a month, at the most." No longer than that. God help her, she wouldn't put up with this for more than a month. If Gran were willing, travel arrangements could surely be made quickly and the estate settled within that time. If Gran wouldn't go . . . well, they'd have to make things up as they went. "When is the physician due to check on her condition?"

The housekeeper's confused expression set her nerves on edge. "I don't—that is, she doesn't wish—that is, I can't really say."

She let out an even heavier sigh. *Saints preserve us.* They hadn't even called a physician! Who knew what ailments Gran suffered and how they might be eased? What if a simple remedy existed? "Please send for one immediately!"

"You'll have to speak with her about that. She's not comfortable with the nearest physician's impertinent hands, she says."

"Oh, I'll speak with her. There must be someone who can see to her medical care properly."

Mrs. Weathers looked for a moment as if she'd been force-fed a bushel of lemons. "She won't like it."

"My grandmother requested that I come see her in her hour of need. Here I am, and I shall see that she receives the best possible care."

The lemons must have multiplied, because the woman's face screwed up even more tightly, as she said, "If you think our care's been inadequate or abusive, I wish you'd come out and say so. I've done my best to tend to the Grand-dame's needs, and it isn't an easy task. My husband and I have been in her service for over thirty years now, and we love her as if she were my own sister. If you want to accuse me of mistreatment, at least be direct about it."

Helena recoiled from the defensive outburst. Taking a step back, she responded, "Oh, no, Mrs. Weathers. Honestly, I meant nothing of the sort! You've always taken excellent care of Gran and seen to her every need. And I remember well her distrust of people outside of our family. But there have been medical advancements, and someone well-trained in modern medicine could make all the difference in her condition."

"Well, as I said, you'll have to discuss all that with her," Mrs. Weathers responded, mollified but clearly not completely convinced.

"Indeed, I shall. Believe me, I have no desire to upset the apple cart here. But new approaches do sometimes improve upon older ones."

"Yes, you would think so. Do as you see fit. I'm sure that's your plan in any case." With that astoundingly impertinent remark, the old woman swept out the room, shutting the door behind her. Helena could hear her mumbling down the hallway about having to start cooking dinner earlier with more mouths to feed.

She hadn't expected a warm welcome, but she couldn't help being distressed by the harsh reality.

The sun was setting as Daniel finally approached his home, dark and solitary. A tall, reedy figure on horseback stood in silhouette against the barn doors. He'd known village gossip traveled quickly, but here was incontrovertible proof. He couldn't see his brother's expression, but his presence didn't bode well. Gordon didn't normally welcome him home. That wasn't their way. They always met at dawn at the Lanfield main barn for work. When was the last time Gordon had set foot on his homestead? And Ruth would have his hide—well, both their hides—if her husband was late for supper.

When he pulled up to the doors, Gordon dismounted and moved to begin unbuckling the cart's harness.

"Heard you were back," Gordon said, his tone gruff and laconic, as usual.

"Aye."

They continued the work of getting Talos unhitched. The only noise for a while was the dull clang of buckles and slaps of leather as they went about their task. Daniel wasn't in any mood to volunteer information. When he turned to lead his tired horse into the barn, Gordon spoke.

"Heard you had passengers with you." Others might misinterpret the flat statement as casual conversation, but Gordon rarely spoke without purpose and direction. This was him being canny.

"Oh, aye." Daniel stopped and looked back at his brother. He cocked his head as he waited patiently for the next comment.

"A mother and daughter, some have guessed."

"You've heard a lot. Since when are you one to go gammering?" When his brother simply waved away his question, he decided there was no point in drawing out the inevitable revelations. Gordon probably already knew their identities, although a do-dance like this wasn't his brother's way. If he had a question, he would normally just ask directly. So maybe Gordon hadn't learned whom he'd brought back. Maybe Marksby didn't know, and the women were still a mystery. But everyone would find the truth of her identity soon; even if she stayed at the Thorton house, her presence couldn't stay hidden for long. "Niece, not daughter. And, in case you haven't yet heard, it was Helena Thorton, though now she's Mrs. Helena Martin. The girl, her niece, is Miss Elizabeth's bairn, nearly grown."

As if he'd mumped his sibling or slammed him in the stomach unawares, Gordon went slack-jawed. He knew the feeling well himself, especially as it related to Mrs. Martin. He nodded in sympathy as his brother began imitating a fish out of water, his mouth gaping, wavering, grasping at words instead of air. Finally, Gordon spoke, his voice hoarse, as if he had to push the words out. "What do you mean? Miss Helena? Returned?"

"For all the world, brother, I wish it weren't so, but I met her by chance in London. When she received a letter from Grand-dame Thorton, she set herself to returning. What do you know of their grandmother's illness?"

"Word is she's near death's door," Gordon said, looking serious, almost reverent. "Never thought I'd see the day."

"She has the heart of an ox, Mrs. Thorton does."

"No doubt," Gordon agreed, gruffly, "but I was talking about that strumpet, Miss Helena. Never thought she'd be so brazen as to show her face here again." His voice held a strange mix of anger and wonder, shot through with bitterness. "Maybe just after she ran off, realizing her mistake, or maybe when her mum passed . . . but it's been so long. Never would've thought to see her again."

"You needn't see her," Daniel replied. It would be best if Gordon didn't, if his shock was any indication. He knew his brother had been devastated by her betrayal, but they hadn't spoken of the woman in years. Gordon's rancor now was palpable. Best for both he and Helena that they pretend she wasn't near. "She's here to care for the Grand-dame, that's all. I already warned her to avoid the village."

"Why did you bring her?" Gordon asked accusingly.

"If you'd told me when I left that I would come back with the likes of her and her kin, I'd have said you were cracked. I still don't gaum how it happened. When her Gran sent for her, she couldn't refuse. She needs to be here. As to why I drove them, I was there when the decision was made. She has very determined, very persuasive friends who said she and the lass wouldn't be safe traveling by rail." He hesitated and decided instantly that Gordon didn't need to know about Mrs. Martin's fears and fainting spells. He summarized, "They were in need, and it seemed only right to bring them when I was traveling to the very place they needed to go. I couldn't turn my back on them."

"Sure, you could," Gordon said firmly. "If that—if she were so determined, she could've made her way on her own. If she had trouble, why, it might've convinced her not to bother."

He considered telling his brother that was exactly what he'd intended. But it wasn't what he'd done in the end so it wasn't worth rehashing. Mrs. Martin was here now, for good or ill. He could only hope the woman would be judicious enough not to draw attention to herself.

"Best keep your distance from the Thortons while they're here," Gordon proclaimed as he stood in the stance Daniel had come to recognize when they were much younger. His brother was laying down the law or at least trying to. He never took Gordon's imperious orders well.

"Think I don't already know that?" he responded, matching his tone to his brother's. "What need have I to seek their company again? You know me better than that."

"Aye, I do know you. And that's exactly why I said it. Does she know about your homestead? About the property line?"

He cringed inwardly. Anyone with eyes could have seen how Mrs. Martin had reeled from the changes she'd seen here.

"Nay. I haven't said anything. She's here to care for her Gran, not the Thorton lands. The knowledge of the land transfer would only bring her pain. And there's naught she could do to change it now."

"That bodes well," his brother said, his voice heavy with sarcasm. "You should have convinced her to stay in London. She doesn't belong here."

"Gordon, be calm. What's done is done, and she won't be here long."

"Easy for you to say, brother. Just stay away from her."

"That's my plan."

Chapter 10

After confirming with Mrs. Weathers that the post office was where she remembered and that the path there was the same, Helena rushed out after breakfast, leaving Vanessa to help the housekeeper clean up and see to Gran's morning needs. Anxious to assure Elizabeth and the children that they'd arrived safely, Helena penned a letter to them the night before. She'd have to be prudent about sending missives in light of her limited funds and her grandmother's need of medical attention, but this letter should go as soon as possible to reassure everyone at home. She'd chosen her words carefully, not wanting to alarm her sister about Gran's severe condition but needing to vent some of her shock at the changes she'd encountered.

So alarmed was she by her grandmother's difficult breathing that she'd spent the night in the rocker by her bed, dozing lightly and awakened by every cough. It reminded her of nights she'd kept vigil over the boys when they caught sniffles. That same post-vigil fatigue had settled into her bones, and every step felt like she was weighed down with stones.

Traversing the fields, she had that same sense of time slippage, as if she were in her youth again. Only occasionally did small changes strike her consciousness as odd, and even then she wasn't sure if they were new or simply not remembered. The small stone bridge arched over the beck where she expected it to be, but it looked and felt a bit different than she recalled. Farther along, on a slight rise, she encountered a low wall she was sure hadn't been there before. Then, as she stepped over the stile, she saw a compact house framed by a grove of trees. A barn sat a few yards beyond it. She was absolutely certain these structures were new, and she looked around in confusion. This was Thorton property, was it not? Who could be living there? She would have to ask Mrs. Weathers about this new occupant.

These new surprising features lent her imagination convenient fodder, distracting her from her body's morning aches and twinges. With each step toward the village, she pictured the stone wall and imagined building it higher and wider and thicker. In her mind, it could withstand any onslaught, any criticism, any insult lobbed at her. This mental exercise had served her well for many years with but a few exceptions. Whatever derision or enmity she encountered in her former hometown, it would not change who she was and what she valued. It wouldn't change the love she'd found and the life she'd built.

When she entered Marksby, brimming with confidence and resolve, the lane through the village was quiet, no man nor beast in sight. As she approached the shop where the post was run, some women exited laden with packages. They stared at her as if she were some kind of museum exhibit, so she greeted them pleasantly and proceeded into the building. She remembered that too, the wariness with which Marksbians viewed strangers in their midst. Isaiah had noted it during his stay long ago, claiming that what made the Thorton household so particularly appealing was their ready hospitality in an area so forbidding. From today's fleeting encounter, she didn't recognize the women, and she was sure they didn't recognize her or else there would have been more explosive reactions, at least according to Mr. Lanfield. But then, she still suspected he'd been exaggerating for effect.

Her interaction with the postmaster was likewise mundane. When he inquired about her business in Marksby, she explained her grandmother's situation, and his reaction was neutral and polite as he wished Mrs. Thorton well. Surely, Mr. Lanfield's perceptions of the village's condemnation must have been clouded by his own animosity.

Just before she left the shop, she heard a low female voice whispering furiously thorough a heavy curtain behind the counter. The postmaster pushed through the divider, saying "Now, now, dear . . ." She couldn't discern the trouble, but she refused to believe that it had anything to do with her. Shopkeepers had many concerns.

As she closed the shop door firmly behind her, she was shocked to find that the main thoroughfare was no longer deserted. Various men and women, some of them in tight groups and others standing individually in doorways, dotted the lane. *How odd*, she thought, as her breathing quickened. Even odder, she couldn't help but notice, was that they all appeared to be watching her. Everywhere she turned, the people along the road were looking at her. A woman at the curb down the way whispered something to her companion, whose eyes widened as she stared and stared. Later, when she recalled the incident in the safety of her bedroom, she would realize that there had been no more than two dozen people out there, but in the moment, they seemed legion. Helena's stomach turned over as she looked around at all the unfriendly faces, and that familiar surge of anxiety shot up through her throat. She turned toward home, focusing on moving her feet forward. Keep walking. One step, then another, then another. Ignore everything else. Just keep moving forward.

"Helena Thorton!" someone called out behind her. She stopped, her heart pounding so hard she feared it would burst out of her chest where she stood, and she turned in the direction of the high feminine voice that carried to her. Her throat dried and seized, but she couldn't swallow. *I'm Mrs. Martin now. Mrs. Martin. I have a family; I have young children who need their mother.* She opened her mouth but couldn't get any words out. An older woman who looked vaguely familiar nodded and said, in a shrill, cutting voice, "I heard you'd come. You should be ashamed to set foot here! Now you can bear witness to the ruin you left behind." With that, she slowly and quite obviously turned until she presented her back. The woman stood with one hand on a thick cane and another on her husband's arm. Yes, suddenly she recognized them, this couple who'd been friends with her parents, although she could not guess their names. The wife must have said something to her spouse because he nodded, looked at Helena sharply, and then very slowly and deliberately turned his back. Then, one after another, without a word, the villagers along the street followed suit. Not a single person spared her a merciful look or gesture. An awful silence filled the air. She'd never felt so mortified.

She rushed out of the village. *Keep moving forward. All will be well. Keep moving forward. All will be well.* Only after she'd crossed a few stiles and several hills stood between her and the village did she stop to lean against a tree and catch her breath. She would not cry, would not allow the village the satisfaction of insulting her. If any hot tears fell, she wouldn't acknowledge them.

When she arrived at the Thorton house, Vanessa asked, "Is something wrong, Auntie? Has something upset you?"

She shook her head. "Nothing at all, dear. Perhaps I'm not so accustomed to this fresh country air anymore. It will pass, I'm sure." The rest of the household need not know about her humiliation. As soon as her grandmother's health was resolved, she and Vanessa would happily escape the confines of this petty, small-minded, vindictive little village.

News tended to travel with remarkable speed through these lands, and so it was no surprise to Daniel when some of the neighboring farmers rode out to meet him as he went along the Lanfield perimeter, reacquainting himself with the flocks. By the time he paused for lunch at the northernmost point, half a dozen men had found reason to greet him and share their perspectives on the return of the pariah Helena Thorton Martin. More importantly, they'd felt it necessary to share their wives' surprisingly strong and vocal objections to her presence in the village. Half a dozen times he explained that she only intended to care for the Grand-dame and that he'd done only his Christian duty in assisting her and that he, of all people, was as irate about her return as anyone else.

A heavy ball of dread settled in his wame as he caught sight of his brother galloping toward him. Gordon handled the books and oversaw the farm's operations, which meant he rarely rode out this far.

"What's wrong, brother?" he called out.

"You need to fix this situation with Mrs. Martin and quickly!"

Daniel resisted the urge to roll his eyes at his brother's urgency. "This was so urgent you needed to ride up here? We had this discussion last night. My association with the woman is done. There's naught to fix." Except for a few concerned neighbors, whom he'd set straight.

"Have you any idea how many people have already been to the house this morning? Prattling like fishwives. If it wasn't the men coming to me spouting things about injustice, it was the women coming to commiserate with Ruth."

"Aye, I got an earful from some of our neighbors along the wall."

"People keep asking about you too. Why did you have to bring her yourself? Let her make her way as any stranger would. Folks are confounded and none too happy with you."

He'd been asking himself the same thing for days now. He thought back to the sight of her helpless and insensible at the Great Exhibition, of her standing vulnerable and defenseless in the courtyard of the inn. Any woman in such circumstances would draw sympathy, wouldn't she? He had cause to despise her, but he needn't turn into a monster and abandon his own values in return.

"It was a simple twist of fate, Gordon. Who would have guessed that, in a city of thousands, I would have encountered her? And in such a time of need?" Unaccountably, he was reluctant to mention her fainting spells. That seemed too personal, not his to share. "The Grand-dame was practically our own grandmother once. Mrs. Martin has persuasive friends in London, and one of their husbands might yet prove to be a fortuitous connection." Even as he said it, he could hear the weakness of his arguments. But he couldn't fully convey the imperative he'd felt in his breast to do her the simple courtesy of a ride in his cart. Gordon's lips quirked skeptically. "You would have done the same, Gordon. Despite everything, you would have brought her here yourself. There were . . . other factors, and it wouldn't have been right to leave her and her niece without escort."

"That damn noble protective streak of yours."

"It's been a long time, and Mrs. Martin has changed, I think. What she did to you was inexcusable, but all our lives have changed a great deal since then."

"She would be wise to stay out of sight as much as possible. Have you heard about her visit to the Wyatt shop this morning?"

As his brother related the story about the villagers shunning her, a chill ran through Daniel. What had possessed her to parade herself in Marksby the day after her arrival? She was lucky they'd treated her so cordially, compared to what they might've done. An unwelcome image of her insensible and injured, even bloodied, flashed before his eyes, and his entire body tensed.

He couldn't help the odd sense of admiration at how Mrs. Martin blithely dismissed the negativity she encountered. She soldiered on. He'd expected her to collapse into a helpless mess and run back to London weeping, but she'd held her head high and faced her critics honestly, bravely.

Despite himself, he appreciated how she'd negotiated a space for herself here. And he had to admit too that his visceral reactions to her reawakened a fire in him that he hadn't felt toward a woman in a long time. Perhaps it was the fact that there was no chance of emotional attachment between them. Perhaps it was his native protectiveness spilling into something more. Perhaps it was the intensity of his animosity seeking a different outlet. Whatever it was, he could no longer deny his body's heightened awareness of her. Nor his increasingly insistent desire to be in her presence, to watch over her, to shield her. A heat he hadn't felt in years surged through him at the thought of her delicate neck.

He shifted in his saddle as a particular body part awakened. What irony that he'd be aroused by this woman. The feel of her hair, her soft pillowing flesh—the memory of even the lightest touch set him alight rather inconveniently.

Chapter 11

Memories of her recent humiliation fresh and vivid in her mind, Helena hesitated in the doorway of the village shop, her hand trembling as she reached for the doorknob. Meeting her niece's gaze, she said, "We shall be quick. No time for frivolities or trinkets."

"Yes, Auntie. As you said earlier, I shall keep to the list and only the list."

She'd warned Vanessa in the most general terms about how standoffish the villagers might be, but she couldn't bring herself to tell anyone about the shunning. Mrs. Weathers had begun to soften toward her, showing her tiny kindnesses by allowing her to help in the kitchen, suggesting things she might find useful in the house, pointing out things she and her sister had left behind that they might enjoy. But perhaps that was a result of the diligence she and Vanessa had shown since their arrival. From sunup to the snuffing of the lights at night, every waking moment was devoted to Gran's well-being, including anything in the household that needed doing in order to promote her comfort. With Vanessa's help, she'd thoroughly scrubbed the sickroom, washed and aired the linens and window hangings, made the windows sparkle. They'd cleaned every inch of that bedroom. All that work did wonders, it seemed. Sun streamed in the windows, no longer impeded by cobwebs and dust. The very air, while still tinged with antiseptic and mustard poultices, was no longer musty and dank. It wasn't much, but it was a start. The doctor's visit was reassuring, and he'd thankfully not advocated any bloodletting. Instead, he'd provided them with several natural remedies for treatment, as well as a list of necessary items for her grandmother's comfort. After he departed, Gran dismissed his ideas as muckment. But Helena didn't think it would do any harm to try.

She didn't miss her niece's precocious tone, and she hoped Vanessa would conduct herself in a dignified manner. This wasn't London, and these people wouldn't understand her forthright, sometimes impish nature. She smiled tightly as she gestured for her niece to lead the way into the store.

Yet again, the past collided with the present. When she'd first come to mail the letter to Elizabeth confirming their safe arrival, she hadn't bothered to look around much, so preoccupied had she been worrying about the reactions her reappearance would incite. Now, she was at leisure to observe. So much of the large room was as she remembered it, the shelves packed to the ceiling, the tables piled with incongruous items. Here was a basket of ribbons next to bottles of lamp oil. There were lollipops next to sewing needles. She hadn't recognized the postmaster. The store used to belong to Mrs. Robinson, but she'd surely be in her nineties by now. That remarkable woman had always known exactly where to find any item in the store, always seen the order beneath the seeming chaos. As Vanessa went directly to the counter with the list in hand, Helena moved quietly toward a corner stacked with fabrics. Perhaps a bright new nightgown or a small pillow might brighten Gran's day. A simple item would take less than a day to sew. She rifled through the materials: cottons, wools, even a silk. A lovely yellow calico caught her eye, and then a simple blue worsted . . . so many possibilities. Immersed in the colors, patterns, and textures, even the distinct scents, she didn't realize how much time had passed until she felt a tap on her shoulder.

"Auntie, our order is ready."

She straightened and made her way to the counter at the rear of the building. A woman she didn't recognize stood packing their items into a crate. As she and Vanessa approached, however, the woman looked at her and froze with a sour expression and narrowed eyes. Helena's stomach dropped, but she continued to move forward. Just before she reached the counter, the woman picked up the half-packed crate without saying a word and went through a curtained doorway into a back room, leaving the remaining items on the counter. The moment the clerk was out of view, Helena heard what she had to assume was the woman's voice, loud and vociferous.

"Louis, can you believe that Thorton strumpet has the nerve to show her face here? Again?"

Louis? That wasn't the name of any of Mrs. Robinson's sons, at least not that she could recall. He must be the postmaster she'd encountered. Now she could only hear the deep indistinct mumbling of his voice, not his actual sentiment. His rough tone was not reassuring. Then she heard the woman say, "Well, if you won't get those whores out of here, I will! They can rot, for all I care."

"Auntie, what is happening?" Vanessa whispered. "She was so helpful before. Is she talking about us? What could have changed her demeanor so abruptly?"

"Undoubtedly, me, dear. My very appearance, as Mr. Lanfield so accurately predicted," she replied tersely.

"What is wrong with your appearance? You are dressed quite normally."

"Oh, my sweet, don't joke. Some people here have very long memories. It is as Mr. Lanfield predicted." She could hardly stand to let the words pass through her lips. He'd been absolutely right.

"What should we do now?" her niece asked.

"What can we do? We wait for her to return. Gran needs those remedies."

They didn't have to wait very long. As another shopper entered, the bell attached to the door rang out, and the clerk poked her head out of the curtains. Her jaw set and her eyes icy, she met Helena's gaze before shifting away to find the newcomer.

"Oh, Mrs. Carter! How nice to see you! I shall be with you momentarily." Then the clerk disappeared into the back room again.

Standing at the counter, Helena spied Mrs. Carter, an older woman she recognized from her youth. "Good morning," she called, and the other woman merely narrowed her eyes. Had she been on the street that day? Had she been one of the ones to turn her back? When the clerk returned, Helena braced herself. That sick feeling in her stomach grew, and heat prickled her cheeks.

"You won't be able to purchase what you want here," the clerk said. "You should go." The clerk moved toward the end of the counter, her attention focused on Mrs. Carter. Helena stepped into her path, equal parts embarrassed and determined.

"May we at least purchase the essentials we need, Missus . . . ?" she asked, dipping her head. She could swallow her pride for her grandmother's sake.

"My name, not that it is any of your concern, is Mrs. Wyatt, and my husband and I run a respectable shop. We reserve the right to decline to serve customers, as prudence demands," the woman replied, frowning and unyielding. "Your money is no good here. I objected to his even taking your letter, but he's a duty as postmaster that he can't ignore."

"But we need at least the mustard seed and herbs and flour for my great-grandmother, Mrs. Thorton," Vanessa interjected. "As you may know, she's very, very ill, and the physician is not hopeful. Her breathing has become labored. We desperately need anything that can give her some ease."

"That is not my concern," the clerk said, but her expression weakened.

Helena whispered to her niece, "If you think you can convince her, I shall step away. Clearly, my presence is the problem. She treated you as a normal customer. Whatever the cost, see if you can at least get what is necessary, for Gran's sake."

When Vanessa nodded slightly, Helena turned to the clerk and said, "Please excuse me, Mrs. Wyatt. I am sorry to disturb you and your patrons." She made her way to the door, bumping against a table in her haste and nearly toppling a lantern on display. She hated the thought of leaving her niece to deal with the transaction, but she was certain there was no way the woman would concede in front of her. She couldn't but notice that, as she wound through the tables toward the door, Mrs. Carter watched her aptly and maintained a wide berth. How lowering.

As she exited the shop, she heard Vanessa pleading quite prettily. Sweet, headstrong girl.

Outside, she took a deep breath, the air refreshing her spirit and clearing away some of the miasma that had pressed upon her in the shop. Mr. Lanfield had warned them; only now did his words coalesce into reality. All the anger and resentment she'd attributed to her parents and the Lanfields—it wasn't just them, and it wasn't just a matter of strong emotion. Emotion translated to action, action that affected not only her but anyone attached to her. She'd been prepared to be treated as a pariah. Yet it hadn't occurred to her that such malice would be extended to innocents—to her vulnerable grandmother, to her sweet niece. Had her parents been thus condemned by everyone? Had her grandmother been abandoned, leading to her condition?

She worried her lip as she waited for Vanessa and breathed a deep sigh when the girl opened the door carrying a small package. It wasn't large enough to hold even half of what they'd originally wanted, but it was better than nothing. One look at Vanessa's pale face raised her internal alarms again, however, and she quickly led the girl in the direction of home. Vanessa's quick but wavering smile only worried her more.

As if by tacit agreement, Helena and her niece walked out of Marksby at a swift pace. Ribbons of fluffy clouds now filled the sky, making odd shadow patterns on the land around them. She saw darkening skies far ahead of them. That was all the day wanted—for them to be caught in a storm on this road.

"I have never encountered such viciousness, Auntie!" Vanessa burst out. "Well, at least not personally. That woman was unbearably rude! It galled me to hand over our money to her."

"Did she insult you again after I left the building?" She could bear any insult against her, but she wouldn't allow her innocent niece to be the target of such ugliness.

"No . . . not really. Not exactly." Her niece's clenched fists belied her words, as did the way the girl's chin jutted out defensively.

"What did she say, dear? You can tell me."

"She didn't say anything to insult me personally, but she defamed you horribly." Vanessa's hands rose in fists, surely without her awareness, and she spoke with such righteous indignation. "She was so bitter and angry and used such coarse language. I've heard worse but only on the streets of London."

Helena could only imagine the woman's string of complaints and epithets. Her stomach twisted at the thought of her niece suffering abuse on her behalf.

"Don't give her another thought. Her words mean nothing to me."

"She called us whores, didn't she? When she was in the back?" Vanessa shot back, indignantly. "No one has ever called *me* a whore. And you are one of the most admirable women I know. She doesn't know a thing about us, and yet she spewed such slander!"

"Shh. It's over now. Perhaps if we need anything else while we're here, we can take a small jaunt to Bradford instead."

"That is how you plan to respond, Auntie? You cannot be run off by such horrible people. That's not right. It's not fair." Her niece looked at her, affronted and resolute.

"Dear heart, as unpleasant as the streets of London can be, you haven't seen this kind of nastiness up close. I can only hope Gran's health will improve soon, and we won't have to seek supplies again. If I've caused so much trouble that it hasn't dissipated over the past twenty years, I don't expect to mend such a massive breach in a week or two. It would take too much valuable energy to combat that level of animosity now. Gran needs our attention, not this ancient history. Believe me, all will be well."

"If you say so," Vanessa replied, as if tired of the conversation. "But it's still not just, and you shouldn't have to suffer it. Oh, look at those lovely flowers! They would certainly brighten Gran's rooms!" With her characteristically swift shift in attention, Vanessa veered into the field and quickly picked a handful. They continued on their way in what Helena hoped was a companionable silence, having left the village and its unpleasantness behind them.

The clouds had thickened considerably by the time they reached the milestone Helena knew was their halfway point. The sun was no longer visible. The gray skies and shadowed hills were achingly reminiscent.

"What are you thinking of, Auntie? You look so far away, suddenly."

"I'm just missing your uncle. We first met along this road to Marksby, you know. Or perhaps you don't. My boys have heard the story countless times with endless amusement, but I don't know if you ever heard it."

"I don't think so. Was it romantic?"

"Hardly, unless mud and embarrassment are now considered romantic. One never knows with you young ones." She flicked a flower petal in the girl's direction and caught a distant, dreamy look in her niece's eye. Was it put there by thoughts of whoever had prompted her parents to send her out of London? All too well she remembered the feelings suggested by that look, and she wasn't exactly in an authoritative position to chastise her niece for developing impulsive romantic attachments. A heavy cloud slipped in front of the sun again, placing them in a small circle of darkness while the rest of the hill glowed. An answering darkness slipped over her heart as bittersweet memories flooded her mind. "I was returning home from visiting my grandmother, in fact. This was when my grandfather was alive, and they lived at the Grove. I'd brought over some of my mother's wonderful pies, and in return Gran sent me back with a package of very special treats she'd received from a friend on the Continent. She assured me they were like nothing Elizabeth and I had ever tasted. She went on and on about them, making me promise to treat them with care."

"Didn't you just want to tear into them on your walk home?"

A pang shot through her. How like Vanessa she'd been!

"Oh, absolutely! It was temptation such that I'd never known before," she admitted. "After all, Gran's words made it such a challenge. What could possibly be that good? But I wasn't a child anymore, so I was determined to behave appropriately." That was perhaps the last thing she'd done back then that her family would deem appropriate. "I never did get to taste them."

"What happened?" Frowning down at the ground, Vanessa picked her way carefully around some large ruts.

"When I left Gran's house, the skies were ominous. Much worse than today. Still, I thought I could get home before the rains began. I was very wrong. I'd just reached this main road when the skies opened. Within minutes, my clothes were sopping, and the package was soaked through." Even now, she could feel the chill and the weight of her waterlogged cloak and skirt. "The rain came so hard and so fast that I ended up walking in mud up to my ankles and was at risk of losing my boots. At one point, I lost my footing, and my left leg got stuck in a deep rut that I hadn't seen because of all the water on the road. The mud was so heavy I couldn't pull myself out." A bitter taste flooded her throat as a flare of panic raced through her. She'd been trapped and alone. So long ago, and yet the sensations were imprinted on her skin. "I remember getting down on my hands and knees to try to work my foot loose. So then I was up to my elbows, my dress completely covered. I could feel dirt spattering on my face as the rain continued to pour. It was so cold and slimy, and that awful mud was everywhere."

A noise of disgust lifted her out of the memory, and Vanessa's horrified expression made her chuckle. If anyone would appreciate the total awfulness of the situation, it would be her fastidious niece.

"Oh, my sweet, it was even worse than you can imagine! I was no stranger to dirt and muck, having grown up on the farm, but this was truly a mud bath. And not the kind of mud bath that's come into fashion recently. It was in no way soothing or medicinal."

"It sounds ghastly!"

"Let's not forget that not only was I practically immersed, I was also immobilized. At one point, I tried to scoop the mud away from my leg, but I still couldn't see very well because of the murky water that had collected in the rut. I could only feel the mud flowing in as fast as I tried to dig it away. " She shivered now at the memory and felt panic returning, rising. Only one thought could calm her. "So you can imagine what a sight your uncle encountered."

"Oh, Auntie, how mortifying! That was how he found you?"

"Worse than that, dear, it was how he almost ran me over in his gig! There I was, bent over, plastered with mud, in the middle of a raging storm. Anyone driving by could have mistaken me for a boulder, I'm sure, if they saw me at all. I didn't even hear or see him until he had passed me and called his horse to halt. When he stepped down, oh, you can't imagine my combined relief and horror. Here was a stranger, a gentleman by his bearing and attire, and there I was, trapped and covered in muck. I was entirely at his mercy." He'd been such a welcome sight! Thinking back, she should have been at least a little fearful of him, given her vulnerable position. But she hadn't been. He'd been her savior, her strong and handsome knight rescuing her in her hour of distress. Yet again, she marveled now at how fortunate she'd been. How many girls had had those same thoughts only to find far too late that it was all an illusion? "When he saw my predicament, he simply yanked me up and out of the hole and asked me where I lived."

No need to mention how he'd reached into the muddy water to gauge the depth of the rut, how her skin had burned at the fleeting stroke of his hand against her leg, how her whole body had reacted to his nearness.

"I tried to tell him that I could make my way home on my own, but he wouldn't hear it. Said his mother would never forgive him for leaving a woman in such a predicament. So he drove me home. By the time we arrived, it was near dark and the storm had grown even stronger. My parents were so relieved that I was safe. They invited him to stay for the night since the roads to Bradford, where he was staying, would be impassable. That was how our courtship began."

No need to tell Vanessa about the heart of it, the way he'd talked with her on that drive as if they were the only two people on Earth, as if her thoughts and opinions mattered, as if he wanted to assuage all her curiosity about the wider world and indulge her adventurous ambitions. Within a fortnight of their meeting, she'd built quite grand plans about traveling Europe with him, about exploring Greek ruins together, about ocean voyages and train expeditions. When he'd proposed marriage a few weeks into their acquaintance, it had felt as if she were dreaming. Even now, it felt as if she'd inhabited a fantasy world. His sweet deference, appearing only in his most private, most vulnerable moments, had completely enthralled her. And everything he'd shown her about himself remained true throughout their marriage. God, she missed him so!

"Auntie! Watch your step!" Vanessa's abrupt exclamation pulled her from her reverie, and she just barely skipped around some muck in the road, pulling her skirts tight against her. She blinked as she took in their surroundings, surprised at how far they'd gone without her noticing. They should have left the road already to cross the fields toward home.

"This way," she said as she led the way into the grass, following a line of trees up over a gentle hill. In the shade, the cool scent of earth and moss brought her back to the present moment.

Vanessa asked, "What's that horrible cacophony?"

Chapter 12

"That sound, Vanessa, means we're about to meet quite a lively party."

As they crested a ridge, the discordant noises coalesced into the natural symphony of what must have been a hundred sheep or more roaming the hillside. At the sight, a hitch in Helena's throat left her momentarily speechless. She was twelve again, she and her mother on their way home from visiting neighbors, watching her father in the saddle talking to the sheep as if they were his children. Now a stray breeze tried to dry the tears welling in her eyes. Those days were long past. These were just sheep, nothing more. Sheep roaming naturally, until such time as their shepherd came to collect them.

An indelicate outburst from her niece caught her attention.

Apparently, a ram had taken an interest in Vanessa's skirt and was now butting up against her, advancing each time she retreated. "Go away, you silly sheep! Oh, do go away!"

"You need to be a bit more forceful than that, Ness! Try an angry 'Shoo shoo!' and perhaps follow it with a gentle push."

She had to stifle a laugh when Vanessa's "shoo" came out more as a whimper than a command. But then she heard "Oh, no, you don't! My dress is not your dinner! You go on and shoo! There's plenty of grass around for you to eat. I'll not appear slatternly because of a sheep who can't tell real flowers from fake ones." That was the Vanessa she knew.

Unfortunately, it still didn't have the desired effect. The animal kept on nibbling, and the strain on Vanessa's skirt became obvious. She rushed over to her niece and attempted to grab the ram, but he wouldn't budge. What she wouldn't give for a turnip to distract the stubborn thing! Vanessa shrieked and fell onto her side trying to free herself.

A sharp whistle pierced the air just as she caught sight of a collie bounding toward them. A moment before the dog came nose-to-nose with its target, the ram abruptly released Vanessa's skirt and turned away with characteristic nonchalance, as if nothing had happened, as if he'd simply become bored with his prey and moved on of his own accord. Hoofbeats rumbled through her, followed by deep chuckling. A deep familiar chuckle. When she looked around, it was hardly a surprise to see Mr. Lanfield dismounting from his ever-present Talos and a young man pulling his horse up alongside. In a well-worn coat and woolen trousers, this Daniel Lanfield looked different from the way he had in London. Larger. Sturdier. With the broad rim of his hat shading his face, he looked more relaxed as well. This man exuded a warm, easy familiarity that confounded her. Despite her better judgment, she felt the urge to respond in kind.

"I suppose this little troublemaker must be one of yours, Mr. Lanfield," she called out.

"That he is. And you're no better now at controlling them than you were at age twelve, Lark," he boomed in reply with a broad smile that lightened her heart. "Your father taught you better than that."

The nickname jarred her. She hadn't heard it in decades, and to hear it from him was completely disorienting. Father's voice. *Since you're up so early, Lark, you can help me check on the lambs.* So often, as a child, she had been the first one awake in the house and would greet her parents with nonstop chatter when they appeared to start the day. Even as she grew into a young woman, the name had stuck. *Give your ma a moment's quiet, Lark.* She'd last heard it the morning she'd left with Captain Martin, her parents unaware of her imminent escape. She nodded and turned away to watch the headstrong ram getting herded away. She swallowed hard, blinking back the stinging in her eyes. The past was much too present today. And she could not, for the life of her, make sense of Mr. Lanfield's transformed demeanor. By the shuttered look on his face now, apparently he'd been just as surprised by his friendly approach as she had.

A frustrated growl from her niece drew their attention.

"Away with you, Meno, you scamp! That's no way to win a lass's good graces," the young man said, fondly, as he came right up to the ram and nudged it away with a short crook. Even then, the beast took some convincing. But the lad's manner remained easygoing. Then he looked at Vanessa with a boyish Lanfield smile that magnified Helena's awareness of days long past. Both the Lanfield brothers had that smile. "Are you well, miss?"

"That beast is a menace!" Vanessa said, not at all amused by the animal. Her cheeks were a bright red, and her bonnet askew. "My skirt is ruined!"

"He's too fond of billowy fabrics. My mother almost turned him into dinner after he got to some sheets she had drying outside."

Despite the lad's kind manner, Helena could see the telltale signs that Vanessa's emotions were running high. Kneeling to examine the skirt, Helena replied, "It's hardly ruined, dear. Not to worry." She could hear brusqueness in her voice and cringed inwardly. Mr. Lanfield's unexpected appearance had disturbed her; he set her emotions whirling in chaos because she didn't know what to make of him or his changed attitude. She needed to take control of the situation, both on behalf of her and her niece. "You're perfectly capable of sewing those tears. It won't take long. A little mending and cleaning and it should be good as new." She turned to Lanfield's companion and said, "Thank you, young man, for your concern."

"But, Aunt Helena—" Vanessa shut her mouth. Helena had long ago mastered the look, that look mothers give their children to curtail undesirable behavior. She was pleased it worked as well on her nieces and nephews as on her own children.

She tilted her head subtly toward the men, hoping her niece would perceive the reminder and compose herself. Vanessa brushed her hands on her skirt and straightened.

"Thank you, gentlemen. I am well, I assure you. No real harm done." Vanessa curtsied prettily, but then whispered furiously, "Auntie, look at these huge holes that beast ripped out of my skirt. Patching them will look ridiculous."

"We can make it a new fashion trend," she replied lightly. "It's just a skirt. And, anyway, it isn't like you to be this flustered over your apparel."

"It isn't just the skirt, Aunt Helena!" Vanessa's voice rose, as did the redness spreading from her cheeks to the rest of her face at an alarming rate. "I am entirely out of my element here. I don't wish to look ridiculous. I have no idea what to do here, how to be of use. I

feel like a fool! And in front of strangers, no less!" Her niece's outburst was so unexpected that she just stared at the girl for a moment,
only now seeing how much of a toll the day—the whole trip, in
fact—was taking on her sheltered niece.

"Ladies," Mr. Lanfield interjected, "may I introduce my nephew,
Henry, my brother Gordon's eldest. Now he shan't be a stranger."
When he introduced them, the lad's eyes went wide.

"Er, pleased to meet you both," Henry said haltingly, his face
turning bright red, a near match to her niece's. Did he know her as
one of the notorious Thorton girls? What had he heard?

"Be a good lad, Hal, and take this lot across to the upper field,
would you? The sky looks nasty."

When Helena turned her attention back to Vanessa, the poor girl
looked to be near tears. "Nessa, dear, I realize this has been a great
change for you, but you are doing quite well. You judge yourself too
harshly."

"It's not just me, and you know it." Her niece looked at her pointedly. "Everything is different here, and those people so unpleasant!"

"Has someone been rude to you, Miss Vanessa?" Mr. Lanfield interjected, jogging the rest of the remaining distance to them, his expression no longer relaxed, his jaw tense. Although her niece didn't
answer, the girl's downcast expression spoke volumes. "What have
they said to you?"

Vanessa looked at her questioningly, but she shook her head.
Clearly, he knew the general sentiments in the air, but they didn't need
to draw him into the conflict directly. She would handle the village's
censure without his involvement. But the twist of her niece's mouth
said she'd come to a different conclusion.

"Vanessa, we should be on our way!" Helena said quickly to forestall her. "Gran will be missing us!"

"Hold a moment, Mrs. Martin, if you please," Mr. Lanfield com-
manded, his face dissected by lines radiating from his narrowed eyes
and tight frown. She bristled, but before she could respond, he added,
"Miss Vanessa hasn't answered my question. And you, in your attempt to brush me off like a fly, have given more than enough of an
answer. What happened?"

"Nothing that need concern you. We really must be going," she
said decisively, as Vanessa wailed, "It was terrible!"

"Mrs. Martin," he said softly. Concern emanated from him as he touched her forearm lightly. "I can help you, if you'll let me."

"Please, Auntie, tell him about that miserable woman."

Her niece had grown comfortable with Mr. Lanfield during the trip, and their combined front now did not bode well. She could hold out against one of them indefinitely, but if they worked together, her chances of dealing with the resentful villagers on her own terms became much, much slimmer. And that hand! The warmth of his hand through the cotton of her sleeve. That slight touch soothed her inexplicably. She liked it too much. It reminded her of other things she liked about his nearness.

"It is of no consequence. The village shop wouldn't sell to me," she admitted. "Vanessa managed to convince the clerk to let us purchase a few things for Gran's benefit. She can tell you more; I left the store to avoid further escalation." Clearly about to burst, Vanessa glanced at her gratefully before launching into the story, full of indignation, her voice growing louder and more strident. Mr. Lanfield responded with sympathy, echoing the girl's sentiments. His nostrils flared when Vanessa mentioned the insults the woman had called them. He would take on the role of avenging angel, if they let him. If she let him. Such a stark change in less than a week's time. When he'd walked away from her at the Crystal Palace, he'd worn the look of a man who'd just avoided getting sucked into a fetid cesspool. He'd turned his back without another glance. Now he looked at her in an entirely different way—as if he cared, as if her well-being mattered to him.

"Naught has changed," he said. "After your aunt left the village, she became Eve herself with all of Marksby being cast from Paradise, or at least the hope of Paradise. The myth was embraced and passed down. Lasses are taught not to be vain or selfish, else they follow the same path as *that Thorton girl*."

"You said people held a grudge," Helena said, chagrined. "I didn't expect it to persevere so vividly. Please tell me, has my family been treated with such animosity all these years?"

"No, your parents, your gran, the Thorton farm, they all suffered as terribly as the rest of the village. Poor and clemmed. They were treated with sympathy instead of hostility."

"That's some comfort, at least!" For so long, Marskby's condemnation had been a distant unpleasantness, just an idea in her mind.

"What about my mother, Mr. Lanfield?" Vanessa asked. "She doesn't talk much about her life before London. Neither of them does." Vanessa looked at her with an open plea.

Mr. Lanfield answered, "I cannot claim to know what your mother experienced. She didn't spend much time in public after your aunt's departure. Whether that was an effect of public condemnation or some other cause, I couldn't tell you." Vanessa seemed unsatisfied with that response, but he continued, "I did warn you."

He gazed out over the flock for a few minutes, but she could tell that he wasn't watching the sheep, that his mind was busy elsewhere. Then he said suddenly, "Did anyone follow you out of the village?"

"No, no one." She was certain. She'd felt eyes on them as they left the shop, and she'd checked behind them every so often as they walked home. "Why?"

He shook his head. "Nothing really. Would you like me to escort you ladies home? In case you might have drawn some persistent attention?"

"There is no need, Mr. Lanfield," she replied. "If anyone was going to follow us with trouble, surely they would have surfaced before now. Your nephew may need your help with the flock. You should go after him."

"Hal's been working the fields since he was out of short pants. He knows the way. But you might have a point. The skies over there look ominous. I don't want him alone if the storm turns ugly. Are you sure?"

"Quite sure. You are too kind. We should all be getting home."

As he turned his horse to follow his nephew, she remembered something. "Mr. Lanfield! A quick question!" At his backward glance, she called out, "Do you know who lives in that new house on this side of the river? I didn't realize my father had built anything there for tenants."

"He didn't," Mr. Lanfield replied. "He sold it. That's part of Lanfield property now. And as for who lives there, the house is mine." With that, the infuriating man pointed Talos away and took off at a gallop.

Chapter 13

Vanessa blinked back hot, angry tears as she picked her way through yet another field, this one full of tall grasses. She'd barely managed not to cry in front of Mr. Lanfield and his nephew. That Henry looked to be only a few years older than Billy. She had resolved not make even more of a spectacle of herself by dissolving into girlish tears. Thank goodness he'd led the sheep away and rode down the hill. He looked at ease on a horse, but then he must be, working like this every day. She hated that the two men had seen her so upset and disordered, so bloody weak!

But really this was too much indignity to bear in one day. Stupid sheep. Stupid shopkeeper. Did she have a target painted on her forehead today to be treated thusly? That shop woman's vicious tongue and heartless demeanor were surely just a rare case of narrow-minded provincialism, or so she tried to rationalize. Not everyone in Marksby would be like that. Mr. Lanfield wasn't. Not really. He and Auntie might snip at each other, but he was much kinder in general. And he'd come to their aid time and again. Mrs. Weathers and her husband weren't. Not really. Maybe at first. But they'd changed almost overnight once she and her aunt had shown they weren't afraid of hard work and could be trusted to do their part in the house.

But . . . was this how people treated a woman who sought to direct her own future? Women who chose their own destiny, defying family and convention to do so?

"Vanessa, watch your step, dear!" Aunt Helena called out, just in time. She'd almost walked straight into an area dotted with sheep droppings. Between the rocky terrain and what the sheep left behind, she couldn't allow her thoughts to wander. But still . . . what would people think of her if she ran off with Billy? She felt the urge to ask her aunt, but it wasn't a question she could ask without tipping her hand. And Auntie would absolutely tell her mother, even if she only speculated about eloping. It wasn't fair, was it? She would only be following in Aunt Helena's footsteps. And see how happily that decision had bloomed into a fairy-tale love story!

Her mind slipped to Aunt Helena's tale of how she'd met Uncle Isaiah. He'd rescued her, for heaven's sake! It was practically love at first sight! Her mother said over and over that such things only happened in fairy tales, but Auntie was living proof, wasn't she? And, oh, how she wanted that kind of love for herself. She thought back to Billy's first overture. Sally had introduced them. He'd said she'd caught his eye. She could picture the way he'd wiggled his eyebrows and said, "Give us a kiss, love," before they parted. It wasn't a fairy-tale beginning, really, but they could still have a fairy-tale ending. Arriving at the Thorton home did little to quiet her mind, nor did the too-vivid image of Henry Lanfield astride his horse. At least by the time they arrived home, she no longer felt like crying.

Chapter 14

"I'll be right behind with the strays. I need Max to round them up, though," Daniel shouted to his nephew, raising his voice more than usual to carry over the storm. His nephew's silhouette nodded. The massive storm had descended before they'd managed to get the sheep to the sheltered fields. It would be best for them to at least have some cover available, in case the storm persisted. He watched Hal walking his horse along behind the group, subtly steering them down to the bridge crossing. Reassured that his nephew had everything well in hand, he turned back up the hill and whistled to the trusty Max to find the others. It didn't take long, with the collie nipping at their heels, for the wayward sheep to return. His thoughts turned to Helena Martin, a wayward sheep if ever there was one. As much as he felt she deserved to be ostracized, he couldn't help but feel sympathy for her. Perhaps it was the fact that he'd seen her at her most vulnerable more than once and knew how delicate she could be, or perhaps it was the fact that he'd met her fine sons, innocent and bereft of their father. Whatever it was, the sight of her and her niece struggling with the rambunctious Meno had drawn out his protective instincts. When Miss Vanessa had mentioned today's incident at the shop, he'd had to quell his immediate desire to hunt down Mrs. Wyatt and threaten to withdraw Lanfield as their customer and supplier. While there were many farms in the area, he was well aware that he and Gordon made a significant impact on the shop's income in multiple ways. Looking back, he couldn't comprehend his own drastic reactions. The villagers' behavior was exactly what he'd warned her would happen, justifiably so.

Hal's sharp whistle drew his attention. Damn, he knew better than to allow his mind to wander at a time like this! His nephew was focused on the flock, which was reluctant to cross the bridge. They massed along the stream as if disoriented by the storm and didn't seem to register his whistled commands. Rain-swollen, the beck nearly reached the peak of the arch underneath the bridge, and debris swirled and slapped against the stones. They'd have to remember to check the bridges on their lands for erosion over the next few days.

He urged Max ahead to steer the sheep across the bridge and didn't miss the relief on Hal's face when they began pouring over the stone archway, as if a gate had been opened. Gordon's son carried the same trait that afflicted all Lanfield men, himself included: stubborn self-sufficiency. They'd all drive themselves into the ground before asking for help. If Daniel hadn't returned from London, Gordon would have managed as best he could alone, out of necessity. All the Lanfields were raised to treat every situation as if alone, as if they should never expect assistance and therefore never seek it.

Daniel caught a glimpse of something white bobbing downstream, and then another white blob, and then another, getting washed away. Light puffs in the murky, churning waters. *Damn and double damn.* He mounted his horse and sped down to intercept the sheep that had fallen in. If luck was on their side, the sheep would get caught in eddies and be easily rescued. If not . . .

Racing along the shore, he found one sheep as hoped, pulled into a shallow eddy by the water's edge, shallow enough that it was already finding its footing and making its way up the bank on its own. The other two weren't so fortunate. They hadn't made it far either, but both had caught on an old tree that had fallen into the beck. Tangled in its branches, the sheep couldn't right themselves, and he could hear their panicked cries. Despite the rushing debris, he nudged Talos down into the frigid water. *Blast, no way to get close enough to the sheep this way.* Sliding into the icy water, he leaned against his horse for stability in the strong current. When he reached the first animal, he made short work of freeing it from the branches and then made his way to shore to deposit the waterlogged beast. In its gratitude, the headstrong thing immediately bolted up the bank and out of sight. At least its liveliness was a good sign. By the time he managed to reach the other trapped sheep, its condition wasn't as promising as the others'. It had been tangled, he now saw, much more intricately and, unfortunately, with its head just barely above water. It had ceased to cry out and made only the faintest attempts to kick and wiggle when he touched it. He had to cut away some of its coat, so entwined was it with the tree's appendages.

When he carried this one back to the bank, he tried to hold it with its head lower to the ground than its tail. Water poured out of its mouth. But it was still listless when he laid it on solid ground. Alarmed by its lethargy, he rubbed its body briskly to clear more water from its lungs and then secured it across his saddle for the remainder of the trip home. Along the walk to rendezvous with his nephew and the flock, he watched carefully for any sights of revival. The sheep bleated a few times and shook itself awkwardly, almost like a human's shiver. But it still wasn't back to normal.

As he expected, Hal had gotten the rest of the sheep across without incident, and, of their own accord, the flock headed straight for a cluster of trees.

"Good work, as allus, Hal!" he said as he slapped him on the back. Water jumped off the young man at all angles from the impact.

"Thank you, Uncle. Sorry you had to take a dip. I should've jumped in the gill myself but didn't see the fallen ones until you'd already followed them in."

"No need for apologies. You were doing what you needed to do."

"Is that one lost to us then?" Henry gestured at the prone sheep, his expression heavy with guilt.

"I think she'll be fine. I'll take her back to my barn, where she'll be warm and dry. She should be back to normal by tomorrow. You've nothing to be sorry for, Hal. You did everything right. Now go home and get some rest. We'll have to check fences and bridges tomorrow after all this."

"Aye, sir. Should I check the west or meet you here to run the whole perimeter together?"

"Check to the west. Then we can meet at the north ridge to check that flock and compare notes. Remember to tell your father that we moved the newer flock to the Pleiades grove. Now go before you worry your mother!"

"Aye, and a good night to you, Uncle!" As soon as the young man turned for home, Daniel carefully mounted behind the still too-docile sheep and made haste.

Surely, Mrs. Martin and her niece would have made it home before the storm descended. He'd have to pay a visit to the shop soon and speak with the owners about civility. Lost in thought, he almost dropped the reins when Talos was startled by a thunderclap. *Focus, man!*

As soon as he got back to his barn, he wrapped the sheep—Lampy the Younger, now that he could see her better—in a horse blanket and began vigorously rubbing her from head to tail. It wasn't long before that blanket was waterlogged, and he had to root around for more. By the time he returned to the stall, little Lampedo, like the Amazon warrior for which she was named, stood and bleated loudly. He tossed a dry blanket over her, relief coursing through him. After he got the newly recovered sheep settled in a clean stall with water and hay, he still had to take care of Talos. He leaned against a post to catch a moment's rest. Talos had been his usual dependable self, even wading into the violent beck undeterred. He couldn't allow his mount to suffer just because he was tired and cold and still sopping. Talos must be all that and more, having carried a double load part of the way.

Just as he was about to straighten up and get to his task, there was a light knock at the barn door. He almost didn't hear it over the rain hitting the roof. Before he could respond, the door opened to reveal a woman in a heavy cloak, her face obscured by the low hood.

"Ruth, what are you doing here? Surely, Gordon and the boys wouldn't let you go out in this mess! Is my brother with you, fool that he is?"

"I'm sorry to disturb you, but I'm not Ruth." Her delicate voice alerted him before she pulled her hood away and showed her face. Helena.

"Mrs. Martin!" He didn't know what else to say, her presence here so disoriented him. In a thousand years, he wouldn't have guessed he would ever see her here, in his barn, on his land. He certainly wouldn't have expected it on a night like this. His heart pounded, surprise mingling with a strange sensation he didn't recognize. If it were any other human being on earth, he might have identified the odd feeling as pleasure. But that couldn't be the case now.

"After we left you, I saw you and your nephew struggling to rescue some of the waterlogged sheep during your crossing," she explained, haltingly. Her eyes kept darting around the room. He'd come to recognize it as a sign of her discomfort, a sign she wished to be anywhere else, perhaps. "I waited at Gran's until there was a break in the storm. Mrs. Weathers made some stew and bread." She raised the basket she was carrying, like a grown version of Little Red Riding Hood. "I thought, with all that trouble, you two would need a warm meal."

She looked so ill at ease, and yet she'd thought to come here, thought to look after him and his nephew. Warmth spread through him; it had been years since a woman—well, a woman other than his brother's wife—had tried to attend to him. Ruth acted like a mother to him, which was laughable since he was almost five years her elder. And maybe that was Mrs. Martin's intent too, a mother's instinct so deeply ingrained. She'd expected Henry to be here too. He shouldn't read anything more into this visit than neighborly concern. He shouldn't. And yet his heart still beat harder, his pulse sounding in his ears.

"Aye, I owe you thanks, ma'am. Uh, the house is open, if you'd be so kind." Even to his own ears, he sounded like a dolt. "I still need to tend to Talos. If you must return home, don't let me keep you. Ah, but you're welcome to sit a bit for warmth before you go." He'd never felt so horribly tongue-tied before. He must be more worn than he thought. This was Helena *Thorton*. And he'd just invited her into *his* home. As soon as the door closed behind her, he set to work, muttering all the while about the fickle hand of fate.

Chapter 15

Helena was relieved to see that the storm remained at bay as she walked carefully toward Daniel's house. Tidy hedges made a pretty border around it. They surprised her. After all, they were ornamental, and she hadn't thought he cared much for fancy trappings. In the darkening, storm-cloud-laden evening, she found it difficult to see details, but the structure looked solid and permanent. Built in a simple style, it had a large window in the front room, a large, impractical window that must let in quite a chill on a winter's night but also must provide a beautiful view of the hills. Someone had taken great care in its construction and built it to last, to be passed down to future generations.

The interior of the house was even more Spartan and utilitarian than Helena had expected. It was a modest home, just large enough for a family starting out. The main room wasn't much larger than some shepherd huts, built in the fields for occasional shelter. It held a kitchen, a table, and an assortment of chairs and benches. A spinning wheel sat in the corner, complemented by a basket of raw wool. She could only guess that the doors on both sides of the central room led to bedrooms. It wasn't much, but then a man like him didn't need much.

After she stoked the fire, put on coffee, and set the stew pot on the hearth, she felt at a loss as to what to do next. Glancing around Daniel's home, she felt like an interloper. How long had he been a widower for the house to have no evidence of feminine influence at all? This house wanted warmth. For a man so reserved, she felt as if she was violating his private life just by being in his home alone.

So she fled the too-revealing building in favor of the barn. The small barn was warm and dry, despite the chill outside. No leaks in

104 • *Amara Royce*

the roof, no drafts. Remarkable construction, really. Not that she would have expected anything less from the Lanfields. Perhaps there was something productive she could do here. Talos stood in his stall, calmly chewing oats, with Daniel nowhere in sight. The horse paused when she approached and put his nose out for her to pet him. So forward. So charming.

Then Daniel's voice drifted over from the farthest stall. Curiosity piqued, she moved quietly through the barn until she could just see him through the slats. Leaning his back against a wall, he sat on the straw-covered floor with a sheep cradled on his lap. He was singing! Whatever the tune was, she didn't recognize it, but it sounded like some kind of lullaby. Such tenderness. It seemed like such an intimate moment that she retreated, afraid to break whatever spell he'd wrought. This was a man who cared deeply but so privately. It was no wonder he'd despised her all these years, after what she'd done to his brother, to his family.

When Daniel finally emerged from the stalls, he had patches of drying mud stuck to his clothes, reminiscent of his younger days. His head jerked when he saw her, and she could have sworn his surprise was tinged with relief and even a little pleasure. After a moment, he nodded to her, frowning slightly, and said, "I didn't know you stayed. You should have gone back to your grandmother's after dropping off the meal. I don't mean to sound ungrateful, but it sounds like the storm has gotten worse. It won't be safe for you to return tonight." He was right. The rains had picked up, and the rumbles of distant thunder were unmistakable.

She knew perhaps better than he how much more severe the storm had become. Even on the short walk between the barn and the house, she would have been soaked through if she hadn't used the heavy cloak she'd found at home. Her boots hadn't fared so well, but she hadn't forgotten that aspect of farm life.

"You should eat something," she said. "I left some things warming in the house. And you should get some clean, dry clothing on as well. You'll do no one any good if you make yourself ill."

"There's nothing for it, is there? You'll have to stay the night. Come along."

Despite her instinct to object, she knew he was right and went to take the closest lantern down from its hook. His hand brushed hers as he moved to do the same. He froze. When she looked at him, he turned away and said, gruffly, "Be careful the wind doesn't knock it out of your hand."

Discomfited by the sudden tension, she snapped at him, "I'm not a child. I've managed just fine getting to and from the house with it. I'm capable of carrying lanterns, for heaven's sake."

He looked weary and stiff as he pushed the door open. Wind and rain took the opportunity to shove into the barn, and the lantern flickered.

"Let's get on with it," he said as he pushed her toward the house, pausing only to secure the barn shut.

Rain poured down in heavy sheets, making it difficult to see the building just a few yards ahead. A strong and sudden gust almost knocked her off her feet, but Daniel caught her, steadied her, and then remained close by as they made their way to the house. She followed him inside.

"Is the barn large enough to hold all the Lanfield sheep on the worst winter nights?" she asked, mainly to break the silence.

"By no means. When it's so cold that we fear injury to the flock, we keep many of them in the big barn on my brother's land. We also have a few smaller shelters out in the fields, ah, including a few of the Thorton barns now. We use mine mainly for strays and the rare quarantines. It's useful to have the extra storage and be able to separate some of the flock when necessary." His reply sounded perfunctory, but then he looked at her and added, "I didn't figure you'd be all that interested in talking about shepherding."

"It's as fine a topic as any. My father was quite proud of his sheep. But right now I suppose food is the real priority. May I?" She gestured toward the hearth, where she'd left a large pot of stew heating. So many questions filled her mind, but they could keep, for now.

"No need. I can serve myself just fine. Thank you. I'm famished, and 'tis a relief to have something to warm my belly."

"Well, Mrs. Weathers provided the food. I haven't done all that much," she replied. The warmth spreading through her midsection couldn't be attributed to food. Or to the fireplace.

She watched briefly as his stiff fingers struggled with the buttons on his coat. That was all the proof she needed. The moment they'd entered the room, she'd become aware of the sodden chill of her clothes in such stark contrast to the warmth of the house on her exposed skin.

If she felt thus after just a few minutes, it was a wonder he could move at all. Her hands itched with the impulse to go to him and undo his coat herself. She could picture his clothes piled on that rush chair, could picture him bare while she drew linen along his arms, his chest, his legs to dry him ... could picture rubbing his thick muscles to warm him in other ways. Would his chest be firm but with a touch of softness? Would his legs be covered with hair? Would he enjoy the sensations as her palms slid along his rib cage? What on earth had come over her? Startled by the uncomfortable turn of her thoughts, she moved swiftly toward the hearth to put her idle hands to some better purpose.

"You've been working for hours in the wet. It's no trouble for me to get you a bowl," she insisted. "Now go sit in front of the fire before you catch ague."

"I'm blathered and should wash before I do aught else," he said tiredly, his accent heavy.

Graphic images crowded into her mind, and she didn't trust herself to look at him, lest he catch an inkling of her thoughts. What wicked demon possessed her? Daniel Lanfield, for heaven's sake! A man who despised her without mercy! It would be more sensible to take her chances out in the storm! Reining in her wayward thoughts, she poured hot water into a basin for him and asked, "Where might I go to give you some privacy?"

"Any room but that one," he said. She had no choice but to look where he indicated. His face was blessedly neutral as he pointed at the room nearest to where he stood. "That one's mine. The other rooms are all unoccupied. Any will do. I'll fetch you when I'm ready." When she met his gaze, the light from the fireplace reflected strangely. It seemed as if his eyes glowed with intent. Surely his words were all innocence. *I'll fetch you when I'm ready.* She had no doubt he could fetch her easily, if he put his mind to the task, especially with such strange thoughts dominating her mind. Yet he had no sensual interest in her, just as she had none in him. Truly.

She hurried into the nearest room and shut the door firmly, leaving her alone in darkness. When had the house become so warm? The sounds of water sloshing sparked more vivid but unwelcome images of him in her mind. What had she done to deserve this torment? A truly depraved voice in her head whispered that she could open the door the tiniest bit to see if the reality matched her imagination. She ignored it. An aberration. A result of years of physical deprivation, perhaps. Was she coming down with a fever? She pressed her head against the door and took a few deep, cleansing breaths.

As Daniel removed his clarty boots and trousers, careful to keep all the mud and muck from scattering through the room, he glanced repeatedly at the thin door separating him from Helena. She'd thought to bring him a warm meal, thought to pour water for him. Her attentiveness touched him. Sure, that was all. But the way she'd looked at him before closing that door . . . he must have imagined it, but he could swear her eyes had roved over him as if he were already naked. He should have been disgusted by it, but that wasn't the sensation coursing through him at the moment. Her swift but intense glance had him burning from his toes to his scalp. Any chill from the past few hours burned away, leaving him aflame and certain parts of his body standing at attention. Once he'd put aside his clothes and rinsed off as best he could, he hurried to his bedroom for fresh clothing.

"You can come out," he called before closing his bedroom door. "I'll just be a few minutes more. You should start eating. No reason for us both to wait."

As he swiftly finished dressing, the muffled sound of her movements in the great room agitated him. No woman outside his family had set foot in this house ever. Those light footfalls and whispers of domestic activity struck him as both comforting and, unaccountably, arousing. How could they spend the night together in this house?

"I've eaten," she replied, her voice carrying through the wall. "I can sleep in a chair or even on the floor," she called. "You've worked so hard today. You really should get some rest in a comfortable bed."

As if he could let any woman sleep on the floor while he used a soft bed and still call himself his mother's son. He quickly finished buttoning his trousers and yanked his door open.

"Today was but a regular day's work on a farm. Naught to speak of. As for you sleeping on the floor, it would be a cold day in Hades, ma'am. My ma would come back from the grave just to shake me for my thoughtlessness." He would not compromise on this point. Gentlemen did not sacrifice a woman's comfort for their own.

"I refuse to banish you from your own bed." She stood with her hands gripping the back of a chair, braced to argue. Her defiant stance perversely charmed him, as did the steaming bowl that sat on the table accompanied by a thick slice of bread and full mug.

"Well, I refuse to have you sleep anywhere else in this house. As a guest, you must take the bed. I'll tie you to it if I must." Did he really just say that? He nearly smacked himself in the head for his idiocy. She should have slapped him. Yet she didn't appear offended. Instead, she looked curious, thoughtful.

"We could share it," she said, watching him carefully. Her cheeks reddened, but she held his gaze.

"Huh?" He couldn't have heard properly.

She was watching him carefully. A bright red crept up her neck and her cheeks, but she held his gaze as she added, "No one need ever know. We both need sleep, and surely your bed would reasonably accommodate both of us."

Now a pang of discomfort shot through him. She wasn't wrong. His bed was plenty large enough to share, and his bones ached from the day's strain. But other parts of him ached in a different way, and those were the parts that made sharing *that* bed a very bad idea.

"We would know." He cleared his throat. "And that's a thing you can't unknow."

When his eyes met hers, the flush on her face grew even stronger. When her gentle fingers brushed against his cheek, he ceased to breathe. Then she said, with a tart smile, "I only mean to sleep. Just keep each other warm."

He had never been a man of many words, but now he could barely eke out a breathless syllable. Her touch burned his skin, and muscles all over his body contracted. Had he caught a fever from the rains? She moved in close to him, and he was struck by the sense of rightness and pleasure. It should feel awkward, shouldn't it? Unnatural. This woman, of all women. It should feel wrong to slide his hands around her waist. Her finely muscled arms should feel like an affront. Touching his lips to hers should feel like burning in the fiery pit of hell. And yet. That inexplicable, irrational sensation overtook him, just like the night at the coaching inn. Her closeness unraveled his brain. Something in him reveled in her softness. Her mouth, her skin, her full hips. A thrill shot through him when she wrapped her arms around his shoulders and pulled him closer. He traced the line of buttons down her blouse with his finger and grew hot when she shivered against him. His good sense had fled, and he could not make himself seek it. One thought invaded his mind: *More*. He feared this overwhelming desire. Even with Nancy, he hadn't felt such over-powering lust, as much as he'd been determined to do his husbandly duty toward her. He'd found her attractive, and his body had performed accordingly, but he'd never felt anything like this.

Chapter 16

God in heaven, Daniel Lanfield was kissing her. Daniel. Lanfield. Helena couldn't believe it. As if those were the only two words her mind could grasp, they repeated over and over in her head until they merged into one constant nonsensical string. *DanielLanfield-DanielLanfieldDanielLanfieldDanielLanfieldDanielLanfieldDaniel Lanfield*. What was she doing? The sensations careening through her were incomprehensible too. Hot and soft and moist and taste and teeth and . . . Even as she clung to him, she couldn't make sense of what was happening. He was kissing her. And she was kissing him back, pressing up on her toes to get closer, to get as close as humanly possible. When he tipped his head, she followed. When his lips parted, she followed. And greedily pulled him closer. Judging by the way he paused and gasped against her lips, he was as shocked as she at the power of their kiss.

No, a voice in her head cried. But it was drowned out by everything else, by all the sensations rioting through her, by the voices saying *yes* and *please* and *more*. At first, the kiss felt pure and achingly simple. Just a kiss. But the wave of need that crashed over her couldn't stop at a little kiss. She needed more. More of his touch, more of this intensity. When she pulled him down to deepen the kiss, the firmness of his shoulders against her arms, of his chest against hers, left her a shaking mass of sensation. She couldn't think, only feel. His lips were so soft, so different from the rest of him, from his calloused hands and his rigid muscles beneath her fingers. So soft and warm and gentle. It wasn't what she'd expected. *He* wasn't what she'd expected. A tendril of warm pleasure unfurled in her belly, blooming as she felt a rumbling groan go through his chest. She could feel his heartbeat under her fingertips. He must be able to feel her quivering. But, oh, she couldn't resist just a little more of this.

By God, his lips against hers, his firm body against hers, growing firmer by the moment from what she could tell through her skirts—she couldn't breathe! Or maybe that was because his lips wouldn't release hers. She pulled back slightly just to take a breath, but it was enough to break the moment.

You cannot do this! He loathes you! He thinks you loose and immoral, and you are proving him right!

When she'd said the words *We could keep each other warm*, she certainly hadn't meant anything like this. She had to put a stop to this insanity.

Suddenly, air whooshed around her, chilled and disorienting. Daniel was at the door, his back to her, his hand frozen on the knob. He looked just as confused and uncomfortable as she felt.

"I don't expect you'll pardon me, Mrs. Martin, but I am sorry for this," he said to the wall, his voice shocked and distant. "I'll make my bed on the floor in the other room."

"That's wise," she said, "but there's no need for apologies."

"Or 'appen, in the barn," he said, as if she hadn't spoken.

"Don't be daft. There's no need to go to such extremes over a . . . harmless misstep."

He turned his face to meet her gaze, his mouth twisting into a grimace that made her wary.

"A misstep," he echoed sharply. "That would be a fine, mild word for it." He stopped speaking so abruptly that she waited a long moment for him to continue. She'd give a great deal to know what he was thinking right then as he closed his eyes, his hands clenched against his thighs.

"Given the rough weather we've had today, literally and metaphorically, it's no wonder we forgot ourselves, Daniel." She tried to make her tone light and casual, but she didn't realize until his eyes flew open with a jolt that she'd used his Christian name. Where on earth had that come from? "I'm sorry. Mr. Lanfield."

His eyes blazed at her correction. "Definitely the barn."

"No! I shall not drive you from the comfort of your own home. You cannot sleep in your barn in the middle of a storm."

"Ah, Mrs. Martin, I cannot sleep here. Because that didn't feel at all like a mistake, even though we both know it was. For a critical moment, I forgot who you are and what you've done. I forgot who I am and where my loyalty belongs. I'll bed down in the barn because . . . if I stay under this roof with you, I've no doubt I'll want to do that again. And that cannot happen."

She couldn't bring herself either to concur with or deny his prediction. *I forgot who you are and what you've done.* He would never forgive her for her youthful transgressions. He would never see her as anything besides the girl who'd abandoned his brother and ruined Marksby. The realization hurt more than she'd imagined it could.

"Daniel! You dolt, open up!" A male voice, deep and jovial, sounded from the vicinity of the front steps. Helena leapt from the bed, disoriented. She sat back down abruptly, dizzy from standing too quickly. The events of the previous night flashed in her memory, and shutting her eyes only made everything worse. A heavy hand knocked at the front door. That was the pounding she'd heard in her dream. There was something familiar about that voice, uncomfortably familiar. "Come open the door, man! Hal told me you nearly drowned over a lamb or two, you fool! Open up so I can knock some sense into you!" Oh, dear Lord in heaven. Gordon! It had to be.

She peeked through the curtains as well as she could without disturbing them. She dare not draw the man's attention. But she couldn't see much of him. She could tell that he was tall. He dressed much like Daniel—practical, warm, sturdy. That was all she could see before the creak of the door told her he'd entered the house. She pressed herself into a corner between the window and the bureau and struggled to right her clothing. She hadn't undressed, but she'd untucked her blouse and loosed her stays to sleep. Even with the laces in the front for easy reach, her fingers fumbled, and a fine panicky sweat prickled her skin. Angels in heaven, her boots were across the room, by the door, still covered in muck.

"Danny!" Gordon called out again. This time, his voice was louder and more anxious. "Why aren't you waking?" His footsteps ranged through the front room but quickly made their way to the bedroom door. What was she to do? How could she face him? Like this? She hadn't seen him since she ran away. What must he think of her? Of all people in this village, he surely had a right to hold a grudge. What would he think, finding her here? She couldn't slip out the window without her boots. If he hadn't heard she'd returned to Marksby, perhaps she could pretend to be a new maid. Perhaps a lightskirt. There must be some such women in the area. A hysterical laughter threatened to burst from her. Perhaps she was finally slipping into madness.

Gordon knocked loudly on the bedroom door but didn't wait for a response before opening it.

"Daniel! Wake up!" He halted just a few feet into the room when he realized Daniel wasn't in bed. "What on—?" He whirled around, calling for his brother. When he caught sight of her boots, he froze. Then he turned slowly, the clock in the front room ticking away each inch.

"Pardon me, miss! I didn't—" He looked confused, almost alarmed. He was taller than she remembered and broader too. He filled the doorway, and a shiver skittered down her back as she tensed. He made an imposing figure, one that likely wouldn't be pleased when he recognized her. "Do you know, ma'am, where my brother is?" His tone was cautious, as he looked from her to the rumpled bed repeatedly.

"I think he's in the barn," she said quietly. She had to clear her throat before she could add, "He slept there last night."

Surprise was evident on Gordon's face. "The barn, you say? Why? No, no need to answer that." He scrubbed his hand over his face and looked toward the door. "I didn't mean to startle you. I feared Daniel might have caught sick from a dunking in the beck last night. I best go see to him. I'm his brother, Gordon. Might I ask who—?"

And there it was. He saw her now. The very air in the room changed as he recognized her. His face shifted to the same steely cold stare she'd seen on Daniel's face at the Crystal Palace when she'd told him who she was. The chilling silence lasted for what felt like an eternity. That telling sour taste flooded her mouth as her scalp began to tingle, every hair alert to sudden danger.

Finally, he said, "I'd heard you were back, Miss Thorton."

"Yes, Mr. Lanfield. I have returned," she responded with a tone she hoped was neutral, masking the fear rising in her chest. "You may not have heard I've been Mrs. Martin for quite a while now." Chagrined, she quickly added, "And it is I who should ask your pardon."

Glaring, he waved away her comment with a gesture of his meaty hand as he stepped farther into the room. His massive bulk blocked her exit, and her level of panic shot up, much like she expected a fox felt when run to ground. "Not my business," he said gruffly. "What is my business, though, is what in hell you're doing in my brother's bedroom at dawn?"

The barely leashed fury in his voice set her stomach churning. She had to get out of here, but she couldn't think. She gaped at him, trying to piece words together that would make sense.

"No, brother, that's not your business." Daniel's voice carried from the front door, and his tone matched the frigidity of his brother's. His heavy footfalls only marginally settled her rioting nerves. His voice grew louder as he approached, adding, "You'd best remember your manners, at least when you're in my house."

"Danny! Thank God!" Gordon rushed out of the bedroom.

Momentarily free from his hulking presence, she took a deep breath. When had she started shaking? She grabbed her boots and shoved her feet into them, not bothering with the laces. It was enough to have them on in case of a quick retreat. The sooner she left this place, the better! As long as she had all her belongings, including her bonnet and her cloak, she could manage something as pedestrian as fastening her boots out on a boulder somewhere. As soon as possible. She exited the bedroom just in time to see Gordon releasing his brother's shoulders.

"I was worried, brother, when you didn't appear in the yard this morning. Thought I'd maybe find you retching your guts out or passed out with fever. Ruth and Hal too both feared you'd gone ill. You know better than to fight that swelling beck for a gimmer or two."

"I'm fine, Gordy, nary a scratch. The wee lambs needed help. They were caught in a fallen tree and wouldn't have gotten out on their own. Lampy's the only one that had trouble recovering."

"You and your naming. I've told you time and again you can't name the bloody things. They aren't pets."

"Lampy the Younger is doing fine, as am I," Daniel said firmly. "No harm done. So you can go about your day. I'll be out in the fields within the hour."

Gordon raised an eyebrow and tipped his head in Helena's direction. "An hour, you say? Time enough to sort out whatever business you have with this one?"

"Gordon," Daniel warned, "I shan't tell you again to mind your manners. Mrs. Martin and her niece saw me and Hal struggling with the flock by the water. She was kind enough to bring me a warm meal, but the storm raged too strong for her to go home safely."

"So you slept in the barn?" Gordon said skeptically.

"Aye, so I slept in the barn," Daniel replied, his chin up.

"And *Mrs. Martin* here was only being a *good* neighbor?"

"Aye. Watch your tone." The curt reply came through gritted teeth, but Daniel wasn't the only one whose ire was up now. She'd grown tired of observing this brotherly exchange, which fleetingly reminded her of dogs bracing themselves to face off against each other. She was no one's bone to bicker over.

"Gentlemen, I am still here. And, yes, whatever you think of me, Mr. Lanfield, I was trying to be a good neighbor. I didn't think your brother had anyone here to care for him, and clearly I was right. I thought he would benefit from one of Mrs. Weathers's hearty stews, seeing as he would be too busy to see to a hot meal himself. I'll be leaving as soon as I can ready myself."

"No use atoning for your sins here in Marksby, bitch."

Before she'd even fully comprehended Gordon's words, Daniel pinned his brother against the wall, a hand to his throat. The unadulterated hatred in Gordon's words and in his eyes as he and his brother stared each other down made her stomach turn.

"Enough, brother! Apologize to Mrs. Martin. She knows she's done wrong, but that was a long time ago, and we've all changed."

Gordon shoved Daniel away and advanced on him. "Seems like you've changed quite a bit in the month you've been gone. The Daniel I know wouldn't forget his home and his family so easily."

"You think I've forgotten anything?" Daniel replied, now toe to toe with his brother. Mirror images, they stood tall, defensive, glaring at each other. "I'm a Lanfield, same as you. I know as well as you what our family has suffered. But I wasn't about to send a defenseless woman out into that fierce night."

"To a Lanfield of Marksby, she's not a defenseless woman." Gordon jerked a thumb in her direction. "She's a bitch and a frow, and she always will be."

Bollocks! That was more than she could allow! She charged forward, catching Daniel's cocked arm and pushing him away. She stood between the two men, unable to recall when she'd been more infuriated.

"Gordon Lanfield!" For the first time since Daniel had entered the room, Gordon looked at her straight on. He stared down at her as if he meant to do her harm, but she would have none of it. He might be entitled to some anger toward her, but he had no right to question her devotion to her husband or her children. "I do sincerely regret the pain and embarrassment I caused you so many years ago. Truly I do. But I *won't* bide you insulting my husband and my family by questioning my virtue."

"Virtue? As if such a one as you has any at all," Gordon scoffed.

She curled her hands into fists and pressed them against her legs, fighting the urge to slap him. Meanwhile, Daniel reached around her to grab his brother by the shirt and bodily whirled him toward the bedroom door.

"Out! I warned you. This is finished. Mrs. Martin will be on her way home shortly, and I'll be about my work soon after. That's all you need to know. Now get out!" He herded his brother through the main room and yanked open the front door. Gordon glared at her malevolently before Daniel shoved at his shoulder. "Go, Gordon. No good will come of this." More gently, he added, "Go home. See Ruth and your children. I'll run the fields today. Just let this bide for now."

She could have cried with relief when Gordon turned his back and stomped out. She slumped against the bedroom doorframe before realizing that her boots were still undone.

"I'll be ready to go in just a moment," she said quickly as she hobbled to a chair.

"We should talk," Daniel replied without looking at her. His voice had a flat, empty quality, but she refused to let herself interpret his demeanor.

"No, Daniel, there's nothing to talk about. I won't darken your door again." He looked as if he wanted to object, but he said nothing. A few minutes later, she walked out. And she refused to be upset that, in all that time, he wouldn't look her in the eye.

Chapter 17

No one was more surprised than Helena to find herself again a passenger in Daniel Lanfield's cart. It had been several days since the unpleasant incident with that nasty woman at the village shop, several days since that disconcerting night she'd spent at his home, several days since she'd sworn to herself that she would avoid this man without exception. What was that saying about necessity and its offspring, invention? Ha. Vanessa and Mrs. Weathers certainly invented some fantastically pressing reasons why she simply had to accompany Mr. Lanfield on his day trip to Bradford. She touched the list of "rare but essential" items that couldn't be acquired in Marksby. Utter rubbish. It was as if everyone meant to torment her.

To be fair, Vanessa still oscillated between indignation and stubbornness. One moment she insisted they couldn't give "that virago" any of their business or their money and the next she declared that they must make daily visits until the shrew gave her aunt the proper respect. But when Mr. Lanfield arrived at the door to fetch Mrs. Weathers for the excursion, it was mortifying to have the woman hem and haw and insist that Helena go in her stead. Helena had sworn she'd avoid his presence entirely. And he'd maintained a neutral stance through the entire exchange, as if it didn't matter to him who rode along to Bradford. But Mrs. Weathers and Vanessa were so peculiarly insistent that she go to Bradford, it didn't seem worth arguing. So here she was, sitting alongside this silent rock of a man. She tried not to look at him, tried to focus on the road ahead, but she was constantly aware of his every move, even the slightest twitch of his hands as he steered. When he finally relaxed into the seat, his thighs flexing beneath the rough fabric of his trousers, her heart was beating faster for reasons she didn't want to explore.

It seemed pointless to try to make conversation, but the silence stretched oppressively over miles and miles, and she had to do something to distract her from this unaccountable sensitivity to his presence. Finally, she blurted, "Why are you helping me?"

"Because of your grandmother." His curt, facile reply irritated her.

"There are myriad ways to provide aid to her without suffering my presence. Why are *you* helping *me*?"

"Because you need it. I've seen enough in these past weeks to know that you couldn't manage this trip without assistance."

"That is untrue!"

"How would you get to Bradford otherwise? Mr. Weathers? It's hard for him to make such journeys these days. And I was already going."

"But you despise me."

"No, I don't," he replied matter-of-factly. She stared at him in disbelief. And, damn him, all he did was stare right back.

"Oh, suddenly you don't? That's news. Care to explain?"

"No, I simply don't. Does an elephant despise an ant? Does the ocean despise a grain of sand? I don't despise you because you are simply too inconsequential now for me to bother."

She didn't believe that either, but she couldn't garner the nerve to confront him about the kiss they'd shared in his home, the kiss that was burned into her memory and made her skin tingle even now. No, it would be better to leave that particular incident unexplored. Better to accept his indifference than to follow that kiss down its mysterious, ambivalent path.

As they entered the city, she found that Bradford wasn't what she'd expected. She'd been a child when she last visited with her parents, and since then, the town had exploded into a metropolitan hodgepodge. The buildings were a mix of old and new and gave her the impression of a colorful flower garden overtaken by imposing weeds.

"Do you think Marksby would have grown this way if the railway agreement had gone through?" She hadn't meant to say the words aloud, and she was as startled as he by the question.

He looked around thoughtfully before replying, "There'd have been growing pains, no doubt. Bradford was already a metropolitan center. Would the village have changed this drastically? Who can say? But I doubt it. I don't believe we would have allowed it to modernize quite so severely."

She nodded but couldn't help wondering if modernization would have benefitted the village as much as everyone seemed to think.

Still exceedingly sensitive to his nearness, she was relieved when he suggested they meet at a designated location in the shopping district after their respective errands. She was even more relieved by how smoothly her transactions went, without the slightest malice or unpleasantness. She didn't even think they overcharged her. But as she exited the last shop, purchases in hand, her senses were jarred by the overwhelming surge of passersby. She stepped back into the shop, trying to catch her breath. Leaning her forehead against the shop window, she closed her eyes and focused on the cool glass against her skin. Surely, she could get to the meeting location just a few blocks away. It was at the edge of a park. She just had to keep walking. As she ran through calming thoughts in her head, she looked out the window and noticed that the crowd had dissipated somewhat. So she took a deep breath and then determinedly stepped out the door, staying close to the buildings so that she could slip into a doorway if a large group of people passed. She just barely managed to keep the anxiety at bay until she found their meeting spot.

As she sank onto a park bench, she couldn't help but notice that it was at a slight remove from the walking paths and traffic but still easily visible from the thoroughfare. When Daniel finally appeared, she was embarrassingly relieved that he came down and tied up the cart.

"We should stop for a meal," he said gruffly. "I was told we should try the inn at the end of this street. Simple but good."

His nonchalance startled her, despite her hunger. He was treating her as he would a friend, and it was . . . disturbingly appealing. But could she manage that kind of environment after struggling just to get to the park? Looking at his expectant face, she felt a strange and unfamiliar confidence. It was only a meal, and it was nearby. And she couldn't bear being so trapped by her emotional reactions. When she agreed, he led them silently down the lane, his presence serving as a calming protection against the rest of the world.

When they entered, they found that the only space left was at a table already occupied by a well-dressed man who was greeted by everyone who passed by. Helena's internal alarms rang in her ears. Too many people. Too much. But Daniel's low voice gave her focus.

"I won't allow any harm to come to you," he said quietly. And she believed him. Just before they reached the man's table, Daniel asked one of the barmaids whether they should join him or wait for another table.

"Go on!" she said brightly, "Mr. Salt is always happy for company. He tends to be quiet, but don't let that dissuade you."

Annoyed by the overly familiar way in which the barmaid leaned against him when she answered, Helena was watching his face carefully for his reaction. So she didn't miss how he cocked his head when he heard the man's name.

"Who is he?" she asked.

"Mr. Salt? I only know what I've heard, which I never count for much." He shrugged but looked at the table intently. "He introduced the import of alpaca here, which has affected the local farms quite a bit." His voice took on a hard edge, but he shifted his jaw as if struggling to suppress his reactions. "He's held important posts here in Bradford too. I've heard he has grand plans to revolutionize conditions for mill workers. In fact, you'd get along with him well, now that I think about it."

The mention of mill conditions did, in fact, draw her interest. She'd spoken privately with so many factory workers in London, young and old, who suffered horrible conditions, even with all the reform laws. It would be fascinating to discuss potential solutions. And the idea that the popularity of alpaca wool affected Marksby reinforced her thinking that more factors shaped the village's prosperity than just her long-ago escape. Focusing her attention on the table ahead, she felt the rest of the room fall away, her anxiety held at bay by concern for those in the mills.

When they approached Mr. Salt, he didn't make much of a physical impression, but then again Helena was fully aware that appearances didn't always convey reality. The man's hair and thick beard looked difficult to tame, and he had a distant look on his face, as if he was working to figure out a complex problem. Hesitant to intrude, she touched Daniel's arm and whispered, "Perhaps we should find another table. The man is clearly occupied, and we shouldn't disturb him."

Her voice must have carried more than she anticipated because, to her chagrin, the man abruptly shifted his attention to them and stood politely.

"Please do join me," Mr. Salt said with a slight bow of his head, his voice low but earnest.

After engaging in niceties and introductions, they were convinced that he meant his invitation sincerely, and Helena was pleased to find him a straightforward and engaging dining companion, especially when their talk turned to factories. As they compared London's and Bradford's situations, she was both excited and horrified by the similarities.

"I'm not surprised," she said, when he described the cramped and deplorable conditions for workers in Bradford. "The Ten Hours Bill marked important progress in fair treatment of mill workers, especially children, but it wasn't a panacea, at least not in London. And those are the tragedies that have been reported. I know of one instance when almost an entire family was lost in a factory fire. The parents and their children all worked in different parts of the building, and only one of the children survived. The poor orphan was taken in by the manager so as not to lose an employee to an orphanage."

"Aye, I've heard similar tales. Deplorable," he said with fervor. "That's why I'm determined to start fresh. I've done my all to keep my mills clean and safe, to pay my workers decent wages, to set reasonable hours, but it's difficult to maintain what seem like reasonable conditions when unscrupulous mill owners will woo them away with the promise of more pay for more work. I believe there is much more to an efficient and effective workforce than constant production. So many workers earn just enough to pay for their cramped, overcrowded tenements and have barely enough to eat, stretching every morsel and going hungry so that the children can be fed. I have in mind a miniature utopia in which to test an entire society constructed to foster happy, knowledgeable, productive workers. I believe focusing on the well-being of the workers, physically but also spiritually and emotionally, will result in the greatest and most dependable output of quality goods. Clean, affordable homes, schools for all, shops and markets offering fair prices—all of these work in concert to foster good, diligent workers. Just as a stallion performs best when well-fed, well-treated, and properly trained, so too I hypothesize mill workers shall thrive under the proper conditions."

"That's a massive and quite intensive project," she replied, awed by his vision. The sour look on Daniel's face distracted her momentarily, but Salt's ambitious idea fascinated her. "You're practically building your own village. You must have a vast network of contacts based on your political career here in order to build all those sectors of society in such accord. I shall keep a close watch on your vision as it becomes real. I know many people in London who would be thrilled to see your utopia succeed. Indeed, it would be wonderful to alleviate the suffering of so many, but it seems we need more proof of how the use of compassionate business practices can benefit revenue more than long hours and intimidation tactics. Factory work must not be so dehumanizing."

"How is it that you know such detailed information and have formed such particular ideas about industrial practices, Mrs. Martin?" Before she could reply, Mr. Salt turned to Daniel, as if just noticing him for the first time. "Sir, are you an industrialist? Your . . . companion . . . seems extremely well informed."

She tensed at the way he referred to her and felt, rather than saw, Daniel recoil from the word *companion*. Really, no word seemed truly fitting for whatever their interaction was now.

"Mr. Lanfield is a neighbor of my family," she explained. "As I am from London, I needed a guide to take me around Bradford for various and sundry items to care for my grandmother."

"Of course, of course. How very good of you to come all the way from London to look after her, ma'am. Perhaps when this new mill town is constructed, you might visit it and see the progress for yourself, assuming that it works as well as I hope. In fact, if you have the time, Mrs. Martin, I would be pleased to give you a tour of the land, idyllic for my purposes."

In her periphery, she glimpsed Daniel's shoulders stiffening at that. She turned to find his expression had grown dark and suspicious as he stared at Mr. Salt. What on earth could possibly make him so dislike the man based on such brief acquaintance?

"Given her grandmother's condition, I doubt Mrs. Martin has time to go traipsing about the countryside," he said. Did she imagine the deep growl in his voice?

"Forgive me," Mr. Salt replied immediately. "I didn't mean to presume. You're both welcome at any time. Send me a note if you wish to see the place, and I'll arrange everything. Now, if you'll excuse me, I do hope you have a safe trip back to your village." He took his leave of them politely, but that didn't relieve her concerns about Daniel's standoffish behavior.

"Mr. Lanfield, that was unconscionably rude!"

"No more rude than his undermining of English wool trade. No ruder than his behavior toward you," he insisted.

She stared at him, baffled by his response, as heat crept up her neck. She was almost afraid to ask, but the words came out anyway. "What do you mean?"

His brows came together as he scowled at her. "I've already told you. He introduced the alpaca trade in this region, and it hit Lanfield and other local farms hard." When he fell silent, crossing his arms over his chest forbiddingly, she found she couldn't let his other observation go. *No more rude than his behavior toward you.* What could make him react so extremely?

"What did you mean about his behavior toward me? He was all politeness."

"He's known to be a private, quiet man. Don't you think it strange that he was so loquacious with you? And he was so quick to invite you to his property out in a remote area."

"If I understand what you're implying, don't be ridiculous. We share a common interest in social improvement. Many people do. And his invitation was to both of us, wasn't it?"

He looked unconvinced. "Didn't you see how he looked at you?"

"Really, Daniel, you're fabricating this perception entirely of air. What has come over you?"

"We're done here," he said abruptly. "It's time to go."

Confused by his curt manner, she left the public house on edge, her anxiety growing as they wove through the still-full tables. Stepping out the door, she felt her lungs expand. She stopped, closed her eyes, and took a deep cleansing breath. She felt Daniel close behind her and admitted, "I'm surprised I lasted that long in there."

He simply nodded and led her to the cart. She could practically see the wheels in his head turning and wondered what path his mind was following. It didn't appear to be leading anywhere good.

As before, silence felt like the safest choice as Daniel drove through the crowded streets. But this time, instead of an empty, vapid silence, the air between them felt tense and bitter. Again. She hadn't realized how much had changed between them until the distance between them stretched out again. Once they were outside of the city, the road became more monotonous. Fatigue crept through her limbs, and she tried every trick she could to chase it away. Twice, she felt her head jerk up as she almost nodded off.

She was startled awake a third time as Daniel pulled on the reins, calling Talos to halt.

"What's wrong?" she asked, her head muddled from that twilight stage of sleep.

"If you're so tired, you should move to the cart and lie down properly," he said in a clipped tone.

"I'll be fine," she replied quickly. His derisive snort transformed all her accumulated confusion and frustration from their trip into irritation. "You seemed to be in a mood. You were much more pleasant earlier, cordial even. What happened to set you off thus?"

"Well, let's see, shall we? First, you make abundantly clear that you wish to avoid my company. Then you absolutely refuse to discuss that brief and baffling intimacy we shared the night of the storm. Then, after striving to assist you and watch for your safety, I find that you're entirely oblivious to a man inappropriately vying for your attention. If that weren't enough, and I'd say it was more than enough, then, despite all my best intentions, you fall asleep with your head against my shoulder."

His catalog of complaints took so much effort to unravel that she didn't realize at first what his words implied. When she did, she felt thunderstruck. Trying to navigate through a minefield she wasn't prepared for, she said tentatively, "I'm sorry to have been such a problem today. It seems everything I do is bound to cause you grief."

"Oh, Helena, you are a problem indeed, but grief is not at all what you cause me." He shifted to face her, and his fierce, intense expression stunned her. "Obviously, I haven't explained myself well. I need you to go sit in the cart because I'm unbearably aware of your every move. I need you to move out of arm's reach because, when you laid your head on my shoulder, all I wanted to do was take you in my arms and kiss you senseless. I hope you, of all people, can understand the conundrum of desiring something entirely untenable."

Any hint of tiredness disappeared. Instantly, she recognized that she'd wholly misinterpreted the energy she'd felt swirling between them. And she was frightened of how strongly it moved her, probably as frightened as he was. Coward that she was, without a word, she immediately climbed down, and she understood all too well why he set down the step for her to climb into the back, assiduously avoiding all contact with her. Whatever this feeling was between them, it was best they pretended it didn't exist.

Chapter 18

Only ten days since their arrival, Vanessa could almost collect eggs from the chicken coop without gagging. She'd never be able to tolerate that disgusting smell. Mr. Weathers insisted he keep the task of cleaning the coop daily, thank God! How these three elderly people got along here without help was a mystery.

She wouldn't admit it to anyone, but Aunt Helena had been right that taking on some of the unfamiliar household chores would be "improving." Even with the stench of the coop, she'd rather be outdoors in the morning sun than endlessly dusting knickknacks. She might even offer to beat the rugs if she could do it out here, with the verdant emerald fields in sight. With the chickens all squawking like eager gossips, she didn't hear the hoofbeats until they were almost upon her. She tried to blow stray locks away from her face, to no avail, as she straightened. She must look a fright, but Granny Thorton hadn't exactly been in a condition to welcome company. Perhaps she could duck behind the coop for a while. She sighed. No, with Aunt Helena gone to Bradford for supplies, she should go and help Mrs. Weathers greet any guests.

"Good day, Miss Vanessa!"

She jumped at the greeting from that deep, energetic voice. Oh, no, no, no. Although they'd only met once, she recognized that voice. And even without turning around, she could picture the handsome dark-haired lad attached to that voice. She was a tiny bit pleased that he remembered her name, although she should probably tell him to call her Miss Addison to be proper. Still, she liked how her name sounded in his lilting accent.

"Good morning, Mr. Lanfield. You're out roaming early today."

"Nay, it's just an average morning. Most days, I'm out on my horse at first light."

She'd had to adjust quickly to the rhythm and schedule of farm life when they arrived. On their third day here, Mrs. Weathers had come knocking at dawn, muttering something about pampered delicate flowers. Since then, Vanessa had made sure to throw herself into helping around the house. She began falling asleep exhausted soon after nightfall and waking while it was still dark.

"Your family must depend on you for quite a lot," she observed.

He shrugged, although a glimmer of pride crossed his face, and he said, "We all do our part, don't we? Need any help?" He dismounted with surprising grace.

"I've just finished. Anyway, I'm sure you have more pressing matters than attending to me and my little chores."

"I wouldn't mind. There's no chore too small on a farm. And, if I may say, you looked a bit out of place when we first met. I hope you're doing better now."

Her face heated at his reminder of her humiliating episode with the hungry sheep. She bristled at his judgment of her.

"I'm fine, thank you," she bit out as politely as she could. She lifted her chin and added, "I'd like to see how you would handle the teeming chaos of London, which is a world away from these bucolic fields."

"Bucolic. I'll have to remember that one." His too-full lips quirked, and amusement lit his hazel eyes.

What was she doing, noticing his eyes? She adored Billy's pale gray eyes, the color of burgeoning smoke.

"I'll grant you, miss, I'd likely be a fish suffocating on land in the great city. I've never been farther abroad than Leeds, which I'd consider unbearably crowded. One advantage of any city, though, is that there are lots more pretty girls, like you." Then he winked at her. Actually winked!

She couldn't suppress a giggle at his ridiculous flirtation, and she was mightily relieved to hear him laugh as well.

"That was poorly done of me, wasn't it?"

"I did expect a bit more finesse." What was she doing? *Stop flirting!* "Now I'm certain you have more important things to do than stand here amusing me."

He nodded and doffed his cap. "In fact, I'm here to deliver some packages from my mother to your, well, great-grandmother, I suppose. We've always just called her the Grand-dame."

"Oh, I like that! It sounds so dignified."

He snorted and then looked repentant. "Er, she's deeply respected. She just, er, doesn't stand on ceremony, if you catch my meaning. She's not one to value dignity over enjoyment. I still remember how she'd come fish with us when my siblings and I were little."

"You're quite fond of her, aren't you?"

"She's like family"

"Well, come on then. I'll give these to Mrs. Weathers and see if the Grand-dame is up for a visitor."

It took little time to deliver the eggs, along with a pie the young man's mother had sent along.

"Tell her that her Prince Hal is here," he called out as Vanessa left the kitchen.

She turned impulsively and replied, "I'm sure you're not as manipulative as all that."

"Only because I've lacked the opportunity," he shot back with another wink. His playfulness was so different from the calculated teasing and innuendo of the boys she and her friends encountered at home. He didn't seem at all predatory. As she made her way up the stairs, she heard him compliment Mrs. Weathers on her pretty ribbons and heard the old woman's answering giggle.

Gran's face lit up when she announced the young Mr. Lanfield. It was a joy to see her so revived. After helping her with a hasty toilette, she went to get "Prince Hal" and left them chatting fondly. When she returned almost an hour later with a tray of tea and pie slices, she found them both belly-laughing. He immediately rose and took the tray from her.

"May I ask what was so amusing?" she asked.

Gran dabbed at her eyes with a handkerchief and said, "Oh, dearie, it would be too difficult to explain. Just us being silly."

Before she realized it, young Lanfield had placed the tray on the bureau and already delivered tea and pie to Gran's bedside. As soon as Gran was settled, he said, "I should be going. You need your rest. I'm so pleased to see you are on the mend. Everyone at home will be relieved to hear it."

The beautiful new blanket draping Gran's bed distracted her. "What a piece of work!" she said in awe. "Is this from your mother?"

"Aye, well, it's more of a family affair," he replied, a blush creeping up his neck. "The wool is from our flock, sheared by our own hands. Mother and the bairns at home did all the spinning. Mother handled the dyeing." He ticked off each step with his fingers. "And all of us took turns with the knitting when we could."

"You knit?" Vanessa said, surprised.

"'Course I do. It comes natural to shepherds maybe. Everyone I know carries a sack or basket of knitting with him. I've always needles and yarn with me in the fields. You know what they say about idle hands and all that."

"This cover is spectacular! My mother and her friends do a great deal of handiwork with yarn and thread, and they would all marvel at this."

"Naught but a blanket," he said with a tilt of his head. "Mother does much more intricate lace and such. That's the really impressive stuff."

"I expect your mother would get along famously with mine!"

Something about her mother triggered a drastic change in him. It was as if a wall had suddenly been erected between them. His expression went blank, his posture stiff.

"It'd be futile to speculate on that now, wouldn't it?" His jaw was clenched. "I'd not wish for my mother to suffer the company of those Thorton girls—" He stopped midsentence, as if just then realizing where he was, and his face reddened alarmingly. He moved to take Gran's hand briefly and said to her, "I'll visit again soon, Granddame. You know I can't stay away from your bonny face."

Gently, Gran patted his arm and said, "Get on with your chores, Hal. You're a good lad." But before he could walk away, she added, "Just watch what you say about us Thorton girls, all right?"

"Yes, ma'am," he said with a bow of his head.

Vanessa went to see him out, but he ran down the stairs too fast for her to keep up. She heard him call out a farewell to Mrs. Weathers as he rushed out the back door.

She couldn't wait to return to London.

Chapter 19

The ipecacuan and mustard blister prescribed by the doctor seemed to do wonders for Gran. Within a few days, her breath came easier, and her color and appetite improved significantly. It felt like a gift to see her rise from her bed one bright morning to sit by the window. How long had she been suffering needlessly before sending for assistance? Helena wondered. How close had the sweet woman come to crossing the veil? Helena shook her head as she took that opportunity to change her grandmother's sheets and tidy up. No good could come of such speculation. Gran was on the mend, and, now that the door was open, she would strive to visit as often as she could. Gran couldn't stay here indefinitely, and she and Elizabeth couldn't give her the kind of regular attention her health must require, not from such a great distance. Changes would have to be made. Still, as she looked at her grandmother's gentle and dimly sad countenance as the woman tilted her face toward the streaming sunlight, she knew such a monumental conversation must wait, perhaps for a time when her sister could be present and all together they could decide the best fate, not only for Gran but for what was left of the Thorton farm.

When her grandmother fondly declared it was time for her to stop hovering and "let a person enjoy a moment's peace," Helena went to join Mrs. Weathers and Vanessa in the kitchen. It was amazing how quickly a day progressed here. With all the cleaning and washing and cooking and spinning and all the other -ings that the housekeeper had heroically been managing on her own, the sun flew across the sky. And there was something satisfying about the rhythm of such a day. Even Vanessa seemed to have acclimated to the routines of the house.

"Come to the public house this evening," Mrs. Weathers said, when Helena brought in some of the wash that had been drying outside. "It'll do you a world of good, I'm sure. I'll be there, and we can tuck you into a quiet corner and simply watch everyone cavorting!"

Such an easy invitation extended. She had to smile. Who would have guessed upon her arrival that anyone in Marksby, including Mrs. Weathers, would seek her company? The thought was quickly followed by the realization that, if she was noticed, there was no telling what ugliness might arise. When she said as much, though, the housekeeper and Vanessa both vehemently argued that she needed and deserved a little entertainment.

"Just so," Mr. Weathers interjected as he ambled into the kitchen. He removed his hat in a charmingly formal manner and said, "Anyone who might mistreat you will have to answer to me and the missus." Although he smiled jauntily when he said it, his eyes said he was decidedly serious. How was she to resist their combined and concerted efforts?

Thus she found herself seated next to Mrs. Weathers and her husband at The Crowing Cock. She'd never been there before, since her father had never been one to drink or carouse in the evenings. But the atmosphere seemed friendly and cheerful. No one seemed to notice her in her shadowed spot, and she soon found that she did indeed feel more relaxed, more carefree, than she had in weeks or even months. As predicted, they sat undisturbed while the festivities and gossip flowed copiously around them.

"That Rosalina is quite the flirt, you see," a female voice said. "She's already broken quite a few hearts among the local boys, but she's a good girl, for all that."

"You remember old Mr. Ackley?" another woman asked suddenly, before launching into the colorful marital history of the man from a neighboring parish. Apparently, he'd been through four wives in ten years, each wife younger than the last, and he was angling for a young Marksby lass, whose parents held split opinions about the possible match.

Helena let the random snippets of conversation wash over her while she took small sips of ale. In the mere half hour she'd been at the pub, she'd been exposed to more people than she'd encountered in Marksby since that dreadful episode outside the postmaster's shop.

A group of men entered the pub, clean and tidy but carrying the scent of horses and livestock. She didn't recognize any of them, but that mattered little. Like Daniel Lanfield, many of these men could have grown up here in the village and only slightly resemble the boys they had once been. As they made their way to a large table, she heard a familiar deep voice—Daniel's voice—call out from the midst of the group, "Mrs. Flanigan! I've sorely worked these men today and regret my heavy hand. Give them your finest brew to ease their burdens!"

The woman laughed and spoke to a couple of the serving girls. One began filling mugs while the other went back toward the kitchen. Then Mrs. Flanigan made her way to the table Daniel and his men occupied and, with a broad smile, made comments that Helena couldn't hear but that elicited bursts of laughter. After spending a few more moments with them, moments during which Helena would have given much to be a fly by their table, privy to the source of their mirth, the woman glided back to the counter. She refused to ponder why the woman's easy demeanor with Daniel and his men mattered to her, but Daniel seemed happy to receive her ample attention.

Turning to Mrs. Weathers, she asked after the Weathers children, but slowly she realized that a hush had fallen over the room. Mr. Weathers tapped his wife's hand and tipped his head to direct their attention, just before a broad shadow loomed over the table. Helena's skin tingled, and she knew whom she would see when she looked up. What she didn't know was how Daniel would greet her, given the muddled way they'd left things after the Bradford trip. Was he angry with her? Would he chase her out of here? Would he leave that to the rest of the crowd after making her presence so clearly known? She closed her eyes, chastising herself for such unfair thoughts. In these past few weeks, Daniel hadn't done her any harm, no matter the occasion. Even at his most furious, he'd kept his temper in check. Even when he'd kissed her, he'd hated himself for it but hadn't taken that anger out on her. And it was impossible to ignore that pulsing awareness of him so close by, urging her to draw him even closer. Damn her wayward emotions.

"Mr. Weathers, 'tis a pleasure to see you and your lovely wife this evening." When she raised her gaze to meet his, he smiled gently and said, "And it's a welcome surprise to find you here, Mrs. Martin."

She struggled to tamp down the pathetic frisson of delight his smile sent through her as she murmured a polite greeting in response. When he turned his attention back to Mr. Weathers, she let loose the breath she hadn't realized she'd been holding.

"I think we could all do with some entertainment, sir! Is it too much of an imposition to ask you to grace us with some songs?"

She'd forgotten that the normally reticent man was a fine and lively singer. People from nearby tables who heard Daniel's request echoed his sentiments, and it wasn't long before Mr. Weathers was cajoled into rising. Then he did a most surprising thing.

"Do you still play the piano, Mrs. Martin?" Mr. Weathers asked quietly.

She was startled by his question and could only nod in response. Then, to her further astonishment, he turned to Daniel, and said, "And I'm sure you haven't forgotten how to fiddle, have you, lad?"

His eyes widened slightly, but he grinned, causing Helena's heart to do an inconvenient little flip. "No, sir! It would be my pleasure to accompany you," he said, with a quick bow.

Mrs. Weathers interjected. "Ah, Helena, you wouldn't know, but Lanfield can do magic with a fiddle!"

Her husband looked at her fondly and said, with what Helena would swear was a mischievous look in his eye, "It's rare that I get to perform with two talented players. I've no doubt Mrs. Martin still has an excellent ear." He named a few songs, and remarkably she knew them all, sweet ballads and folk songs she'd learned well in her youth.

But the thought of going over to the piano at the other side of the room and being the center of attention froze her body. She looked up at Mr. Weathers helplessly as that familiar fear shot through her. Hot tears of frustration welled in her eyes. No! She couldn't be this weak, fragile thing!

She felt warm breath against her neck before she heard Daniel's low voice in her ear. "You're safe here," he said. "We won't allow anything to happen to you. If you don't want to play, you don't have to." The combination of his deep rumbling voice and reassuring words calmed her. Then he added, "But if you truly wish to accompany Mr. Weathers, which I think would be a rare treat, both for you and for him, then all you need to do is take my hand."

And there it was—his large, beautifully callused hand—just waiting for her.

Just then, Mrs. Flanigan stopped dead next to their table and focused a bright smile upon her. "Ah, Helena Thorton! Heard you were back! You had the voice of an angel. Come and entertain us!"

The proprietress glared when someone grumbled behind her, and Helena suddenly felt the urge to laugh at the absurdity of the situation. Even at home, she hadn't sat at the piano since . . . she couldn't bring herself to finish the thought. She used to love playing for her family and friends, entertaining them, rousing them to join in. Music brought them together and lightened their spirits. But she hadn't even wanted to play since . . . Isaiah. Now, however, she felt the stirring appeal of the piano and the way it allowed her to throw all of her emotions into the spry movements of her hands. And at least a small host of people here seemed interested in letting her do so.

She took Daniel's hand, allowing him to help her stand. Then she followed the two men to the instruments. She felt so exposed and conspicuous as she played a few trills to acquaint herself with the piano keys, but, to her relief, her partners took places in front of her, partially obscuring the audience. Once Mr. Weathers began to sing, however, her anxiety was drowned out by his jovial and charming resonance. He began with a simple, familiar shepherd's ballad, and soon everyone in the room was singing along. It didn't matter if her fingers faltered once or twice; no one would hear her mistakes over the concert of voices. After a few rousing songs, people cleared a space to dance, and the atmosphere grew loud and jocund. She was relieved when Daniel suggested that she and Mr. Weathers take a break as he played a reel that had everyone on their feet. Marveling at how she could be so inconspicuous and feel so unperturbed amid all these people, she sat back and watched the party. Daniel glanced back at her and winked without missing a note, and the subsequent burst of pleasure in her chest surprised her. His enthusiastic movements gave him a boyish air, his uncharacteristically expressive face showing that he reveled in the moment. He grinned as he danced the bow across the strings and ended a spry piece with a dramatic flourish before diving into the next. How long had it been since she'd felt so light and carefree?

Too soon, he turned to her and Mr. Weathers and said, "'Appen these folks could use a rest? Should we do a lullaby next?"

Laughter and teasing responses flew through the room, and Mr. Weathers said something about being parched and needing his wife's loving attention. She smiled at how startling the old man's demeanor was. Such a quiet man, and yet here he sang, he laughed—comparatively, he spoke volumes here, and yet she didn't think it had anything to do with the flowing ale. He felt uniquely at home in this pub with these neighbors, and she was thankful to have seen this side of him. Without him shielding her, though, everyone could see who she was. Some whispers flitted through the room, and she recognized the Wyatts from the shop as they stood and exited.

Yet Daniel wouldn't be deterred. "Come on, Helena, play something soothing for us all!"

One song immediately came to mind, and her throat slammed closed. It was much too real to her, too intricately woven into her own experience, and yet it seemed too perfect to ignore. When she reached the pause after the first few notes, she heard him gasp close behind her.

"*The Poor Old Weaver's Daughter?*"

She met his dark, questioning gaze and nodded, swallowing hard. No words could explain what had possessed her to play the song about a man trying unsuccessfully to woo a pretty maid with gold. When Daniel took up the melody on his fiddle, her relief was palpable, and she focused her attention on the song itself. She knew people would recognize the song so it was only natural when some began to sing softly. As the lyrics shifted to the girl's refusal, following her mother's advice to marry for love rather than money, she felt the song echoing through her. She'd wanted everything, love and money and the world, and, unlike the lass in the song, she'd turned her back on her family to get it. Her face went hot as the song continued. What would her life be if she'd made different choices all those years ago? Such a question shouldn't be worth thinking, not now, but the song stabbed directly into all those choices she'd made. Daniel's fiddle began to enliven some spaces in the song with lively trills and vibrato. Again, he brought her back to the present moment, and she followed where he led, transforming the sad, nostalgic tone of the song into something sweet and optimistic. They played surprisingly well together. He seemed to anticipate her shifts, hanging back at some points to let her playing lead the song and then picking up in others. As they came to the end of the song, the room hushed. But this silence was markedly different from the others she'd encountered in Marksby. Moving to stand beside her, Daniel bowed to the crowd. Hoots and applause rose in the air, along with calls of "One more!" and "Again!" But she shook her head at Daniel, and he nodded in understanding. She was done.

As he called one of his companions up to take his place, she made her way back to the table occupied by the Weathers. She'd had enough of this emotion-wringing stroll through the past. She needed to clear her head and take hold of the present. Mr. and Mrs. Weathers offered to bring her back to the Thorton house, but she hated the thought of cutting their evening short for her sake, especially when they were so clearly enjoying themselves.

"I'll be fine walking back. The moon is bright tonight, and I know the way," she assured them.

"I'll take you, Mrs. Martin." Daniel's voice came from behind her. Of course. "I was just leaving myself."

Before she could respond, Mr. Weathers said, "Aye, that's a good lad! You'll be in good hands."

Surely, the sweet old man couldn't mean the same inappropriate thing that ran through her head. *In good hands.* The emotional overload of this evening wreaked havoc on her mind. Without looking at Daniel, she replied, "I'd hate to be even more of an inconvenience to you."

"It's no inconvenience. I'm going in that direction anyway." While his words were cordial enough, she detected a strange undercurrent of insistence in his tone. When she twisted and looked up at him, she became acutely aware that he was in the grip of the same emotional chaos. Whether they should want this or not, whether it was wise or not, an undeniable need pulsed between them.

"You are too kind, Mr. Lanfield."

They slipped out a side door, as music and laughter spilled out behind them. Whatever lay ahead on this clear starlit night, as the moon bathed the hills in a silvery glow, Helena felt new doors opening. For the first time in a long, long while, she welcomed the unknown.

Chapter 20

As they rode in silence, the sparkling darkness beckoned to her in its vastness, and long-buried memories clamored for attention. She'd last seen this swath of sky the night she left with Isaiah. It had been full of promise then, and she felt a shimmer of that same heady optimism now, as if her whole body were taking a long, bracing inhale.

"You can't see the stars in London," she said, sweeping her arms wide and throwing her head back to stare straight up, immersed in the richness of the view. "It's been so very long. I'd forgotten how many stars one could see here. So much has changed here, and yet all this is as I remember it. Like a velvet blanket sprinkled with diamonds."

"There's a spot near my home that provides the most amazing view of the night sky. It's so perfect I built a kind of nest in order to do some stargazing comfortably. Would you like to see it?"

Her *yes* was out of her mouth before her brain fully processed the question. She'd missed this view and couldn't resist the chance to immerse herself in the inky sea of stars. When they left Talos and the cart, she realized exactly where his viewing nest must be located. It was at the very top of a nearby rise, and she could picture the rocky remains of an ancient watchtower there. In her youth, she'd slipped out of the house on more than one occasion to stargaze there. And it was where she'd met Isaiah one night to plan their escape. Conflicting emotions rioted through her as they climbed.

At the sight of the jumble of stones, déjà vu swept over her. Here. In the darkness. With a man she—Her mind stuttered; she had no way to end that thought now. Daniel beckoned her closer, and she saw that he'd created a smooth, raised area, nearly like a couch . . . or a bed. He covered it with horse blankets and spread his arms in invitation. As she settled at one end, he gently tapped under her chin, directing her gaze upward. The glittering endless light blending at its edges with the quiet landscape left her breathless. How silly of her to be so enamored of the sky she made herself dizzy, for heaven's sake. That was the cause of her dizziness, surely. It had nothing whatsoever to do with the man whose light touch made her whole being tingle.

He didn't speak and didn't put his hands on her again, but his nearness felt disturbingly comforting. She shouldn't like it so much. Soon he would say something cutting, something condescending to remind her of what a terrible person she was, and this moment would be tarnished. She wouldn't tolerate his judgment anymore.

"What's wrong?" he asked. He sat more than a foot away, and yet his voice made her feel as though he embraced her.

"Nothing," she repeated with a shiver. He took off his coat and wrapped it over her shoulders. His warmth radiated from it, and she yearned. But this momentary truce couldn't last. "I don't know what you mean."

"You were enjoying the night sky. Very nearly immersed in it, I thought. Then you tensed as if you expected something nasty. What happened?"

When she turned from the heavens to look at him, he had a peculiar expression.

"You think me simple for missing the stars," she said. Surely, he could appreciate directness, and it was honestly one of the myriad thoughts that disturbed her in this moment.

"Not a bit," he insisted. "Even during my short time in London, I felt bereft without this sight. That fog is no myth. The city felt unnatural, despite all its fine buildings and modern lights. This . . . such a night is a lover's embrace, endless and full of magic. How could one not miss it?"

Gone was the distance, the superiority, he'd maintained during the trip. Was this the genuine man? Had he set aside his family's grudge against her? *A lover's embrace?*

"I didn't know you had a bit of the poet in you, Mr. Lanfield." She tested the waters.

"You flatter me. Truly, though, I understand what you must feel," he said. "This is a sight without compare. The aurora borealis might appear in the coming weeks, in fact. Can you see it in London?"

Oh, to see that again! She shook her head and became all too aware of his proximity. And she had to accept that she wanted his arms around her. She looked away from him, fighting the urge to burrow against his chest.

Tilting her head up to the stars again, she said, "I have heard that one may catch glimpses of the aurora borealis on the outskirts of London on a clear night. My neighborhood is not an ideal viewing spot."

"I'd forgotten this, too," he said, his voice low. "All I need to do is look, but I haven't simply looked up at the stars in a long, long time." He turned away and dug something out of his pocket. Whatever it was, small enough that she couldn't see it in his hand, he raised it to his lips and then said, "My brother and I sometimes sat on the porch in the evenings and spun these crazy stories about the stars, cobbled together from what we recalled of Greek and Latin stories and our own fancies."

"Tell me one of your stories," she said softly, wondering if he would acquiesce. It felt like an unguarded moment. Maybe he didn't despise her anymore. Her body canted toward his. He grasped her shoulders again and gently turned her until she was facing away from the moon. The heat of his hands through her clothing spread in cascading waves down her body. What was the matter with her?

"You don't want to hear me rambling."

"I wouldn't have asked if I wasn't interested. I could do with a bit of rambling."

"See that one?" he said as he pointed to a constellation. Orion. Easy to recognize from the stars that made his belt.

When she nodded, he continued, "Gordon and I understood that it was called Orion after the Greek myth. But we agreed that it looked more like a barn cat in mid-leap." His mouth made a wry twist as he added, "Well, a cat with a fancy belt around it. We wove lots of our stories in the stars. We had one about an ancient and powerful chieftain who, rather than see his village pillaged and destroyed, set fire to it all himself. The embers rose to the heavens and became ours stars, we said."

"What a terrible story. Wasn't the story of Orion tragic enough? Why would he purge everything rather than be defeated?"

He shrugged. "Just a silly tale we cobbled together. It meant naught, just a boys' game." This was not the same man she'd traveled with from London. It couldn't be. Perhaps he had been kidnapped and replaced by a fake. The intimate companionship of this Daniel called to her in a way she hadn't realized she needed. For the first time in quite a while, she felt at home. It wasn't just the dissonance of returning to Marksby and being away from the life she'd built in London. Since Isaiah's death, nothing had felt right or comfortable or peaceful. She did everything she could to present a brave face for her boys, but she felt tense and hollowed out all the time. In this moment, under this sky, the desire simply to be held in a warm embrace felt . . . normal. It was a gift, and it left her speechless.

If Daniel found her silence odd, he didn't show it. When he finally spoke, his deep voice was barely a rumble, more felt than heard. "My wife, Nancy, didn't die. She left me, left Marksby. I could tell that she wasn't happy here, even from the beginning. After a few years, she began to complain that I lacked imagination and ambition. She hated that I had no higher aspirations than to live here and work Lanfield as long as needed."

His revelation in that quiet, resigned tone tore at her. For a man who showed so little of his feelings, his pain reverberated between them.

"I don't remember her," she said quietly.

"You wouldn't. Her father kept her close to home when she was young, and I didn't meet her until she was of marriageable age. At first, she bustled contentedly around the house, planting flowers, putting up curtains and trinkets." He looked around, but it was clear he wasn't seeing their surroundings. "She took the strangest things with her when she left me. That was how I knew. Initially, I thought maybe she went to visit her parents and take some time away. But there was a small crystal bowl in which she kept dried flower petals and herbs. She always said it made the room smell more pleasant, but to me it smelled only of decay. Still, I tolerated it and all the other knickknacks for her sake. The fancy silver candlesticks, the caps made of French lace. I thought these were harmless and would be enough to brighten her life here. She took all of it with her. I was blinded by the idea of her as my ideal helpmate, an extension of myself. I didn't see her. I didn't recognize that her wants and needs were much greater."

"There's nothing wrong with being content with your place in the world, being satisfied with the life you have," she pointed out.

"That's what I've always said, what my family has always said, but she wasn't happy here."

"But," she added gently, "there's also nothing wrong with wanting something different from what others expect of you."

"You would say that."

"Can you truly say that you have never wanted anything more than to run Lanfield? You've never wished to travel? Never wanted a different career? I remember how good you were at tinkering. You had a knack with mechanical objects and puzzles. Do you still design those wooden puzzles? The sculptures that have to be pieced together just so?"

He nodded. "When I find the time. There's too much work to be done here. Nancy did what she could, but, by the end, she did it all grudgingly, as if this world wasn't worth her time and effort." His voice faded. He turned away from her, and she almost missed what he said next. "I don't hate you, you know?"

"No? That's quite a reversal. Rather, I suppose you would say you don't hate anyone. You're too decent and moral for that."

"Don't glorify me yet," he said. "I'm no stranger to darkness. I know what it is to fear, to envy, to hate. And I don't hate you. I don't know what I think of you now, to be honest. Not yet. But I mean to learn."

"Why?" She was genuinely curious, especially since she was finding it difficult to tell what she thought of him now.

"We rarely get second chances in this life. Seeing you here again, I believe you will make the most of yours. There is hope in that." He stared at her intently.

Ensconced by the intimate darkness of their surroundings, it felt only natural for her to lean in and kiss his cheek, a simple gesture of affectionate thanks. She kissed her brother-in-law and her boys in just such a way. As soon as she touched him, though, she couldn't deny the difference. He inhaled sharply. The muscles of his arm tensed under her hand. The stubble of his cheek grazed hers with a pleasant rasp. *Oh, dear.* A hot, sharp sensation she'd laid to rest years ago shot through her. Surely, she'd imagined it. After the constant tension of the past few days, her nerves were unpredictable. But no matter how much she tried to brush it away, she recognized the tingling under her skin all too well after years of marriage. It wasn't just comfort or companionship. It wasn't anxiety. It was the low but insistent burn of want.

So close. His breath mingled with her own. A faint scent of brandy. They might as well be kissing, his lips were so close to hers. Her mind skittered away from the thought, from imagining the sensation of his mouth on hers. As their lips parted, a beautiful sense of awe whispered through her. She dropped her face to his neck and breathed in his scent, earthy, animal, real.

"What?" he asked, his voice rougher than usual rumbling through her body.

"What what?" she replied, unable to resist jabbing at him.

"You sighed," he said, as his hand rested between her shoulder blades. "What?"

"If you must know, I'd forgotten the pleasure of a good kiss."

He grumbled. "Is that all it was? A good kiss?"

Before she could respond, could explain that good meant so much more in her mind than it sounded, he tipped her face to his, and his mouth took hers. The pleasure intensified, heightened, sharpened to a fine edge that left her breathless and wanting.

"So . . . was that only good?"

"That was"—she took a deep breath—"that was heaven. Good is not commonplace or inferior, you know. I couldn't have wanted more from that first kiss. It was pure and beautiful, and I'd forgotten how completely wonderful such a moment could be. It was that good. I could kiss you for days."

"I must say I've never understood the appeal of kissing." He kissed her again. And then again. Each kiss was unique, varied, as if he was testing new possibilities. "Now I see."

"Surely you've kissed women before. You've never liked it?"

"Not especially. So I did it as little as possible. Fortunately, Nancy didn't seem fond of the act either, or at least that's the impression she gave. But maybe that's another way in which I failed her."

"No," she whispered and then kissed him gently. "Not now. This time is for the two of us. No one else is welcome here."

"You could kiss me for days?" She felt him smile against her mouth. "I would let you. I could drown in you." Then there were no more words. His mouth devoured her, and she took her turn greedily.

Their groans mingled as they both gasped for air. If he felt even a fraction of the pleasure that spiked through her, it was a wonder the blanket beneath them didn't spontaneously combust. His hands gripped her hips, demanding. Just as she felt herself slipping into mindless sensation, Daniel pulled away.

"I wanted you to suffer when you returned," he said in a rush. He held her, but his gaze focused on the sky. "I wanted you to feel shame and humiliation and remorse." Guilt laced his voice, and she understood all too well his inner conflict.

"I did," she admitted. "It wasn't just you. It's clear that I am not welcome in Marksby. At first, the rejection caused me such pain, such humiliation, but I must own the consequences of my actions."

"You don't believe in regrets, though, do you?" His eyes glittered as he leaned closer.

"Of course I do. I feel them as much as anyone else. But I've spent enough time living in the past. I know what mistakes I've made. I know all the ways I've failed, and I've lost much. But I also know there are choices I've made that I wouldn't change for all the world, and I refuse to regret those choices just because others deem them wrong."

"What about the effects of those choices on others?"

"I am not God. I make many decisions every day for the benefit of others. But I am not omniscient, nor am I omnipotent. We all have hard choices to make, and sometimes the consequences are difficult. I can no more regret leaving—and having the life and family I cherish—than I can regret returning now."

She met him halfway, raising to kiss him, and marveling at the feel of his body. Then, the most unexpected thing utterly deflated her. Without realizing it, her hand had found its way to his hip. She felt muscle and bone, but something nagged at her consciousness. Isaiah had had a raised scar there, a souvenir of the injury that ended his military career. Confusion swept through her. She didn't want to think of Isaiah at this moment. Didn't want these unintended comparisons. What she had with Isaiah was sacred. This was . . . purely physical.

"Where did you go?" Daniel whispered against her lips.

"What do you mean?" she replied evasively. "I haven't moved." He tilted his body away and simply looked at her. She touched his face, his stubbled jaw scratching her hand, and said more gently, "I'm right here."

He didn't pull away from her, but he frowned. "You disappeared. Your body was here, but it was as if you were no longer part of what was happening, what we were doing."

"I have . . . reservations," she admitted.

"I do too," he admitted before gently touching his lips to hers and then softly kissing her cheek, her jaw, her neck. Such whisper-soft touches. It was shocking to realize how much she had missed such tiny intimacies. It was equally surprising to realize that Daniel, so rough and ragged, touched her with the gentleness of a butterfly's wings. "I have bushels of reservations. But they don't seem to be very strong ones, not here, not now."

So tempting. *Too* tempting. Mere days ago, he'd felt nothing but contempt and rage toward her. Shrouded in darkness, a cacophony of thoughts assaulted her. She slipped away from him, steeling herself as she anticipated his objections.

"I cannot," she said. "This is . . . you are . . ." She shook her head, unable to voice the words, unable even to complete that sentence in her mind. It had been so long, and in all those years, she hadn't felt tempted, hadn't felt this keen pull of desire. Until now. And she hadn't missed it. Until now. That part of her life, so sweet and intense, had been buried with her husband. She couldn't do this.

A frisson of wicked freedom, just a hint of it, shot through her. It had been so long since she could trust someone to look out for her, so very long since her mind could rest even for a moment. The luxury of it made her dizzy and impulsive. In the space of a breath, she silenced her rioutous mind and practically launched herself into Daniel's chest, his arms wrapping around her from the impact. She should have been furious with him, with herself. He resented her. He'd lied to her about his wife. She'd destroyed his family, his livelihood. He, of all people, was the last person with whom she should be sharing such intimacies. In fact, she was furious! But her anger was caught in a tidal wave of emotions, a froth of heady desire. His weight against her, the faint whiskey-laced scent of him, the bulk of his broad shoulders, his massive chest, his body hardened by the necessities of the family farm—all of it overloaded her senses. The feel of his broad shoulders beneath his shirt, of muscles flexing and contracting as he pulled her closer, made it impossible for her to breathe. Or perhaps the breathlessness was due to the fact that their mouths had been locked together for so long.

"So, so long, it's been—" she stammered. Her own voice sounded so strange, so breathless yet thick and heavy. She pulled away, taken aback by her forwardness, by her wanton irrationality. Guilt and self-loathing crept up her spine. She couldn't betray Isaiah like this. But his hands locked on her wrists. She met his eyes and froze at their stormy intensity. Could he be caught in the same maelstrom? She pulled her lips away but continued to cling to him as the feel of his body against hers made words impossible. Sensations ran riot through her, feelings she barely recognized, heat and longing she couldn't comprehend. She squeezed her eyes shut and tried to rein in her response. She even managed to unclench her fingers and press her palms against his chest to gain some distance and composure.

Then his breath danced across her neck, hot and ragged as it brushed past her ear, and she was lost. Such a small gesture, and yet it was an intimacy she hadn't known she'd craved. A delicate, delicious sip of water in the desert. When his teeth gripped her earlobe, she shivered.

"Make that sound again," he murmured into her ear.

"What? What do you mean?" She barely got the words out. The feel of him, of his lips on her skin, of his coarse jacket, of his solid thighs even through her skirts, all of it drove rational thought from her mind. She hadn't felt such overwhelming passion in so very long, and she hadn't realized how very much her body missed the attention, the surging desire, until this moment.

A low laugh rumbled through him, felt through her palms rather than heard. "Didn't you hear yourself, love?"

"I—no, I—what?" She forced her eyes open and found him pulling his head back to look down at her.

"You make the most arousing noises, my dear. Are you enjoying yourself as much as you seem to be?"

As she stared up at him, bile rose sharply in her throat, the bitterness flooding her mouth. This man was a stranger to her. How could she engage in these ... acts ... with someone she didn't love and couldn't trust? With someone who, until very recently, despised everything about her? How could she lose herself so completely? She'd kept such absolute rein over her emotions, over her affections, since her husband had been taken from her. The loss of him had devastated her so completely that she couldn't bear for people to touch her, with the exception of her children. Her stomach twisted at the thought, and she yanked her body away. Her husband was the only man she'd ever been with, the only man she'd ever loved. She'd known when he died that this part of her life, the physical, was finished. This was some twisted aberration.

"No," she said firmly, as she loosened her grip. "No, whatever madness this is, I am not enjoying it." As if repeating the denial would make it true.

He released her immediately. He stared back at her, his face obscured by the darkness. Yet she could see an echoing struggle within him.

"Nancy was the world to me," he said, gruffly. "She was the only woman I wanted to spend my life with. As her feelings for me faded, I tried harder and harder to convince her to stay. But nothing worked. Everything was too plain, too simple. She wanted things I didn't even know existed and couldn't even begin to give her. When she left, my heart ceased to function." His tone shifted as he continued, "I know too well that one can enjoy relations without involving the heart at all. Or rather the body can feel fleeting pleasure, release at least, without attachment."

She ought to be shocked by what his last statement implied. Such thoughts, pleasure for pleasure's sake, were selfish and sinful. She ought to be disgusted by the suggestion of engaging in such intimacies without affection or even possibly without respect. But she wasn't shocked or disgusted. She was intensely, overwhelmingly curious. So horribly curious she cursed herself for wanting to explore the invitation that loomed in his words. *No!* She pictured Isaiah, pictured him laughing and cajoling. He was the only man she'd ever desired. *Isaiah, my love.* Whatever this errant feeling was, it wasn't real. After feeling so hated for so long, she was relieved to be accepted. That must be all this was.

"I can't," she said. It was all she could think to say.

Hands clenched at his sides, Daniel said gruffly, "I should take you home." Still, she hesitated. His breathing ragged, he added, "Before we do something we'll regret."

Chapter 21

As Gran responded positively but slowly to the treatments, Helena's days developed a routine, of sorts. Despite all the potent memories that lurked in the house, tucked in drawers, hidden behind curtains, she found comfort in being here, in making herself useful here. A whiff of Mother's perfume or her father's pipe would bring her to tears, but it was no longer an unwelcome shock; instead, she embraced each grief as it came and let it run its course.

A thump against the window startled her. She'd left windows open in the back bedrooms to let in some much needed fresh air, and she looked around warily. She saw nothing unusual, inside or out, but couldn't relax. The sound sparked some vague memory, one she didn't want to uncover, but she couldn't forestall the bitter taste in her mouth or the ringing in her ears. Or the darkness at the edges of her vision. No, no, no! Then she caught sight of a gray object on the floor, small, the size of a child's ball. When it twitched, she shrieked. She pressed her clenched fists against her forehead as she struggled to master her unbalanced reaction. In a blink, the poor bird hopped and then took off, only to crash into a window again and then another, growing more frantic as it sought the open air. On one detached, disembodied level, she could sympathize with its impotent struggles, but as it screeched and thudded against the arc of windows, her senses overloaded, and she dropped into a crouch against the wall, hands over her ears, as the banging transformed in her mind.

Rocks pounding against wood, against flesh, against bone. Blood covering Isaiah's face and hands even as he called out for calm and reason. Isaiah's voice drowned out by a mindless throng. And the thudding, over and over and over. No, no, no. She couldn't stop it. It would never end.

God only knew how much time had passed before she realized a trembling hand stroked her head. Gran stood over her looking weak but determined. "I heard a crash. What happened?"

"Nothing, Gran! Only me being clumsy." She looked at the windows, some of the curtains tattered by the bird's struggles. It was ridiculous to try to prevaricate. Clumsiness couldn't possibly account for how her grandmother had found her. And Vanessa stood in the doorway, watching, waiting, wringing her apron.

She rested her forehead on her folded arms, hiding her face.

"What happened to you, Lena?" her grandmother asked, gently. "What happened to the inquisitive little girl who wanted to go everywhere and meet everyone and feared nothing, not even her parents' wrath? You've always had a good heart, but anyone can see plain as day that you're broken. Well, anyone who knows you. You're afraid of everything, it seems."

"I am, Gran. I am terrified, and I don't know how to change that. I don't think anything can."

She heard her niece moving carefully through the room toward the windows. At the girl's gasp, she looked up to see Vanessa cradling something dark in her hands. That damned bird. Others might see it as portentous that a lone bird, probably seeking food or companions, essentially trapped itself for days and may have destroyed itself trying to get free from its self-imposed glass prison.

"Oh, no!" Helena said, "Please no! Tell me it's not dead."

Vanessa looked unsure but, to her credit, didn't waver.

"But why, dearie? What made you so very frightened? You seemed fine when you arrived. A bit skittish perhaps, but that's understandable considering how foolishly folks around here carried on about your elopement, as if that were any of their business. I thought—I hoped—that after you'd been here a few weeks, you would feel at home again."

"I see now that this will always be my home, at least in spirit. But the village has gotten no better in all this time. I'm a scapegoat for all the ills that have befallen this land."

"Aye, well, women have carried the blame of the world since Eve. You used to know better than to credit all that nonsense or else you wouldn't have left."

She looked up and met Gran's gaze. Out of the corner of her eye, she noticed that her niece had moved toward the windows. For once, she needed her family to understand her choices.

"I always took it to heart, Gran, but my husband mattered more to me than any of that; he mattered more to me than my own life. None of the vitriol from our little community touched me then, not when I could have a life with him."

"That look in your eye says it all. He meant the world to you, and now you've lost him too."

Gran squeezed her hand with surprising firmness, and she closed her eyes tightly to rein in the sudden surge of emotions. Lost him. He'd been taken from her, brutally, and she was the one who was lost. Now more than ever.

"What happened, dearest girl? What made you so afraid?"

"It's the crowds, Gran. I cannot abide too many people close around me."

"But why? You've not had such difficulty before."

"How much do you know about the circumstances of my husband's death?"

"Not very much. The newspapers reported mill riots in the South, and we saw his name among the injured. Later, railway gossip filtered from into the village."

"I don't know how much detail the papers would have provided here, but if ours were any indication, the news depended very much on which side the publisher favored. I was there with him. He wasn't even a party on either side. We were simply passing through the town on our way home from a trip to the ocean. It wasn't a riot yet, simply a gathering of people in the town square to air their grievances. When he saw the crowds and heard the angry grumbling, his aim was to pacify them, lest anyone be harmed. He tried to mediate between the mill owners and the workers."

"And look what that got him," Gran said quietly, neutrally, as if reading her own thoughts.

"Exactly! Foolish, foolish man. I told him not to stop. That it wasn't our business. But he believed he could help, believed he could be the voice of reason. He waded into the crowd toward the raised platform at the center of the town square. I tried to follow him, but the crowd became too thick. I remember he called to me and said, 'Go back! It will be safer for you at the edge of the crowd.' But I couldn't bear to be so far away. Watching him make his way, pausing occasionally to convince men here and there to let him pass, I knew in my bones something was wrong. I should have fought harder.

"I don't know what prompted it, but..." She stood and began pacing, touching things around the room. She was in Marksby in her childhood home. She was safe. "It happened so quickly. One large stone flew at him out of the mass of people. I don't know if anyone could have known what direction it came from. I only saw Isaiah's head recoil from the impact. He raised his arms, but I couldn't hear what he said. Then another rock hit him, and then another, and another. I remember screaming, and I remember the crowd around me tightening and surging forward. He dropped out of view, and I tried so hard to get through that mass of people. I begged and cried and shoved. All the while, the crowd tightened around me as everyone strove to get closer to the action. At some point, a constable was trying to get the people around me to disperse. He must have thought me mad as I babbled." She looked out the window at the patchwork rise and fall of the fields around them. In the unreasoning madness of the mob, it was a wonder she had survived.

Gran came to her side, the older woman's grasp on her hand impressively firm. "He died doing what he felt was just. He wouldn't have left you alone by choice."

"A kind couple who owned a shop nearby saw me pass by in hysterics. I was informed later that I only agreed to take shelter with them when the constable promised to find out my husband's condition. I waited there for so very, very long."

Thin but strong arms wrapped around her. "Go on, my lass. I'm here with you."

Helena couldn't hold back the sobs that punctuated the rest. "Isaiah never woke again. The doctors and surgeons there did what they could, to no avail. Soon, they agreed we could do no worse by returning home so the boys could perhaps see their father before he passed on. That was the most harrowing ride of my life. I watched him like a hawk for the entire trip, terrified that each breath would be his last. Terrified that each jolt caused him unspeakable suffering not visible to the human eye."

"It's never easy to see our loved ones go, is it?" Her grandmother spoke softly, as she would to a child. "No matter how they pass, we're never truly ready to let go. And to lose your husband so young, to be alone in all that violence, oh, my sweet Lena, I wish we'd known."

Helena leaned into her grandmother's unyielding hold and let the tears come. All the terror and helplessness and frustration and loss poured through her. When the flood of emotion receded, she was able to explain how Isaiah's gruesome death still haunted her.

"Since the incident, I have found it increasingly difficult to be amid large groups of people. Being here, able to walk the fields without a soul in sight for miles, has been heavenly. In London, I find it harder and harder to leave the house. At first, I felt mere discomfort, but the feeling has grown over time instead of diminishing. These days, I find myself suffocating when surrounded by people. Even the very thought of being in the midst of a group can leave me paralyzed with fear. I've begun fainting. It's really quite pathetic." She finished with a wry smile. "Some might say we received our just desserts."

"Anyone who would even think such a thing is inhuman!" Daniel! At the sound of his furious voice, she whirled to face him. How did he manage to appear at her lowest moments? She hadn't heard his footsteps approaching, and suddenly here he was, filling the doorway. If she were a fanciful person, she might think he looked like an archangel, massive and righteous and larger than life.

"Daniel! What are you doing here?" Helena asked as Gran moved to greet him.

After responding to Gran's welcome and asking about her health, Daniel held her grandmother's hand in his large one and said, "I came to see your grandmother. Gordon's wife sent along a basket, which I left with Mrs. Weathers. She told me that Mrs. Thorton was expecting me."

He looked uncomfortable, and she feared how much he'd heard of their conversation.

"*That* was when your spells began?" he blurted out.

"You were eavesdropping? How very ungentlemanly of you," she said, without heat. She looked at him warily. "How much did you hear?"

"Enough," he said simply. "I heard enough to fit the pieces together. We should talk."

Gran interrupted, "My fine lad, help me get back to bed and then take my granddaughter out for a turn in the air. I suspect she's not fully recovered from that wee birdie that confused indoors and out-doors."

"I'm fine, Gran. Mr. Lanfield came to visit you, not me."

"Well, and he's seen me, hasn't he? Let people fuss over you a bit for a change, Lena. In any case, leave me a moment's peace." Gran's parting wink discomfited her and reassured her simultaneously. The woman was quite fond of teasing her family; the twinkle in her eye attested that she was getting back to full health.

As she led Daniel down the stairs, she whispered, "It was exceedingly kind of you to come, but you needn't stay. I'm certain you have important things to attend to."

"I do indeed," he said, with a determined gleam in his eye. Then he took her hand and pulled her out the front door with him.

"Where are we going?" Helena asked.

Daniel wished he had an answer, but, in truth, when he'd taken her hand, he simply wanted to take her *away*. When he had entered Mrs. Thornton's room, he should have announced his presence immediately, but he'd thought they'd hear him coming up the stairs. The agony in Helena's voice had frozen him on the staircase. He'd been nearly overwhelmed by the urge to rush to her side and wrap his arms around her like a human suit of armor. Even now, the impulse to simply cocoon her loomed large. She wouldn't accept that. Now he just wanted to get her away from the memories that troubled her. Away from the past that hung over her. Just away.

Since he couldn't give her a direction, instead he asked, "You've been better, haven't you? Since you've been here, I mean. You had no problems during the trip to Bradford."

He didn't miss her hesitation as she chose her words carefully. "I believe I have. It hasn't escalated, which is a wonder when you consider all the unfamiliar and even hostile situations I've been in recently."

"Let's follow the Grand-dame's advice," he said impulsively. "She's never steered me wrong before. Come for a walk with me, not for errands or tasks, but simply for enjoyment."

He half-expected her to say no, to give a heap of excuses why she couldn't spare the time. He was all too adept at that himself, devoting his attention to everything that *had to be done*. But he wanted her company. After hearing of the real reason for her spells, he wanted to see her safe and to ensure that she found her tenuous equanimity again. An odd sensation built in his chest when she said, "I know exactly the place to go!"

He wasn't a bit surprised as their path led up to his stargazing nest. She hadn't seen the watchtower ruins in daylight, and it clearly held powerful reminiscence for her. The all-encompassing view was stunning in its own right, giving the impression that one could see all of England from this perch. One could feel all the promise of creation here—the fields, the forests, the beasts, even the puffs of smoke from distant factories, all of it lay at one's feet.

Without the benefit of blankets, the stone slabs were unforgiving. He removed his coat and laid it down for her to sit on, despite her protests.

"Well then, you must at least share it with me!" she insisted. "I cannot sit on your coat while you suffer the chill of this stone, especially when there's plenty of room for you here."

That, he could do. He'd been a cad and an ass, and he wouldn't impose upon her weakness or her kindness. He could stifle his body's perverse reactions and just sit with her, if that was what she wanted. They talked of nothing important—changes in the landscape, new and old residents of Marksby, sheep and other cattle whose antics she didn't seem to tire of. She nestled closer to him and rested her head back against his chest. When she began to shiver, he had nothing else to shelter her with but himself. He wrapped his arms loosely around her shoulders as they both slipped into a companionable silence.

"I should get you home," he said, after a few moments. "You must be cold."

"No," she replied in a low but firm voice. "No, I'm not cold at all."

"But you're trembling. I've kept you out here far too long."

"No," she whispered again. "That's not why I'm shaking."

The odd tone of her voice—*That's not why I'm shaking*—puzzled him. When she turned to meet his gaze, the intense expression on her face brought every inch of him to attention. A light in her eyes bespoke not just affection but need. A need that echoed and amplified the very same complicated yearning he'd been trying to suppress. He couldn't tell who initiated the kiss this time, but when their lips met, he was engulfed in the glorious sensations of her lips, her eyelashes brushing his cheek, her scent, her quickened breathing barely audible. The luxury of these sensations teased at his mind, a siren's song luring him away from good sense. He wanted her with desire so intense, so severe, that he couldn't make himself release her. If she hesitated, if she pulled away, he would honor her wishes, but he couldn't be the one to break their connection, wherever it led.

His arms around her were gentle but firm and warm, as were his lips. To Helena, this moment felt inevitable. Daniel had just held her, uncaring of the hour or the passage of time. And she'd slowly realized how much she'd missed this closeness—this sense of compatibility and rightness—just as much as she'd missed more intimate physical relations. There was no pressure or escalation, not even when she'd laid her head on his chest, reveling in the moment. His hands had stayed lightly wrapped around her. She was not trapped or cornered; she could leave at any moment. Her mind had stopped racing, as she felt his heartbeat. Her pulse slowed, along with her breathing. It was the most tranquil she'd felt years.

And now her pulse was racing again. With absolute surety, she knew what she wanted—who she wanted—here and now. But the intensity of her feelings threatened to consume her.

"What are you thinking?" she whispered, pulling away slightly, afraid to spoil this fragile peace.

He tapped her chin, and she was reassured by the ardor she saw in them.

"I'm thinking of the night we looked at the stars." His fond look turned serious as he added, "I'm wondering if I'm destined to be Perseus, saving Andromeda from the monster, or Orion, relegated to a plaything of the gods and dying at the hand of his beloved Artemis."

She laughed at his somber admission. "I am neither a helpless maiden nor a virgin goddess. I haven't been a virgin for quite some time." She let her hands roam his chest and his massive arms. She felt, rather than heard, his muffled groan as the darkness of his expression transformed into heat. "You would compare favorably with both of those men, though. Strong, fearless, intelligent."

"Is this what you want?" he asked, pulling her against him, the feel of her soft body through the layers of her skirts tormenting him.

Now was the time. She could end this. She knew that, if she said no, he would listen. More than that, he would accept her decision without question. *Is this what you want?* She closed her eyes and gauged her heart. She had to be clear.

"Daniel," she said, "I cannot promise you anything more than here and now."

"Agreed," he responded, waiting patiently.

"This is what I want," she replied, shaken by her own vehemence. "I need this. Need you."

Even watching him close in upon her, she was surprised by the soft touch of his lips against her shoulder. She tilted her head to give him better access as he dotted kisses along her collarbone and up her neck. His hot breath tickled her ear as he whispered fiercely, "By gow, I need you too."

Together they struggled to get her skirt out of their way. His movements stayed gentle but not tentative. Neither of them cared to be patient. He seemed surprised when she moved in his lap to place her knees on either side of his hard thighs and even more surprised when she helped him unfasten the flap of his trousers. Did it matter if he thought her wanton? Too late for such worries now. She needed him with her, inside her, with a desperation that overpowered all good sense.

Her eyes fell shut as his fingers found her and guided their bodies together. They fit so well. And he was so gentle, so gentle. Even the way he worked himself into her needy body was restrained and tender, as if he feared harming her. The feel of their bodies joined, of him moving within her as she rose and fell, was beyond comprehension. He groaned as they found their rhythm, and his hands gripped her, pulling her down to meet his thrusts. Too soon, his movements quickened and grew rougher. He gasped and bucked, suggesting his crisis was fast approaching. If she wanted to go over with him, she would have to take matters into her own hands. She reached down and touched herself, brushing her fingers against that sensitive nub.

Maybe it was the movement or her low moan that caught his attention. He stopped, mid-thrust, and said, in a gruff, lust-heavy voice, "What are you doing?"

She opened her eyes to find him staring down their bodies, obscured by their clothes. "You are about to spend, are you not? I mean to finish along with you." She hadn't stopped her hand, and she rocked her hips to encourage him to continue. It took an effort to force out words as pleasure built within her. "You need not attend to me. Just keep going."

He pulled back and stared down at her, his face contorted with passion and confusion. "What do you mean?"

"See to your own pleasure," she said quickly, "and I shall see to mine. Just don't stop. Heavens above, don't stop!"

With his brows furrowed, he looked almost angry. But he did as she bade, picking up his rhythmic motions even more forcefully. He glanced down again, and her fingers brushed him, making him grow even firmer and thicker within her. She would have to hurry.

Just a few more thrusts, and he stiffened beneath her with a harsh shout. She closed her eyes, blocking out the sight of his face twisted in a semblance of exquisite agony, and focused on the sensations tightening at the locus point beneath her fingertips. She gave herself over to the paroxysm that rushed through her, muscles tightening, back arching.

As she struggled to breathe normally again, she opened her eyes to see Daniel staring at her. His moods and expressions were such a mystery. Was he disgusted by her? The fleeting ecstasy evaporated, leaving her chilled and shaken. After all her self-doubt, after all her reservations, she'd felt a sense of rightness as their bodies met. If he didn't feel the same . . . if he regretted it . . .

Still astride him—his softening cock still inside her!—she felt a chill that had nothing to do with the weather. She stood and straightened her skirts, keeping her eyes averted from him as she heard him fasten his pants. Her vision blurred as she looked out over the hills, but she couldn't let him see her cry. What stupidity. *Damn, damn, damn.*

His touch was gentle, though, as his hand caressed her damp cheek and urged her to face him. He still looked angry, troubled, but his face held worry too.

"Helena, tell me, are you able to fetch yourself like that often?"

"I—" She shook her head and looked away again. What had seemed so instinctive a few moments ago, a natural part of her sexual life with Isaiah, now seemed strange and possibly wrong in this light. Many people condemned such actions as a sin. Was he one of them? If so, he was more of a hypocrite than she could have imagined.

"Please, I need to know," he insisted, quietly but ferociously. But she couldn't bring herself to speak. She shook her head as more tears burned her eyes. Finally, he added, "I didn't know women could experience the same end as men. In ten years of marriage, I never . . .

my wife never . . . I didn't even know to try to give Nancy that kind of pleasure."

"Never?" A guilty niggle of relief whispered at her. He didn't recoil from her but rather from his own inner turmoil.

He shook his head slowly. "I had no idea," he said with wonder in his voice.

"Women . . . that is, I can, yes." She considered how much to admit. How much would be too much? He'd raised the specter of his former wife already. "My husband," she said, faltering, "my husband was older and, as you might suspect, he was much more knowledgeable than I regarding what goes on in the bedroom. He sought my enjoyment as much as his own. He taught me ways to . . . bring about my pleasure . . . ways to explore what felt good."

When his face paled, she had more than adequate confirmation that she'd said too much. She turned away, all too aware of his disgust.

"I should have known. I should have tried harder," he said, with fierce recrimination. "I didn't think women were made that way. I—she—"

With sad relief, she realized that he'd turned his condemnation upon himself, and she hated seeing this good man mired in self-loathing. She explained, "Many couples don't experience *that* and still enjoy being together, physically." It was exceedingly strange to stand there, out in the open fields, talking with him about something so very intimate, despite what they had just shared. Dear Lord in heaven, they'd done *that* in open view in the middle of the day, on a stone slab!

It was disconcerting to offer him reassurance when she so keenly felt the tenuousness of their relationship now more than ever.

"Teach me," he said firmly, distracting her from her spiraling thoughts.

"Pardon?"

"I find I want to feel that again." His thumb brushed across her lower lip. "It's been ten years, and I've never felt it this intensely before."

"Ten years? You didn't seek a lover after she left?"

"No. At first, I was sure she'd return. She'd realize what a terrible mistake she'd made." His voice trailed off, but she didn't want to push him. She waited silently until he added, "As the years passed, I couldn't let go of the idea of her and her betrayal. No woman appealed to me. Even had I time, I had no desire." His voice faltered. "I took release occasionally when a kind and willing lass crossed my path, but it was rare and fleeting and . . . empty." Guilt and anguish laced his tone and twisted his face. "I didn't even know this was possible, this immense pleasure, especially for women." He sounded genuinely shocked, and then he sat up abruptly, tense with dismay. "Is this why she left, do you think? Because I did not see to her pleasure?"

"Daniel, such speculation can only bring pain, not resolution. She had her reasons, but you might never know the full extent of them. It is entirely possible her leaving had less to do with what you gave her and more to do with what she wanted for herself. We cannot be all things to all people; I've come to believe we cannot fulfill all of someone else's needs. I loved my husband, and we made each other happier than I could ever have imagined. But he needed things I couldn't simply give him—a sense of purpose, a sense of duty, a sense of accomplishment. And I too needed things he couldn't just present to me in beribboned packaging, things no one could give to me. I needed to find my own sense of purpose, beyond what other people expected of me. I was fortunate to find that sense of self working with the Needlework for the Needy Society and even more fortunate that Isaiah supported my efforts wholeheartedly."

"You are capable of anything, I'm sure. And later we will talk of this Needlework circle and how it relates to the factories and all of that. Much later. Now I want your undivided attention. I have been in the dark about the pleasures of the flesh for too long." The slide of his body against hers as he moved downward, as his breath skated down from her ear to her neck to her collarbone, curled her toes in anticipation. The "pleasures of the flesh," indeed! But then he paused, his warm breath teasing through her clothing. She couldn't bring herself to speak.

"I want you to teach me, Helena. I want you to show me all the things I didn't know, all the ways I can make you feel good, make you feel *that* good."

"I don't know all the ways."

"Whatever you know, I want it. I want to make your body shake with desire. I want to make you throw your head back in pleasure. I want to make you scream in ecstasy."

"I—I—how ambitious of you," she whispered, finding it difficult to breathe.

"You have no idea." He glared at her with a ferocious determination. "I want it all now. Right now." Then his mouth captured hers, his hands roaming her breasts, and she shuddered at his sudden intense focus.

"Daniel, wait!"

"More," he said, his voice gruff and demanding. "Tell me. Show me. I want more."

"Look around you! This is madness. We shouldn't have done anything out here, at the top of the world, for heaven's sake! We cannot continue this now!"

His hold on her loosened as he took in the landscape around him, awareness dawning in his eyes. He muttered a rough curse and moved a respectable distance away from her. She'd give anything to soothe his tortured expression.

"I'm sorry," he blurted. "I shouldn't have taken advantage."

She had to stifle a laugh, but his serious tone took her aback. Taken advantage of her? "Don't do that. If you took advantage of me, then it's safe to say I likewise took advantage of you. I wanted this just as much as you. And if you want more, I am willing. But we cannot be foolish and adolescent about this. We cannot continue this here. It cannot be now. We've risked too much already."

"Then give me a time and a place." He stood tense and stiff, his jaw clenched, as if he was struggling to keep himself in check.

"Tomorrow night. Near midnight, when I'm sure the house is asleep." He wasn't the only one struggling with his desires. He wasn't the only one who needed more. Anticipation curled along her spine, strange and complicated. The clamoring of her body was a mystery to her, but she couldn't deny it. "I'll come to you."

Chapter 22

Helena couldn't believe Gran's miraculous recovery. It was still painfully slow, to be sure, but, when they'd first arrived, she'd feared her grandmother wouldn't last the night. To see her, mere weeks later, sitting in in the parlor, humming softly as she read her Bible, felt much like a miracle. The sight closely resembled the Gran of her memories. Helena refilled a nearby vase with water and fresh flowers to brighten Gran's room, just as she'd done every few days for the past few weeks.

"Stop hovering and fussing, Lena. Come here and make yourself useful."

Yes, that was the Gran she knew.

"Do you need anything?" she asked, automatically.

"Just come in. I have a thing to show you." Gran pointed to the window seat at the far end of the room. "You recall that seat is also a chest? The key for it is under the flowerpot over there on the sideboard. I've been saving some things for you."

Her curiosity piqued, she did as her grandmother instructed and found the window seat filled with leather-bound ledgers. More than two dozen of them, she estimated at a glance. "There are so many. Which would you like?"

"Find the most recent one. I think it's the right most one. You'll find the year on the first page. Should be 1840."

1840. The year Mother passed the veil. Helena's insides clenched, and for a moment she felt ill. One of the regrets that would follow her to her grave was not seeing her mother before she died. She swallowed hard as bile flooded her mouth, and she had to blink back tears. As she searched, she heard Gran move to her side. The books darkened from right to left, fading as they grew older. She wondered how far back they went. More than that, she wondered how much this conversation would hurt. She lifted the volume on the right and looked at the first page to confirm the year.

"Do you know what those are, dear?" Gran was watching her carefully.

"It looks like a record book." And then the memory clicked into place. "My father used to keep notes in such a book. He'd record profits and losses and special events. He used to write in one at the end of every week." She could see him at the desk, bent over a book like this one, asking Mother to confirm various details as he wrote. Such a mundane task, and yet, looking at a random page, she felt her father's presence, if only for a moment.

"Not just him," Gran explained. "Your mother did too. The Thortons have kept almanacs for generations. These are just some of the ones your parents made."

"I remember Father checking these on occasion, especially when he was planning something, like whether to do the shearing early."

"Aye, the rains and drought, the level of the beck, the conditions of the flock. All manner of farm facts. But your mother and father recorded much more than that. You should read them." Pointing to the book in her hands, Gran said emphatically, "Start with that one."

A tightness in her throat made it difficult to swallow, but she nodded.

"Go on, dear, and have a look. I need to go up and rest, but I'll see you for dinner." Just before leaving the room, Gran added, almost so quietly she couldn't hear the words, "I should have given you those the moment you arrived."

She went and kissed her sweet grandmother gently on the cheek. "You had much more pressing concerns. I'd much prefer to have you whole than to have a stack of musty old notebooks."

"Just read it, dear. I hope it can . . . shed some light for you."

She felt compelled to sit at her father's desk and spread out the ledger, its dry pages yellowed by time. The cover creaked as if it hadn't been opened in a long time. Most of the notebook held factual observations about the farm and the flocks, along with business records. Yet interspersed among all these statements were more personal and informal thoughts. Sometimes they were written as letters, never to be sent. She stumbled upon bits of poetry, some with a renowned poet's name underneath and others signed by her mother or left unattributed. She hadn't known her mother wrote poetry. She occasionally found news clippings and postcards tucked in. Her parents' voices came back to her as she turned the pages, glimpsing bits of their everyday life. Her vision blurred as she read one of her mother's brief poems about a lamb washed away by a flood. She had to close the book when fat tears landed on her arms, lest she damage the fragile pages. She sat back in her father's chair, her breathing ragged. But she couldn't ignore the pain and regret coursing through her. Regret for so many lost years without them. Pain that they were lost to her forever. How she wished yet again that her boys could have lived in the warmth of their grandparents' company. She would give almost anything to have that time back, to have her family welcomed into the Thorton circle. But those choices hadn't been hers alone to make, and neither her mother nor her father had ever given her an opportunity to reunite. It wasn't fair that she'd had to choose. It wasn't fair that there was no way she could ever make amends or obtain their acceptance. And it wasn't fair that she'd lost her beloved Isaiah anyway. Tears flowed freely down her cheeks, soaking into her clothing, and she gave in to the sobbing she'd been trying futilely to control. She heard her own rough, gasping sobs and buried her face in her hands to stifle them, but nothing could stop the tide, and she let it take her.

She didn't know how much time had passed when Vanessa found her. The tears had finally stopped, as had the wrenching hiccups that resulted from her unchecked grief. Long shadows crossed the room, marking late afternoon.

"Has there been news, Auntie?" her niece said, fearfully.

"No, Ness, nothing like that. This is an old mourning that has been a long time coming." Vanessa must have noticed her hoarseness because the dear girl went and got her a glass of water. Helena gulped it down gratefully. Even after finishing the drink, her throat felt parched. Her eyes were filled with sand and felt hot and swollen to the touch. She longed futilely for all the things she'd sacrificed and all the things she'd lost. Only thoughts of her sons, her sweet boys, gave her the strength to compose herself and attend to the needs of the house. What good was mourning a past that couldn't be changed? Her boys were worth the losses, the sacrifices. She couldn't regain the love and joy she'd had in her youth, but she still lived. And she needed to believe she could create a new future for herself, one that didn't involve hiding in the safety of her home. She needed to explore new paths.

Chapter 23

By the time she entered Daniel's home that night, she was made up entirely of raw, exposed nerves. Reading the family almanacs had gutted her. That she still wanted to keep tonight's assignation spoke volumes because she wouldn't have thought herself capable of physical desire after such an emotional day. But she found herself drawn here, not out of lust, but out of a desire for his company. Strange that he, of all people, had become a person she trusted for solace.

"I feared you'd change your mind," he said abruptly. Whatever he saw in her face made him reach for her and pull her into his arms. "Shh, love, I've got you."

He sat her in front of the fireplace. Mugs of tea sat steaming on the table. He'd known she would come. For a while, he simply let her sit, absorbing the heat of the fire. No pressure, no expectations.

"It's been a topsy-turvy sort of day."

"How bad? Did someone hurt you?"

"No, nothing of the sort. Too many memories. They haunt my every move."

"You can still make new ones."

"What I did . . ." No, she would not taint the memory of her life with Isaiah with any semblance of guilt or regret. "My marriage to Isaiah was the defining moment of my life. It made me. For the first time in my life, I knew what I wanted and chose to take my future in my own hands. I knew there would be consequences, and I accepted that the freedom to choose wouldn't be easy or idyllic. But it was worth all the consequences to follow my heart and grasp at my own happiness."

"Even leaving your parents?"

"I would have left their home eventually, wouldn't I? And I never truly let go of them. Until they died, I sent them letters every month with news of their grandsons. I don't know if Elizabeth did the same, but I never received any responses. None. Their rejection cut me to my soul, but even worse was their refusal to acknowledge their grandsons. I would have loved for them to know my boys—for Father to teach them how to carve and how to fish—but if I hadn't chosen a life with Isaiah, I wouldn't have my sons. I wouldn't have had those glorious years with my husband. I wouldn't have the life I have known—one of love and purpose and joy."

"How do you know you wouldn't have come to love my brother or borne him equally fine children?"

"I'd known you and your brother all my life. I admired him; he was a good man, respectful and hardworking."

"So what was he lacking?"

"It wasn't a matter of lack. What I realized with my husband was that it was a matter of suitability. Seems like such a weak word, but Gordon and I didn't suit. When I met Isaiah, as improbable as it may seem, we fit. I don't mean anything crass or physical. I mean that we were uniquely compatible. He understood me, and I him. With him, I felt safe and encouraged and bold and true." She'd known from the first moment they spoke to each other that she couldn't marry Gordon. Even if she hadn't eloped with Isaiah, she'd become too keenly aware of how out-of-joint she and her betrothed would be. They might have made a stable and respectable marriage, but they wouldn't have made each other whole.

"From the first moment we met, Isaiah made my heart soar. With him, I felt safe. With him, I felt I could be bold and honest. Your brother was always proper, always decent, and so was Isaiah. But your brother never showed that passion for life that I craved. I didn't even know how deeply that craving ran until I met my husband. I have no doubt Gordon is a fine husband, and I am so pleased he built a good life for himself, but I doubt very much that we could have had what I had with Isaiah."

He listened so patiently and yet . . .

"Daniel, I'm sorry. This wasn't what either of us intended for tonight."

"This night is whatever you and I wish it to be. The way you de-

166 • *Amara Royce*

scribe your marriage and your husband—I've never had that, never felt that with another person. You've given me tantalizing glimpses of the kind of love we read about in poetry. There's a pleasure in sharing these quiet moments with you, even if we never go further."

She stood to face him, and the weight of his eyes on her made her heart race. *"I need you."* She couldn't tell if she'd said the words aloud, but she felt them deep inside, her core tightening in response.

"Show me," he whispered with eager conviction. "Teach me how to touch you, how to bring you to that point. I want to know everything."

"This . . . what we're doing . . . this goes beyond . . . it isn't just . . ." She didn't know how to say what she wanted to say, but suddenly she wanted some sign that this was more than a tawdry night of sexual education.

"This isn't simply lust, is it?" she asked, feeling suddenly insecure.

"No, Helena, it isn't. I don't know what it is, but there is nothing simple or base about it."

His confident response reassured her only slightly. She looked at him pointedly, but he refused to look down, refused to acknowledge the interest so obviously stirring again below his waist.

"It is not," he repeated more firmly. "This isn't some rash, mindless coupling in a haystack. I want to keep you in my life."

"That isn't possible," she said, but this time, when he wrapped his arms around her, she didn't pull away. The beat of his heart beneath her cheek was strong, as she nuzzled into his embrace. They could still enjoy this companionship, however temporary. When his hand stroked along her spine, she arched her body against his. That was all it took to light the flame.

"Put out the light, would you?" she asked quietly when they moved to the bedroom. She didn't even look at her own body much anymore. She was no longer young and fresh, and her flesh bore the evidence of childbirth and age. Internally, her body tingled with anticipation and an intense need she hadn't felt in so very long, but she didn't know if she could go through with this if he could see all of her. The sensations felt exquisite, but her mind kept intruding. *Don't. What of your marriage? What of your vows?* She couldn't quiet her thoughts, but her body was equally insistent. *Now. Please. I need this.* Darkness might keep it all at bay, if only for a little while.

Daniel didn't hesitate as he snuffed out the candles. When he went to the window, he left the curtains partly open, just enough for faint ribbons of moonlight that made the bed linens seem to glow.

"Is that sufficient?" he asked, a low, disembodied voice in the shadows.

"Yes, it's enough," she replied, moving gingerly in the direction of his voice, unbuttoning her blouse as she went. The dim remaining light would be sufficient to guide their way.

Once she'd passed through the beams of moonlight into darkness again, she slipped off her top and let it fall to the floor. Her eyes closed as shame and insecurity rose within her. His deep intake of breath was her only warning before his hand touched her waist above the band of her skirts. That small touch consumed her attention—the heat of his palm, the roughness of his fingertips, the gentleness with which he slid his hand around her. As he stepped closer, the warmth of his towering body radiated through her. All thought ceased as she reached for him and became a creature of feeling, consumed by stunningly keen need. Wrapping her hands around his thick shoulders, she pressed against him from chest to knee and pressed her lips against his. He responded with a passion that left her breathless. She couldn't say how much time passed as they explored each other; she simply wallowed in this overwhelming sea of pleasure, of want. Before long, she'd shown him everything she knew, everything she fantasized about, and he'd returned the favor.

"Helena! Come out to me, love! You must see this!"

She stared around the bedroom, disoriented by the gloom, and realized Daniel was calling her from outside. What on earth? The strangeness in his voice made her rush to don her shift and one of his jackets. He didn't sound alarmed, but his tone was one she couldn't recall hearing from him before. A mix of excitement and awe. What on earth could agitate him so?

The moment she stepped outside, she knew. Glowing ribbons of pale green, shifting from emerald to peridot, shimmered and rippled in the night sky, illuminating everything in a soft, surreal light. She stopped a few feet away from him, enraptured even more by his rapt

expression, his eyes fixed on the heavens than by the lights themselves. "Aurora borealis," she whispered. Decades ago, the first time
she'd seen it, from her family's garden, she hadn't had a name for it.
She knew now what it was called, and yet the words seemed less like
science and more like an incantation. Shrouded by the fog and lights
of London, she never expected to see this sight again. And Daniel appeared as delighted by them as she felt. She stared up, letting the
breathtaking phenomenon wash over her.

"You are so lovely." Daniel's words, low and close, seemed to
come out of nowhere and took her breath away. He slipped behind
her, and his arms stole around her waist, bracing her so she could tilt
her head back even farther. She felt enveloped by the luminescent
night. Could she truly feel the heat of his body behind her? Surely,
that must be a trick of her imagination. She closed her eyes against a
surge of emotions she dared not recognize. She had to be clear-
headed, had to be reasonable. Just like the fleeting light show above
them, whatever this was between them couldn't last. It was a beautiful illusion, but still an illusion.

"I must return to my family soon. The day after tomorrow appears
to be our best opportunity to take the train from Leeds."

"I can take you and Vanessa back myself next week," Daniel said
in a strangely diffident voice. Before she could respond, he continued, "I thought perhaps I could even stay in London for a time . . . if
there was cause to do so."

His suggestion immediately alarmed her, but she couldn't pinpoint
why. His arms stiffened around her, and she could tell he'd noticed her
hesitation. Gently, she said, "No, you mustn't. You're needed here. I
couldn't, in good conscience, take you away from Lanfield at such a
crucial time." Before he could reply, she pressed one hand to his chest
and admitted, "I am a changed woman from the one you met weeks
ago. You cannot dream of how terribly I feared the future I saw un-
folding before me. Every day it seemed I was sinking further into a
quicksand of fear and immobility. Every day I came closer and closer
to never leaving my rooms. Every day regretting how I was robbing
my sons of so much life, how I was fading into a shadow."

"You would have come to see your grandmother even if I had not
crossed your path."

"No, I don't know that I would have. I would have wanted to, certainly. But, that day, when you came to offer your cart and your company, Elizabeth almost convinced me not to leave London. I was already terrified, and she knew it. She knew all my greatest fears and made them plain. She wasn't trying to hurt me. I needed to know what to prepare for. But when she articulated all the chaos, the activity, the people, I really wasn't sure I could do it. It would have been easier to stay there, easier to control my environs and stay with my boys. But that wasn't what I really needed."

"I agreed entirely with your sister that you shouldn't take such a trip. From the little I knew about your condition, I thought it would be too much of a strain and too upsetting for you to see her under the circumstances."

"Your reaction ultimately convinced me to go. I needed to prove to you, to all of Marksby, that I could return undaunted and unashamed."

"I expected you to be brought down a peg or two when you arrived," he admitted, pulling away from her. When she turned to look at him, she could see the pain and guilt in his entire being, even in the dim lights.

"I know," she said. "You were honest and direct about your harsh feelings against me, and you accurately predicted how people in Marksby would react. Your feelings weren't without cause. I don't fault you for them now."

"By gow, I want you, right this minute, more than I've ever wanted anything in my life."

"Here? Now?" She said it teasingly, but the moment she said the words, she was overcome by the desire to be joined with him in full view of the night sky. To meld with him as the beauty of the aurora borealis shone down upon them. Oh, yes, she wanted that.

"Lord, yes," he whispered fervently, and he pulled her down to the ground with him unceremoniously. He yanked off the jackets they wore and spread both out on the damp ground, and then they celebrated the natural wonders of the heavens in stunningly creative ways, ways she'd never imagined. At one point, he coaxed her astride him, her back to his front, and then drew her down to lay upon his chest. Oh, the sweet majesty as they both stared up at the undulating skies, which matched the rhythm of their bodies, their skin slick and hot as the pleasure flowed over them in beautiful waves. The scent of earth and crushed grass and arousal combined with the visions above and his groans in her ear to shoot her to an unbearably intense zenith. Her screams must have been heard for miles.

"Dawn comes too soon, love. I am loathe to let you go." Daniel said, as he stroked her hair. It was all the activity he could manage as the first threads of light wove across the sky.

"Gran is recuperating rapidly. Her heart is still weak, but she gets stronger every day. She keeps telling me to go, but I cannot. Now that I see her, it pains my heart to leave. Isn't that odd? I never, never thought I'd see this village again. Yet now, even with my sons, with my friends, with my work—all I have worth going back to—the thought of leaving destroys me."

"You miss your boys?"

"With all my heart! I received a charming letter just yesterday from them. My sister has them practicing their writing." She smiled. "They sounded fine, still enjoying the novelty of staying with their cousins. Surely, they are staying up too late." She shredded more grass. "I feel that if I go, I will truly never return. All I have left of the Thorton family will be gone."

"The house and remaining property will surely go to you and your sister when the Grand-dame finally gives up the ghost."

"Ha! She'll probably outlive us all. Anyway, it would be impractical for us to keep it from so far away. We'd best sell it." Her voice cracked before she could get all the words out. "How morbid! Talking as if Gran is at death's door."

"These past weeks, you've had to prepare yourself for that possibility," he said. He tucked a stray lock of hair behind her ear, and a shiver of pleasure skittered down her back.

"So much has changed, Daniel, and yet this is still my home. Every day, the truth looms that I will lose all this . . . lose her . . . far too soon."

"You could rent it out. Then it would still belong to you, and you could gain revenue from it."

The idea of strangers living in her family home, working her father's field, turned her stomach. "We know nothing of landlording. And we couldn't manage the tenants from afar."

"You could sell it to Mrs. Weathers."

"No, if you can believe it, she's already said her family is plan-

ning to move closer to Manchester. Her children are determined to go
for work."

"I could keep it for you." He seemed as shocked as she by his suggestion, but he continued, "'Appen one of your boys or Mrs. Addison's children may want it someday. You couldn't sell their legacy out
from under them. Anyway, we own the rest of the land. It wouldn't be
much more to manage."

Shock upon shock. "Daniel, you couldn't do that."

"Why not?"

She sputtered and grasped for responses. "You have your own
land, your own home, to manage."

"We took over much of the land years ago. What's left wouldn't be
much more to manage, and it could remain yours. I could live there
and let Gordon's oldest boy have my house. He's old enough."

The thought of Daniel living in the Thorton house warmed her, although she couldn't begin to imagine why. She refused to delve into
those murky corners in her mind. He'd serve as an excellent caretaker. He'd walk in her footsteps, in the footsteps of her parents, and
the home would be preserved. Suddenly, the image of him leading his
future wife through the house, perhaps a woman with whom they'd
grown up in the village, struck her with a sharp bolt of emotion. The
vision of him taking the faceless woman's hand as they ascended the
stairs—no, no. That wouldn't do.

"I could not ask that of you. It would be unreasonable to yoke you
to our property, especially if you were to remarry. Your bride would
want control over her home, over its furnishings. She wouldn't want
to live in someone else's home. And I couldn't bear . . ."

She'd meant to say that she couldn't bear to have her childhood
home altered, her family's things removed, but that wasn't entirely what
she meant. She couldn't bear the thought of him remarried. And that
was a horribly sparkling gem of truth newly unearthed—she didn't just
desire him. She cared for him. Such a strong, honest, beautiful man—
why shouldn't he marry again? Why shouldn't he build the family he
hadn't had with his first wife? He deserved better. He deserved more.
But the thought of him with that fictional other woman, that fictional
family, tore at her—the sharp-beaked eagle tearing at the gut of
Prometheus, helplessly chained to a rock.

"Do you think, after the taste I've had of marriage, I would seek that misery again?"

"Not all women are like her." His bitterness tore at her heart. He was such a good man, and he deserved more than this solitary, work-driven life.

"I don't place all the blame on her. Clearly, I was a terrible husband as well. I have no need and no interest in such a future. I would only be your family's caretaker, and I can just as easily work Lanfield from there."

"Have you ever wanted to do anything else? The stargazing, for instance?"

"That's a pastime. It's entertainment. The farm's in my blood. It's me. I owe it to my brother, to my father—I owe it to Hal and the other bairns."

She wished it could be otherwise, for his sake. What, after all, was owed to him?

"This . . . with you . . . this is very different from what I had with . . . my husband," she admitted. "You know, for a time, I felt his death, especially the way he died, was a betrayal. He'd sworn to be by my side, to devote his entire being to me—but in the end, his dedication to the cause, to his ideological fantasy of harmonious labor, mattered more than I did, more than our family did. At least, that was what I thought back then."

"I blame her too." Blame. Present tense.

"As well you should, though. She actually did betray you."

"You talked of fit. Of suitability. I knew she and I were flawed from the start and took her to wife anyway."

"That doesn't excuse her faithlessness."

"It was clear that she wanted more than the farm, more than this country life. Like you, she had the spirit of a wanderer, but she found no encouragement in me."

"She chose to wed you."

"It wasn't as if she had much choice."

She observed, "We always have a choice. They aren't always easy, and sometimes none of the options are desirable. But we always have a choice to do the least harm."

"I think she gambled that I would become unsatisfied with my life and become more like her. She told me more than once I should get out from under my brother's thumb. We never truly understood each other. I can only be thankful that children didn't enter the picture. It was best that she left."

"I do believe you've just said more words now than I've heard you say in the past three weeks combined."

"I envy you."

"What do you mean? Why on earth?"

So many reasons, he thought. *I envy so much of your life.*

"Because you had the love of your life. Because you are bent by your grief but not broken. Because you chose a difficult path but have no regrets."

"You make me sound . . . I was a selfish girl. I wouldn't trade the life I had, but the way I behaved was terrible. Immature. Selfish. What you all must have thought of Isaiah. He was such a good man, such a noble and kind man, and I do have regrets. I regret that the way I left, the actions I chose, made it impossible for people here to see his goodness, for my parents to welcome him into the family properly. It all could have been so different, so beautiful, if I hadn't run away like a petulant child."

"Will you come to me tomorrow?" he asked, loath to leave her side.

"This isn't something we can keep a secret for long, not in a town like this. Your brother would be furious beyond reason if he found out we were engaged in an affair."

"He needn't find out."

She scoffed. "After he found me in your bedroom, I'm sure he must already harbor suspicions."

"Let him. I don't care. What I care about is learning how to please a woman."

"I would say you've achieved that. It seems you're a quick study."

"Call it a point of pride. If there's something I wish to master, I'm highly motivated. But I'm sure I need more practice in order to excel."

"What makes you think I have any interest in your tutelage?"

"I may be uneducated in this area, but my instincts have not gone completely awry. I see your pulse throbbing at the base of your elegant neck. I see the pretty pink that flushes your face when I mention pleasuring you. Plus, you have a natural incentive for me to improve."

"Just once more," she agreed.

"Speaking of once more . . ."

As he practiced what she'd taught him, her moan clawed through him, dragging across his nerves. Yes. This was what he wanted, her splayed out before him, completely open to him. But not just bodily. She'd exposed herself to him, made herself vulnerable to him, and his entire being reveled in her trust. The heat of her skin seared him wherever they touched—lips, chest, hips, everywhere.

Even as the voluptuous sounds walloped him, he refused to shut his eyes. Helena. No one else. No other memories would intrude on this moment. Her first peak eased some of his unrelenting drive to claim her. His thrusts gentled as she breathed deeply and slid her hands across his shoulders, down his arms, along his chest. She smiled up at him, an expression so unexpected he froze. His lungs forgot their function. When she levered her head up so she could touch her lips to his, the world resumed spinning, but at a faster rate than normal. He deepened the kiss, pushing her back down to the pillow as he devoured her mouth and moved deep inside her. Quick, hard pulses that made her body convulse every time he rubbed against that magical spot within that made her cry out. He ground against her, determined to wring every drop of pleasure from her body. When she moaned, her back arching against him, her nails digging into his forearms, his hips jerked harder against her body as his control slipped.

Her body loosened as her head lolled against the pillows. When it became clear that he wasn't done with her yet, she said, haltingly, "Too much . . . I can't. . . . It's so . . ." Then she could do nothing but moan and whimper.

"I need you," he said. "Look at me, Lena."

When she opened her eyes and looked at him, her gaze remained unfocused, hazy with pleasure. "I . . . I . . . oh . . ." And then, "Yes. Take me. Take what you need."

The roar in his head drowned out all thought. He pounded into her, and feminine gasps and cries fed the bonfire that raced through him. When she screamed his name, he cried out in triumph before the waves of ecstasy drowned out all his senses. His last thought before losing consciousness was *Stay*.

* * *

As she drifted back to earth, the silence was interrupted only by the occasional and remarkably expressive bleating of sheep in the distance.

"Such a simple life they lead, those sheep," she said, idly. "They're guided from birth, kept from going astray, protected and well-fed. Feeding and wandering and playing without fear of being lost. These sheep knew nothing of loss or want. Only the beauty and freedom of open space."

"Don't paint too pretty a picture. We've had lean years. We've had losses."

"But have they felt the losses, you think, beyond the moment, beyond fleeting instinctive hunger?"

"They're not as mindless as you might think. I've seen the ewes worry for their lambs—seen them give their own food to their young. I've seen them mourn their dead. At the end of last year's lambing, we lost a ewe when she wouldn't stop searching for a lamb we sold. She kept escaping, and one day we couldn't get her back. It's not always easy looking into the eye of a mother after having lamb stew, I'll say."

"You don't just see them as cattle, do you?" She remembered. Even in his youth, he'd had a tendency to name all the animals. In a flock of hundreds, he'd know each sheep by name.

"Men must harden their hearts for slaughter when needed."

Women too, you dear man. Women too. She straightened her spine, knowing she had to be firm, possibly even cruel. But she had to shear herself away from this man and this town. And she had to start cutting herself away now. A clean cut with a sharp tool. The chill of the night seeped through her shift, and she rolled away from him to cover herself more completely.

"Daniel," she said hesitantly, trying to gather her resolve and find the right words, "you have been an invaluable help to me, but we have no future together. Look at this place. We live worlds apart. You belong here, and while I am overjoyed to again be welcome, I belong in London. That is where my heart lives."

"You are where *my* heart lives. I know you feel the same. Admit it," he insisted. "In your touch, in your eyes, in the way you watch over me and anticipate my needs, in the way your body responds to mine, I see that you care for me deeply. Tell me what you feel. Even if we cannot be together, at least give me the truth."

She shook her head. She dared not say the words. If she said them, this would be real. It couldn't be.

"Marry me." His tone made it a statement, not a question.

"Don't mock me."

"I am not. Marry me."

"That's ridiculous. Why?"

"Because you love me." His conviction squeezed her heart. She couldn't say it, couldn't allow it.

"I don't."

"You do, whether you are willing to say so or no."

"I don't."

"I could make you admit it."

"You . . . wouldn't."

"And that is why you love me."

"No, that's not it. I love you because—"

"Aha!" A blend of triumphant joy and abject relief filled him. "I knew it! Now marry me."

"It wouldn't work. My life, my family and friends, everything is in London."

"You've managed to make the trip more than once now. And I hear there are these remarkable machines called trains that make the trip quite speedy. Indeed, they are a modern marvel of efficiency." He clasped her hand in his, his grip warm and firm but careful not to overwhelm her. Could it be that he was trembling? When he lifted his other hand to stroke her cheek, she definitely felt a fine tremor. She could so easily gut him, but she had no choice.

"People need me there," she said quietly.

"I need you too, Helena. I need you, and I have never needed anyone. I don't want you to give up the life you have, I swear I don't, not if it makes you content. But there must be a way to fit me into your life as well."

She shut her eyes as if she could shield herself against his words. No, she couldn't do this. It simply wouldn't work—for either of them.

"My sons . . . I cannot uproot them," she said, her voice sounding weak even to her own ears.

"We can spend the bulk of the year in London and return here for the weeks when I'm needed at Lanfield. Gordon's sons can help him with the daily work. We can come for lambing and shearing. It would do your citified boys a world of good, you know."

She couldn't ask that great a sacrifice from him. The farm was his life, his home. Literally, he'd built his home there with his own two hands. It was true that she couldn't simply relocate her family, but she also couldn't possibly uproot Daniel. Not now. Not when she had seen for herself how drastically her selfishness had once before devastated so many people. She shook her head and pulled away from him. "Do not ask for what I cannot give."

Chapter 24

Creak. Creak. Creak. Auntie Helena had returned. Hours earlier, when she'd heard her aunt creep stealthily down the stairs, Vanessa had been able to glimpse through the bedroom window a cloaked figure moving in the direction of the stream. Not a woman inclined to a midnight dip, her aunt could only be going to one destination. Now the moon still shone through the curtains, but she could hear early birds calling to one another.

When the footsteps reached the landing, she quietly opened her bedroom door and blocked her aunt's path. "Where have you been, Auntie?"

Stifling a scream, her aunt replied, "Nowhere, dear. I couldn't sleep and so I decided to take some air."

"You were gone for hours." She wasn't such a naïve girl as to be fooled by that weak story. She'd told lies infinitely more believable than that about her outings with Billy, and her parents had never suspected. It was strange that she hadn't really thought much about Billy in recent days. She missed him, of course, but then he didn't need to occupy every waking moment, did he? Her aunt's irritated stammering reclaimed her attention.

"I—you—Vanessa, really! You should be in bed asleep, not spying on me. I'm an adult and have no need for a nursemaid. Now get back to bed!"

She nodded but otherwise didn't move. "I love you, Aunt Helena, but now I have a sense of what my parents must feel. You cannot run out into the fields in the middle of the night. It's dangerous. You could be injured, and no one would know. We wouldn't even know where to find you."

Her aunt ducked her head. Oh, that was a telling clue.

"Or is there someone who would know without a doubt where you were? Someone of whom you've grown quite fond? Someone who lives nearby?"

"That's quite enough," Auntie snapped uncharacteristically. "I do not need to report to you or justify my behavior. We are not equals, my dear niece, and I do not answer to you. Now go back to your room."

She backed away, alarmed at the ferocious tone, and hot tears welled in her eyes. She blinked rapidly and couldn't meet her aunt's gaze. When she was back across the bedroom's threshold, she whispered, "I'm sorry for my forwardness, Aunt Helena. It's only that I was concerned about you. I couldn't bear to see you hurt . . . in any way."

Her aunt gave her a grim smile before tapping her chin affectionately and saying, "You're a sweet girl, Ness. No need to worry over me. All will be well."

She'd heard that refrain countless times from her aunt, her mother, and all the Needlework ladies really. This time, more than ever, she hoped it would be true. In her aunt, she saw all the signs of a girl's growing infatuation with none of her typical caution or deliberation. She felt a new sympathy toward her mother at being able to see inevitable heartbreak and yet being helpless to prevent it.

Chapter 25

Daniel felt as though he'd been gutted. Not that he knew what being gutted actually felt like, but he thought the sharp, stabbing pain in his belly, along with the contradictory feeling that he'd been hollowed out and sucked dry, might be a close approximation. He turned the paper over and over in his hands, wanting to tear it to shreds, wanting to toss it in the fire, wanting to stomp it into the ground. But he couldn't bring himself to do any of that. He looked around the room, stripped of all signs of his faithless erstwhile wife, and still he couldn't destroy this single sheet of paper. He cursed long and loud as he read the letter yet again.

My Dear Mr. Lanfield,

First and foremost, I must beg you to forgive me for being such a terrible wife to you. I prostrate myself before you in apology for leaving the way I did. I must own that I knew as well as you did how poorly we suited one another, and I despaired at the thought of spending our future so unfulfilled. I should have spoken with you rather than running away like a criminal. I hope the intervening years have made the farm a great success and brought you the satisfaction that I was never able to achieve.

I write to you now not only in remorse but also in supplication.

For many years, I wished simply to be free of Marksby. I strove to live as an adventurer. I have engaged in activities both exciting and life-threatening, to my exceeding joy, yet they are experiences you never would have allowed your wife to seek. I only hope you feel such unadulterated excitement and joy in your life, in your own way. In all this time, I never sought or had any expectation of affection, and yet I recently found someone with whom I can share this love of exploration.

We wish to go to America for a fresh start. If you have maintained any hopes of our reconciliation, I am deeply pained to say with certainty that it will never happen. I beg of you to grant me a divorce a mensa et thoro. I am told this would nullify our marriage in the eyes of the church without the exorbitant cost of a divorce through Parliament. I would willingly swear upon a stack of Bibles that I shall never remarry, as my lover and I seek simply to build a future together, without legal encumbrance or formal labels, unorthodox as that may seem.

As you and I have not shared bed nor board in a decade, I dearly hope that you will see fit to grant this request, the only request I have made of you in all the time we've been called husband and wife.

In the hope of your compassionately affirmative response, I remain your humble and imploring,

Mrs. Nancy Lanfield

As he neared the end of the letter, he felt ravaged, eviscerated, the pain as devastating now as it had been the day Nancy deserted him. Shadows lengthened as the sun set. Darkness filled the room, the dwindling fire in the fireplace too weak to defend against it. His mind noted the minute changes in the room, but none of it registered. He sat and stared at the paper in his hands.

Gordon burst into the room with an air of urgency. "Danny, I need you to make a run to Leeds."

"Now? It will be dark before I get there."

"Yes, now. I received a contract by post; it must have been delayed because the order is due in Leeds by tomorrow. It's lucky that we have the wool to fulfill the order right now."

He hesitated. "I've a commitment tomorrow. I need to be back here in the morning."

"All the more reason to leave immediately. Whatever this appointment is, surely it can keep for a day, if worse comes to worst."

Fine. He'd take the bloody load to Leeds. He'd do whatever anyone damn well wanted him to do because the Fates obviously had no love for him.

*   *   *

Every step that brought her closer to Daniel intensified her anticipation but also her dread. Just catching sight of his candlelit windows from a distance brought her bittersweet glee. Their last night together. Every night she'd spent with him, she'd cursed the dawn. How much harder would it be tomorrow, when she had to leave for good? Letting herself into the house, she spied him sitting in the rocking chair in front of the fire.

Something wasn't right. He didn't stand to greet her, didn't react at all. Perhaps he felt as conflicted as she about this final tryst. With his back to her, she couldn't even see his expression.

Then a chill shot through her as she realized . . . it wasn't the right Lanfield.

"Where is Daniel?" she asked hesitantly.

"That's quite familiar of you, calling him by his Christian name," Gordon replied. He still hadn't moved from his seat. "My brother is on his way to Leeds."

"That's peculiar. We recently discussed the possibility of him driving me and Vanessa to Bradford in the next day or so. Why didn't he say he was already going to Leeds?"

"It was an urgent matter that came up suddenly," he said firmly, as he finally stood, a shadowy bulk outlined by the firelight. An ominous sight that only a fortnight ago would have sent her into near-hysteria. "I can't say whether he'll be back by tomorrow. You and your lass will need to find someone else to cart you around."

His snide, bitter tone lashed at her. Something was very, very wrong.

"Gordon, since you are here, there is something I feel I should say to you." She braced herself. This had been too long in coming, and seeing him face-to-face didn't make it any easier. But she owed him this. "I never wanted to hurt you. I wish you could understand—it would have been so much more of an insult to you if I had stayed and married you without affection, especially after having that first brilliant taste of bliss. Did I place my happiness above yours? Yes, I cannot deny it. Yes. But I also meant to free you to find your own happiness. You would not have found joy with me as your wife. And I swear I did not know how terribly my departure would affect the economic future of this village."

"If you had known, would you have stayed?" he asked, his voice neutral.

She couldn't meet his eyes, but she saw his hands clench and unclench at his sides. Her exhaustion overruled her fear. "I cannot say. I'd like to think I would have pressed Isaiah to slow down and court me properly over a more acceptable period. I would have tried to cajole and convince my parents. In the rashness of youth, I couldn't bear to be parted from him. I was a silly girl, afraid he would forget me when he moved on to other towns and saw other, prettier, more accomplished girls. I could have stayed at least temporarily."

His jaw hardened. "So, had you stayed, you still would not have married me?"

"When did you know, Gordon?"

"What?"

"When were you made aware that the land merger and the railway deal essentially hinged upon our marriage?"

"What does that matter?"

"It matters a great deal. When did you know?"

In a tortured, impatient voice, he replied. "Remember the day I said we should have our banns read in June?"

She remembered. An echo of that shock ran through, the stunning shock she'd felt when the amorphous future marriage to Gordon coalesced into the cold, hard fact of a wedding date on a calendar. It was one thing to think of being Gordon's wife as some abstract possibility in the distance and quite another to think of an interminably monotonous existence on the neighboring farm. As his wife, day in and day out, her life would be circumscribed by the needs of the farm. Then, too, she'd felt the rush of infatuation with Isaiah, riotous emotions and sensations the likes of which she'd never, ever had any hint of with her betrothed.

Would having a station built in Marksby have made a significant difference? Somehow, she doubted it. Both families might have benefited financially for a time, but Gordon now was functionally the same man he'd been then. A good man, undoubtedly. Dependable, hardworking, responsible. But he had no aspirations beyond the farm's success. He'd never wanted to see or do anything more. She didn't fault him for that. In fact, she almost envied his singular focus. But she would have died inside, one day at a time.

Gordon cleared his throat and said, "My father informed me that morning. He said that the consolidation of our lands would be a strong inducement for the rail representatives. He didn't order me to do anything specific, just gave the clear impression that a marriage sooner rather than later would be advantageous."

She'd already been smitten by Isaiah at that point. She recalled how she'd clung to him, distraught, when he'd met with her a few days later. He'd been agitated when he'd arrived, and that was the night he'd first suggested they elope. The timing was too perfect to be a coincidence, she realized. Isaiah must have known about the arrangements. To him, there were other towns that would do just as well for a station. She'd been tossed back and forth like a child's ball. But, no! She'd made her own choices. Isaiah hadn't kidnapped her. Had she known of these emotionless financial undercurrents, would she have still gone with him?

Even now, when she looked back, she couldn't believe she'd taken such a mindless risk. It all could have gone so wrong. If Vanessa or really any of her boys or her nephews and nieces tried to do such a thing, she'd be among the first to barricade them in their bedrooms and nail the windows shut. But she'd eloped. And she'd found a loving, devoted husband, a doting husband who'd indulged her desire to see the world. They'd made a beautiful family. When she'd said, "All will be well," she couldn't in her wildest dreams have imagined her life with Isaiah would flourish that wonderfully well. Until the day he had been taken from her.

"I'm sorry, Gordon, but I wouldn't have married you. I didn't love you, and you deserved someone who did."

"You were always so blind to my feelings," he responded caustically. "I'm sure you couldn't have known, but I *wanted* to marry you and not just because of our families. We'd known for so long that we were intended to be together. I suppose I developed expectations. I built my own vision of what our future together would be like, and I wanted it. Your prediction wasn't so different from my own—I imagined coming in from the fields for dinner to be welcomed home by you smiling and surrounded by all our beautiful bairns. But my vision was a lovely thing to me, not the prison you pictured. No, this work doesn't make for an easy life, I'll grant, but I find it deeply satisfying, and I believed you would too."

"You were born to this life," she acknowledged, "and you are uniquely suited to it. I knew then that you were meant to keep the Lanfield farm thriving, and not just because it was expected of you. I knew this was the life you craved, and you were so lucky to have found it so directly. Not everyone finds their path so clearly aligned with their happiness. You needed someone who would feel as at home here as you do, someone who found joy in the land and the beasts and the labor just as you do. I would have tolerated it, but you deserved more than just reluctant acceptance."

"Daniel's done playing your errand boy . . . although he made quite a show of it."

"What are you saying?" she asked, a cold fist squeezing her heart.

Gordon's eyes narrowed menacingly. "You're a smart woman. I'm surprised you didn't ferret out the scheme yourself, especially after I found you in Daniel's home the morning after the rainstorm. He warned me not to be too theatrical, but I knew better. He was afraid I'd drive you off then, but he doesn't know you like I do. I knew my affronts against your man would make you dig in your heels."

"You know nothing about me!" she said, grasping at the first thing she understood. "You had a scheme? To what end?"

"You should have suffered terribly for your desertion," he replied, every word loaded with bitterness. "And yet you look hale, you speak of a happy life with a pretty family, and you lead a life of luxury compared to how we scrape and scrabble here with no guarantee of security from season to season."

"What was this scheme?" she asked again, enunciating every word with growing indignation.

"Married or no, you broke your troth and abandoned this village. Your reputation here was already ruined long ago." At that, his mouth twisted into a grotesque smile. "The problem is that you still show no remorse. You have no shame. So it wasn't enough for someone to bed you; such a faithless slut would be easy to seduce. No, you had to be convinced of some deeper emotion, some romantic commitment. You had to be wooed. And Daniel did his job quite admirably, though I can't account for how he could stomach touching you."

Gordon's harsh words stabbed at her, every syllable another shiny finely honed blade slicing through the core of her. This was exactly what she'd feared. She'd forced herself to suppress those instincts, those alarm bells, in order to trust his word. *Fool. Desperate mindless frowsy ninny.* There weren't enough words she could heap upon herself. But focusing on the words was the only thing that kept the horror at bay.

Had Daniel's kindness all been an act? Had his passion been fabricated as well? How he must have laughed at her. Her face burned, even as a chill surrounded her heart. No. He wasn't lying to her, she was sure of it. He wouldn't. His intensity, his open affection, his tenderness—he wouldn't fabricate those. The Daniel she knew wouldn't play such games with someone, not even for revenge. He would be straightforward in his approach, instead of masking his true feelings.

"That's why you're here, isn't it? A midnight tryst. Danny has you panting after him. Didn't need much to catch your eye."

"I don't believe you. Daniel abhors lying and duplicity. He felt contempt for me when we met in London, and he wouldn't hide it, not even for the sake of polite society. He wouldn't toy with someone's affections, certainly not after the way his spouse played him on a string for so long."

"Poor woman, you tell yourself whatever pretty tales you need to tell for comfort. Nancy was exactly the spark to this cleansing little flame. By doing to you what she did to him, he can obtain retribution and restore his manhood. Revenge and rejuvenation in one fell swoop."

He took an ominous step toward her, and she felt the doorknob dig into her back as she retreated.

"It's best you go, Mrs. Martin. Whatever business you had here this evening is for naught." His tone implied that he knew the personal nature of her intended *business* with Daniel. Her face heated. No, she couldn't believe anything Gordon said. Daniel would return in time as promised, and everything would be made clear.

"Good-bye, Mr. Lanfield. I wish I could say it was a pleasure seeing you again."

"Likewise," he said as he followed her to the door and slammed it behind her.

Yet again, Vanessa rechecked the bedrooms to make sure they weren't leaving anything behind that they might need. She checked under the bed, behind the wardrobe, in every drawer, including drawers she knew they hadn't used. She even peeled back the sheets and remade their beds, twice so far. She had to do something while they waited to leave. Aunt Helena didn't look well, no doubt weighed down by the stress of traveling. What would happen if her aunt had one of those spells again—or another awful trance like the one in the cart? She couldn't whistle worth a farthing, but it was more than that. Mr. Lanfield had a calming way about him. No matter what the occasion, during these few weeks, his harmonizing effect on her aunt had become increasingly clear. Could they truly make this trip without him?

"Ness, stop fussing up there and come down, lass," Gran called. "Come and spend a wee few moments with me before you go. How will you miss me properly otherwise?"

She grinned. Such a singular woman. She could only imagine what it must have been like to be raised in this home, with Gran's guiding hand. She'd be happy to leave behind the filthier chores, but she'd miss that old woman.

"In a blink, Gran!" She took a final sweeping look around the room. She'd thought it so worn and outdated when they'd arrived. So foolish and shallow-minded, she had been. Every piece in this room had a history—the quilt on the bed made from scraps crossing three generations of Thortons, the pillows her great-grandmother had stuffed with goose feathers, the lace curtains knit by a grandmother she had never known. It was no wonder Mother and Father berated her for being a slave to fashion. She'd thought them miserly when they refused her extravagant fabric choices and flashy accessories. Shame washed over her as she recalled her petulant complaints about having to reuse the fabric from outgrown dresses. She traced the circular pattern of the quilt, wondering if her mother knew this one. If her mother would let her come back, maybe Gran could teach it to her.

In the sitting room, Gran stood by the side table, turning the pages of a book filled with tiny, cramped writing. When she touched the dear woman's shoulder, Gran pulled her into an emphatic hug, her thin arms amazingly strong, especially for one who'd so recently been bedridden.

"My sweet lass," Gran said, her voice tremulous, "it was such a pleasure to meet you. I'll miss your sweet smile."

"Not as much as I shall miss you," she replied as she fought back tears. It was a losing battle, she knew, as Gran's sentiments served to heighten her own. Before long, they'd both be one great emotional puddle.

Gran stroked her hair and then turned back to the book she'd been perusing. "Look here. I have something for you. It's one of the Thorton almanacs; your grandparents wrote down many particularly fond and amusing entries about your mother this year, and I think you should have it." Gram's voice dropped to a whisper as she added, "In the spring of this year, your mother experienced her first infatuation with one of the village lads. Oh, how your grandparents fretted and fussed over it. I needn't tell you she didn't end up with that one, but I believe you'll find it illuminating to read accounts from her parents' perspective."

Joy filled her as she gingerly picked up the leather volume. "Oh, Gran! I cannot wait! I was just thinking upstairs that it would be wonderful to have a token by which to remember this visit, and I couldn't imagine anything this special, this momentous! Are you sure you wish me to have it? This must be the only copy!"

"Aye, Nessie, this is yours now. I'm sure you'll take great care with it. Something tells me this particular volume belongs with you." Gran winked knowingly, and heat spread through her as she looked down to the table. "I'm sure that your mother will likewise enjoy the illuminating observations of her parents back then. Now you can take a piece of us with you to London, which would please me greatly."

"I wish I had something to leave with you too!"

"You have, my lamb, you have! You're burned into my memory. To see you here in these rooms, to hear you squawking back at the chickens—aye, I heard you!—to feel your warm embrace as you looked after me. You leave me all those wonderful moments. I'd hoped to see your mother return with your aunt, but your visit more than made up for her absence. It is impossible to miss how you favor her, not just in face but in action. It's been a blessing to see her through you."

Chapter 26

It was amazing how even Helena's view of Bradford had changed since her last visit mere weeks ago. Still crowded and smog-filled, it felt more chaotic and precarious. She sensed Mr. Weathers and Vanessa both watching her as their cart crept through the city streets, which were clogged with vehicles, cattle, and pedestrians. A faint but constant tension gripped her belly; it didn't intensify as she'd expected, though. When Vanessa touched her hand, she attempted to smile.

"Soon, we'll be home," her niece said quietly. The warmth and tenderness in that simple word—home—made her throat tighten. So much had changed in such a short time! Yes, London was her home. And yet. She'd thought she'd lost Marksby forever, cast out and condemned. But this visit had given her more than she'd dreamed possible. The Thorton house was her home again, and she would be ever grateful for this glimpse of redemption. Even if she never saw Daniel again, her home and her family were whole again.

She couldn't believe the terrible things Gordon had said. Wouldn't believe Daniel capable of such cruelty and manipulation. He simply didn't have that ugliness in him. How had this man become so dear to her? Their physical indiscretions aside, she truly cared for him as if he were family. She appreciated his kindness, admired—nay, adored—his strength. She saw now the quiet depth of his intellect and his heart. And she would miss him in every cell of her being. Surely, her heart couldn't physically tear apart, even though that was exactly how it felt. She couldn't wait to see the boys, to hear their laughter, yet Daniel's delicate touches on her hand and her shoulder still burned her skin. In their wake, Daniel had become one of the few people she trusted, one of the few with whom she'd felt truly at peace. She never thought she would experience that communion again.

A month ago, she could not have faced this environment. She knew her corner of London well enough, and now she could see that this city, with all its cramped, looming buildings and its crush of strange people resembled London in tenor, if not in physical appearance. Being a complete stranger in this moment should have set her spiraling into panic. Those deep-seated fears were still there, stewing in her mind, but she could see past them now. She could look upon the crowds and see families, see earnest working folk, see goodness and beauty and hope again. She could breathe. She could be in such an environment and laugh again—not entirely unguarded or carefree—but open in a way she hadn't been for far, far too long.

"There's the station ahead," Mr. Weathers said.

As the moment of their parting loomed, she couldn't convey any of the delicate sentiments swelling in her heart for this man and his wife, both of whom had been devoted to her family since before she was born. She'd promised to return as soon as she could, and to bring her boys with her, but no one could predict the vagaries of time. All she could say was, "This visit has been more than I could have hoped for. I shall cherish every memory and keep you and Mrs. Weathers in my heart!"

When the cart came to a stop, Vanessa's arms wrapped around her from behind. "Me too, Auntie! So very much." Vanessa gave the old man a buss on the cheek and promised to return.

"Time to go, dear," Helena said through the lump in her throat.

As the train slowed, Helena couldn't begin to process how much had changed in the weeks she and Vanessa had been away. The return trip to London had been remarkably swift and astoundingly uneventful. Even changing trains in Birmingham had been easy, even though the station had seemed even more crowded than the streets of Bradford had been. As they made their way out of Euston Station into London's bright fog, Vanessa exclaimed, "Goodness, it's a relief to be in Town again! Ah, to be home!"

"My dear, as near as we are, you cannot tell me you found no joy in the country."

"Of course, I cannot, Auntie. Marksby is so quaint and charming in its own way." The girl's airy, dismissive persona resurfaced so quickly. How unfortunate. This was the girl whose parents had wanted her away from the city. She searched for any sign of the other girl, the one who'd marveled at the tranquility of the rolling hills and the kindness of her kin. Nothing. Vanessa's demure expression, the coy quirk of her lips, the air with which she walked, everything about her demeanor suggested the dangerously selfish and flirtatious young woman hadn't changed at all. It was really too much for any of them to expect that a few weeks away would effect a total transformation. But then the sweet girl linked arms with her, and she heard Ness quietly add, "It is a different world there. I am so glad I accompanied you. Great-Gran is so remarkable. It was such a bucolic place. I can picture you and Mama as children there, and I shall hold many fond memories of our visit. Thank you for taking me with you."

Overcome with emotion, she could only reach with her free hand to squeeze her niece's arm in response. She would hold many memories of the visit, but she wasn't sure she would ever label them as fond ones, not after all that had happened.

After all the walking they'd done in Marksby, they agreed that there was no need for a cab. Indeed, winding their way through London was remarkably entertaining for its novelty. Streets teemed with life, for better or worse. And while Helena had a few moments of tension when passersby crowded in upon her, she never came close to a concerning level of panic. Soon enough, they arrived at her sister's front door. She had to pause at the bottom of the steps to brace herself. There would be questions, not all of which she could properly answer.

Vanessa squeezed her hand and said, "The boys will be so thrilled to see you! It's good to be home!"

Before either of them could knock, she already heard Tommy yelling, "They're here! Mama's home! Mark, she's home!"

When the door swung open, sure enough, Tommy rushed over and wrapped himself in her skirts. "Mama! I just knew you would return today! Auntie 'Lizbeth said not to get my hopes up, but I knew. I don't know how I knew, but I was sure of it!" She couldn't even take a step into the house with his small arms wrapped so tightly around her, and his exuberance brought tears to her eyes.

"My darling Tommy! How wonderful to see you!" she cried, as she hugged him tightly. In the corner of her eye, she saw Mark coming down the stairs as well.

192 • *Amara Royce*

"Welcome back, Mother. Tommy did just say this morning that today was the day, but he's said it every day for a week now," Mark said. He looked well enough, but he remained at a distance. "You were away much longer than we expected." A mix of emotions played on his face. Surprise and relief washed over by wariness and—was he angry with her?

"Come here, Mark, so I can hug you properly. You boys have both grown like weeds!"

He took a few slow steps, then paused and asked, "Why were you gone so long?"

Her heart ached at the vulnerable tone of his voice, and for a moment, she could only shake her head, so overwhelmed was she by memories of her trip. "Your great-grandmother was very ill, near death in fact. And so I am unspeakably pleased to say that she has made a full recovery. It took longer than anyone expected."

Tommy tugged on her sleeve and asked, "Where is Mr. Lanfield? He promised us he would keep you safe. Is he outside with his cart?" He moved to pull her toward the window, but she stopped him.

"No, sweetling, he isn't here. Vanessa and I returned on the train. In fact, I think we should take a train trip sometime soon. It would be a great adventure for us all."

Mark rushed down the remaining stairs, and he and Tommy stood before her with matching frowns. Damn, the mention of trains hadn't caught their attention at all. She braced herself.

"That snake!" Mark exclaimed. "He gave us his word that he would see you safe." Tommy nodded in solidarity.

"Have I not returned safe and sound? He provided safe transport for us to Marksby, but he had important work for the family farm. He couldn't possibly spare the time to drive us back."

"I like him," Tommy said.

"You liked his horse," Mark retorted.

"Yes, but I liked him more." Tommy's chin tipped up firmly. "I knew he would watch over Mama and protect her."

"Now, Tommy, I don't need protecting," she assured him, as she ruffled his hair.

"But—" Mark interjected.

Before either of them could explain all the ways they hadn't seen that statement to be true, she cut in, "I know I have been weak in recent years, but this trip has revived me. It was precisely what I needed to give me the confidence and fortitude I once had. And Vanessa and I made our way back from Manchester just fine without any help."

"I would feel better if he were here," Tommy replied, his voice quiet.

Wouldn't we all? She threw a mental blanket over that thought and said, "Well, now that I'm here, we should go home. You've been in Aunt Elizabeth's hair long enough. Go on and pack your things."

"But we have a surprise for you, Mama!" Tommy looked at his brother expectantly, and at Mark's nod, he burst out, "Bart is home!"

Bartholomew wasn't due back for several months, at least! What had brought him back to London so early? Her mind immediately jumped to the worst possibilities.

"What on earth is he doing back here so soon? Has he been injured? Has he been discharged?"

Elizabeth, who'd been observing the exchange, said, "He's completely fine, Lena. Safe and sound. They had good winds, he said, and his ship should be here a few more days." She addressed Mark and Tommy, "There's no rush, boys. You'll stay with us until after dinner, surely. Bart will join us if he's able." Then her sister stared at her for a moment, as if working out a puzzle. "And, you, my dear, should at least take a few hours' rest after the ordeal you've had. You know you can all stay as long as you like." Her sister led the way upstairs and sent the boys off to find their cousins and clean up their belongings.

"You can nap in the nursery. It should ensure you the most solitude and privacy, and I shall ensure that you are not disturbed."

"That's not necessary, Lizzie," she said, although the strain of the journey, of everything that had happened, suddenly felt like a crushing weight. She followed her younger sister, despite her protestations.

"My dearest, I'll be blunt," Elizabeth said softly, with a hint of smile. "You look awful. And your letters were cryptic, at best, about anything but Gran's condition. You can be sure I plan a full interrogation very soon about the treatment you received in the village . . . and about whatever transpired between you and Mr. Daniel Lanfield. But it wouldn't be sporting of me to begin the discussion when you appear ready to drop where you stand. So here we are." She concluded her little speech as they entered the nursery and gestured toward the small bed.

How could she resist the promise of a few quiet hours? The bed indeed beckoned like a siren, promising the luxury of sleep. The noises from the street made clear that she was no longer in Marksby, and yet they and the sounds of the children below were faint. Just a few hours of forgetfulness. A handful of minutes to keep her thoughts at bay a little longer. She could manage that.

"Sister," Elizabeth said, her voice tentative, "do you need anything else?"

When she turned to look at Elizabeth, at the naked worry in her sister's eyes, she couldn't hold back the wave of emotions any longer. Couldn't stop a tear from slipping down her cheek. That one tear broke the dam, and she fell to her knees sobbing. Within a blink, Elizabeth was kneeling next to her, holding her close, whispering soothingly.

"Was it so terrible there, Lena? I knew I shouldn't have let you go back."

She looked up at her sister and shook her head. "No, Liz. You don't understand. I don't regret a moment of that trip. There were hard moments, especially in the first few days, but . . ." She took a few deep breaths before she could continue. "It was wonderful too. Almost like starting a whole new chapter of my life. I didn't even know I needed it. And now that I've returned, I have no idea what to do with any of it. I feel as if I've been given a fresh start, fresh eyes, and I am overwhelmed. I don't know what to do with myself, and I am terrified to go home."

"Why, sweetheart? You love that house. It's been your sanctuary for so long."

"That's exactly why. What if this has changed me too much? What if I return to that house and find it lacking? What if, when I walk in, I lose my taste for all the things I loved about it? What would that say about my fickleness? About my lack of abiding love?"

"You're simply overwrought and need rest, I'm sure. You are anything but fickle. You never turn away entirely from that which you love. And your family defines your home, not the things within. Rest now. Everything will be clearer once you've had a good sleep. Trust me."

"Elizabeth, I'm in love with Daniel."

Her sister blinked and then moved toward the door. "We will talk later. I'll come check on you in a couple of hours."

* * *

As she prepared for church, Vanessa wondered if today would finally be the day when she saw Billy again. He hadn't been in any of the places she expected to encounter him, and he hadn't tried to communicate with her at all since her return. Busy with work, she told herself. She'd been busy too. So perhaps she'd been as much to blame for their missed reunion as he.

When Mother called up to her, she did her duty, rounding up her siblings and making sure they were all presentable. With the way they clomped down the stairs, you'd think they were a herd of rambunctious goats.

Billy would be by the park entrance. Waiting. She'd make some excuse about stopping to talk with friends. They'd have a moment behind the tall hedge to speak privately.

Since she'd returned with Aunt Helena from Marksby, unanticipated ripples of guilt flowed over her at odd moments. She loved him, didn't she? He was industrious and bold and full of cunning energy. But then, Hal's quiet confidence and easy manner would come to mind, and she'd waver.

Vanessa wondered what had happened between Aunt Helena and Mr. Lanfield. The precise reality of physical intimacy was still an obscure mystery to her, but she hadn't missed her aunt's appearance and demeanor on the moonlit nights when Auntie had snuck back into the house. Her aunt probably couldn't tell, but her emotions had shown easily on her face during quiet moments at the farm—those fleeting seconds of faraway thought, of blushing heat, of tiny and maddeningly enigmatic signs.

Since their return, though, Aunt Helena was a changed person. She hadn't had a spell since Marksby, even though she was going out of the house more and more these days. Auntie's newly acquired confidence was remarkable. This was the vibrant aunt she remembered from her childhood, the one who would take her and her cousins to play in the park on a whim.

Her aunt still had moments of hesitation and still sought to avoid crowded areas, but she seemed determined to focus on life and energy and happiness.

Still, she couldn't ignore the occasional look in her aunt's eye—the longing, the sense of something missing. It wasn't new, really—Auntie had carried that look for a long time after the death of Uncle

Isaiah. But there was a difference now—a new sense of urgency, of regret. She couldn't help but think it had something to do with Mr. Lanfield.

Was it just the midnight assignations? Were they so significant?

Mr. Lanfield had been nothing but respectful and considerate toward her in the brief time she'd been in his company, but he'd obviously felt strong antipathy against Aunt Helena, as strong as any of the other villagers, at least at first. How did one trust such a drastic change in feeling? Yet he'd been kind, as his nephew Hal had been kind. He'd been protective and caring, and Auntie was obviously drawn to him, whether she willed it or no.

Could you desire someone you didn't like, didn't admire, didn't trust? Could you give your heart to someone even knowing there was no future in it?

Was that what she was doing with Billy?

He wasn't at his usual waiting spot.

A girl she'd thought was her friend shared some gossip about Billy being sweet to other girls. Whether the rumor was true, she couldn't find it in herself to care. Such coy and fickle games were a waste of her time.

As she returned home, Hal's open smile hovered in her mind's eye. Hal said what he meant. He was kind and attentive and didn't push. Hal was someone who inspired trust. She wondered what he was doing right then. Would he be walking amid the flock or galloping along the Lanfield perimeter? Would he be chasing that impudent ram and quelling mischief?

Hal was the kind of person who would respond if someone wrote him a letter. That thought bolstered her. She hurried to the writing desk, relishing the texture of the paper and the weight of the pen as her thoughts flew. She wanted to know if he thought of her, if he missed her, but mostly she just wanted to communicate with him and capture some of that companionship she'd felt between them during her brief visit. It didn't matter when she crossed out lines and words and started again; he might even be amused to see the workings of her mind that way. Hours and pages later, she felt a lightness she hadn't known since leaving Marksby.

Chapter 27

Sharing tea with the Needlework ladies above Evans Books, Helena continued to rebuild her shattered heart. Her work and her friends served as another supporting layer, reminding her of where she belonged, of how she was needed. Bartholomew was home with the boys for a few days longer, and she could immerse herself in the trials and tribulations of the less fortunate. Her life was complete, and she wanted for nothing. She didn't need the strong arms and gentle blue eyes that pierced her dreams and left her tense and panting. She didn't need his stalwart presence bolstering her spirit, soothing her panic. Not anymore. Since her time in Marksby, her debilitating fear of the world had eased. She'd attended a performance at the Lyceum with Marissa, and she'd even braved the Lowther Arcade, as a treat to the boys, without any assistance from her dearly protective coterie. She didn't need a man, any man, to be the head of her household. Not even a man who'd, in many ways, brought her back to life.

Honoria appeared in the doorway with an odd expression. Then again, odd expressions had been characteristic of her friend since her return—small, intimate smiles when Honoria thought no one was looking and a generally unguarded effusiveness. The woman carried herself with a new and reassuring sense of contentedness. And it was no wonder. Her dear friend was in love. With a viscount, of all people. She supposed that if someone like Honoria, who'd been so wary, so detached, could fall in love again after the loss of her husband, surely . . . No! She raised a castle turret in her mind to block that line of thinking.

"Helena, someone is here to see you," Honoria said. Were her eyes dancing? Must be a trick of the light. She tried not to notice the way her pulse quickened, the way it pounded so strongly she could feel it in her temple.

"Is it one of the boys?" she asked, as she moved toward the stairs, even though she knew it was a silly question. If it were any of her sons, he would simply come up with Honoria.

"No, I don't recognize the gentleman." With a small grin, her friend paused dramatically.

Helena corrected herself; her friend had been mesmerized or possibly possessed by a demon. She tried not to notice the tiny flip her stomach made. "Did this gentleman give you his name? Isn't it exceedingly odd that someone would come to find me here?"

"Lanfield, I believe his name is."

When she tried to respond, nothing came out. Her chest felt so tight she couldn't breathe. Yet this wasn't the same type of panic she'd experienced before. Daniel had come for her! She rushed down the stairs, unsure of what to say or what to think, and almost stumbled near the bottom in her haste. Forcing herself to slow down, she gripped the railing tightly and considered the moment. She was being ridiculous. This solved nothing. She couldn't leave, and he couldn't stay. Pasting a polite smile upon her face, one she hoped wouldn't show her inner turmoil, she pushed through the curtain and stepped into the front of the shop.

"Good afternoon, Mrs. Martin. It is a pleasure to see you."

Despite everything she'd told herself about the impossibility of caring for Daniel Lanfield, her spirits crashed when she saw the man at the counter. Gordon Lanfield stood there, twisting his cap in his hands. Her disappointment was so acute that she couldn't bring herself to speak. A petite woman next to him took the hat from him and grasped one of his hands firmly. She couldn't see the woman's face, nor could she hear the words the woman spoke to him.

"Hello," Helena croaked. Pathetic. She must seem like a fool.

"Pardon us for surprising you thus. I contacted your sister when we arrived in London, and she told me we could find you here. We want to speak with you. But, first, please allow me to introduce my wife, Ruth. I should have done so while you were visiting the Grand-dame, and I beg your pardon. You might recall Ruth from our younger days."

His demeanor was surprisingly deferential, especially considering their last confrontational meeting. What could he and his wife possibly want with her now? How else could she atone?

"Of course," she said, tamping down her unruly emotions. "I remember you fondly, Ruth!" And she meant it. She could still see the sweet, meek girl she had been; the passage of time had given her a mature grace that suited her.

"And I you, Helena. I'm sorry we didn't meet during your trip. There never seemed to be a fitting time," Ruth said warmly, coming close and giving her a buss on the cheek. Her surprise at the affectionate greeting must have shown on her face because Ruth added, "All these years, I have owed you a great debt. I cannot thank you enough!"

Surprise transformed to shock as she tried to decipher Ruth's statement. Everyone from Marksby hated her, the Lanfields more than anyone else in the village. She'd had no false expectations about being welcomed with open arms. Gran's unconditional acceptance had been more than she'd even dreamed. But for someone to thank her?

Gordon interrupted her thoughts, saying, "How are your children? I'm sure being separated from them was difficult, and I trust they missed you something awful."

"They did, yes, but they're fine," she said cautiously. "My oldest is back from sea for a few days."

He cleared his throat and said, "How nice." Ruth returned to his side and tugged him down by the shoulder so she could whisper in his ear. He cleared his throat again and said, "I never thought you'd be back, not after everything. It was a shock to see you."

He sounded sincere. She couldn't detect any of the bitterness or anger she'd seen at Daniel's home. If anyone had a right to be angry, a right to ignore her or berate her, it was Gordon.

"It's a joy to see Ruth with you," she responded honestly. "You dear lady, you were a lovely girl, and I've no doubts you're an excellent partner for Mr. Lanfield. Exactly what he needed." *Exactly what I couldn't be.* "And I thank you for your many kindnesses to my grandmother. Time has taken such a toll."

He nodded and looked down at Ruth with a fondness so intimate that she felt mildly uncomfortable witnessing it. "Ruth's a good woman, better than I deserve."

"I'm sure that's not true. I'm sure you two are well matched. You've always been a good man yourself. And you needed someone who would be devoted not only to you but to the Lanfield farm."

He stiffened, as if she'd insulted him. Only then did she realize the resentment was still there, a faint but unmistakable undercurrent.

Ruth spoke gently in the breach. "That is why I owe you thanks. If you hadn't run off so impetuously with your handsome and worldly captain, I never would have married Gordon." She touched his face fleetingly and looked up at him adoringly as she said, "You caused my sweet husband pain, and yet I cannot fault you for it because your elopement ultimately led him to my door. We have strong, beautiful children, and we've built a wonderful life together. None of it would exist but for your decision to follow your own heart. You allowed me to follow mine."

"I don't deserve your thanks," she replied. "If you please, why are you both here?"

The woman raised a brow at her husband, and he said, "We decided to visit London. We've never been here, and the farm is all in order." When he seemed reluctant to continue, Ruth jabbed a finger into his chest. He took his wife's hand and met Helena's gaze, his expression free of the rancor he'd exhibited in Marksby. "Fine. The truth is . . . Daniel has not been the same since you left. We—well, Ruth—thinks he cares for you deeply and suffers the loss of you. We—well, Ruth—would like you to communicate with him. Send him a letter or perhaps a package of sweets or even one of these damn books." He gestured wildly at the bookshelves.

"Gordy," Ruth said, a warning in her voice.

"Sorry, love. Sorry, Mrs. Martin." He looked suitably regretful.

"Tell her all of it."

"I lied to you, Mrs. Martin. Daniel had no malicious intent, no dastardly plan to engage your emotions. I didn't trust you, and it pained me to see how you could so easily hurt him. I thought it best to force a clean break between you, but it hasn't worked at all. . . ."

When her husband trailed off, Ruth came up to her and took her hands. "My husband has a good heart, and he only wants what's best for Daniel. Now it seems that what he needs most is to have you in his life. You couldn't have known this, but during your stay, he was more alive, in a way I hadn't seen since his wife abandoned him. You brought him back. And now he's drifting back toward that flat detachment he'd fallen into. We cannot lose him again." Throughout her plaintive little speech, Mr. Lanfield periodically bobbed his head in agreement.

Something in her chest tore at the thought of Daniel alone again in that isolated house.

"You both came all this way just to tell me that?"

"As surprising as it may sound, and to my husband's disappointment, Daniel seems to need you."

"Your anger is justified, Gordon. I wish there had been some other way, but were I in your shoes, I would have protected my sister with tooth and nail from someone I perceived as a threat."

"As if I need validation from the likes of you?"

"How can I make amends? After all this time, Gordon, what must I do to earn your forgiveness?"

"I want nothing from you. My wife and children need nothing you could provide." But then his voice and expression softened, as he drew Ruth's hand to his chest. "There is one thing I believe you can do that might bring my family joy. Give Daniel a chance. Open your heart to him. Send for him. We've seen how changed he is with you, and we want him to have the same kind of happiness Ruth and I have."

Chapter 28

Two months earlier, Daniel would have sworn he'd never visit London willingly. He'd go to improve the family's business prospects, but he'd never relish it, never enjoy the rush of the great and terrible city. But now everything was changed. He fought his desire to urge Talos faster and weave through traffic, his anticipation and trepidation growing in equal measure as he inched closer to Helena's home. The overriding need to see her, to touch her, to hear her unbridled laughter and pleasure beat in his pulse. He needed to immerse himself in everything about her, and he could only hope to convince her that they could have a future together. Thankfully, he found traffic eased on her street. Hastily tying up Talos, he raced up the steps, trying to sort out how to begin. Good God, were his palms sweating? What should he say? Perhaps they wouldn't need words. God willing, perhaps she'd missed him as much as he'd missed her, and they would be in perfect accord. In that endless moment before the door opened, he tried to imagine every possibility, hoping beyond hope that she would simply throw her arms around him in welcome.

What he hadn't anticipated was the young man who opened the door and glared at him. Even at a glance, one could see this was another of Helena's sons. The same coloring. The same eyes. The same hair. Perhaps his masculine jaw and his broad shoulders came from his father, but generally he was Helena through and through.

"I—Where is—Are you—" He coughed and tried again. "My name is Daniel Lanfield. I've come from Marksby, and I'm here to see your mother."

"My mother is not at home, sir. Good day to you." The lad's tone could have frozen a beck in July. When the young buck went to shut the door in his face, Daniel blocked it with his boot. Whatever this boy knew or thought he knew, Daniel wasn't about to be deterred so easily.

"I'm a family friend. In fact, your mother's grandmother sent some packages along with me," he explained, adding with a tinge of challenge, "Hospitality dictates that you should give me the opportunity to wait for her or at least take my card."

"I don't know when she'll be returning. You wouldn't want to waste your day waiting. If you wish to leave a card, there's the tray for it." The man-child flicked his hand at the table in the entryway. "In case you are unaware, my mother is still grieving over the loss of my father. She hasn't yet chosen to accept visitors. So, as a *friend*, you should be aware that your visit comes at a bad time."

Daniel felt a pang of sympathy for him. Although the customary period was over, it was the family's prerogative to determine the length of their mourning. And this family grieved terribly. Helena's eldest son was now the man of the house, protecting his mother and his family. "I am well aware of your mother's situation, and I am truly sorry for your loss. She must be overjoyed that you've returned from the sea. You must be Bartholomew."

The young man's hard expression softened infinitesimally as confusion crossed his face. "I am, and she is. What business do you have with her?"

"Your mother has recently returned from Marksby, and I have some unresolved concerns to discuss with her related to her visit."

"Feel free to leave your card. I'll see that she gets it." But his stony look wasn't entirely reassuring. "It seems my mother has told you a great deal. She is rarely so forthcoming with people outside our family circle."

"Mr. Lanfield! I heard your voice! Did you bring your horse?" Tommy came bounding down the stairs, running to meet them and stopping only when his eldest brother placed a restraining hand on his chest. He stood bouncing on his toes, clearly bursting with energy and excitement.

Daniel patted Tommy's head fondly and said, "Yes, of course, Talos is my trusty companion. He's outside."

"May I see him? Please please please!"

"That's for your mother to decide," he replied, looking at Bartholomew pointedly. "Now," he said through gritted teeth, his patience stretched beyond reason, a filament to which he vainly clung, "if you please, where might I find your mother?"

Bartholomew continued to glare at him, one alpha male's challenge to another, but he'd known enough rams and stallions, and their human counterparts, to be baited. He knew better, too, than to place Helena in yet another position where she had to pick either love or family. At this point, he didn't like his odds.

Bless his bright and shiny soul, Tommy piped up, "Mama's at the bookshop! I can take you!"

"No, you can't!" Mark and Bartholomew said as one, Mark's tone scoffing and Bartholomew's forbidding. Mark came down the remaining stairs, as he and Bartholomew scolded Tommy at the same time. "Don't tell this man anything! We know nothing about him or his intentions, and Mother has been heartbr—" the eldest brother railed until he swallowed whatever he was about to say. Meanwhile, Mark asserted, "Tommy, you can't possibly know how to get there! I'll take you, sir! It would be faster if we take your horse!" Out of all that chaotic commotion, Daniel obtained one clear overriding impression: hope.

"Boys, how has your mother been since her return? I was sad to see her go, but she missed you and needed you so. I have no desire to distress her."

With fervent conviction, Mark said, "She's been crying at night when she thinks we've fallen asleep. She's her usual self during the days, but in the evenings, she seems to pine for something lost."

Bartholomew flinched as if struck.

"What was that?" Daniel had to ask.

"It's much like the pattern she followed after Father crossed the veil. I remember. She tried to keep her grief hidden. I didn't realize Mark had seen." The young man spoke in a neutral tone, but, judging by his troubled expression, he struggled to make sense of it, to reconcile past and present. He turned to Mark and asked, "Did the trip back to Marksby dredge up memories of Father's death?"

"Mr. Lanfield would know best what transpired there," Mark pointed out. "Mother wasn't well even before she left. She . . . it's hard to explain. . . . This will sound foolish, but she reminded me of that turtle you had for a while, Bart. Whenever someone startled him, he retreated into his shell. Tommy was still a babe, and he got hold of

Shelley and scared the creature so much that it wouldn't leave its shell at all."

"I remember," his brother responded soberly. "Nothing worked. I was convinced he would come out when he got hungry." Bartholomew met Daniel's eyes with a dawning and wary comprehension. He explained, "Poor little Shelley died that way. Nothing would coax him out of his shell after that. He just shriveled up and ceased to function." He gripped his younger brother by the arms and said, "What do you mean by this?"

Catching the way the middle brother winced, Daniel had to step in. "Easy, man. Your brother can't talk with you shaking his brain."

Bartholomew released his brother immediately, obviously regretting his rough behavior.

"I think I have a sense of what Mark is saying. Based on several accounts from those closest to her, your mother has become increasingly fearful of crowds and public exposure. So fearful that she's prone to fainting and to attacks that render her virtually catatonic. I have witnessed such occasions myself, and I feared greatly for her safety . . . and her sanity."

Bartholomew scowled, and Daniel was certain the young man was contemplating newly popular treatments for people diagnosed with some version of madness, namely some kind of electrical shock treatment. "Why are you here?" the young man asked bluntly. "What do you want from our mother?"

That brought him up short. What could he say to that? He wanted to be a part of her life. He wanted her to be a permanent presence in his. But there was still Nancy. How could you tell a woman's children you wanted her to be your wife but you weren't free to marry her? How would that look to them? Bartholomew's shields had only lowered partially. He'd be terribly offended by such a proposition . . . and well he should be. Daniel had nothing to offer her but himself, and that was a meager offering, at best.

"I care for her deeply, Mr. Martin, and I wish the best for her. As I said, we have unfinished issues to resolve. You can be sure I mean her no harm."

"Of course not, Mr. Lanfield," Mark replied dismissively before his brother could say a word. "You kept your promise, and she returned safely home. I think she'd be happy to see you. Bart is just being . . . well, Bart. I'll take you to Evans Books."

"Over my dead body," Bartholomew declared. "Nothing good can come of your presence." His voice dropped to a snide whisper. "I'm not a child, and I'm well aware of how men think. Leave my mother alone."

"There's simply no way I would agree to that, Mr. Martin, because I love your mother and intend to spend as much time in her presence as possible. So you may choose to assist me and encourage your mother to seek joy for herself and not just for others, or you may stand aside. I have no desire to sully your father's memory or replace him in her affections. But your mother still lives, and she deserves happiness still. Do you think it's right that her spirit be extinguished when she's already lost so much?"

Something he'd said must have finally resonated with Helena's eldest son, for the young man nodded slowly. While his expression remained stoic, he affirmed, "She does deserve happiness. She hasn't had much of that in recent years."

"She tries," Mark interjected. "For our sake, she tries." But the child's slumped shoulders said what his words didn't. The boy shouldn't have to feel so resigned. These boys deserved the return of a mother who was vigorous and ardent and at ease. He'd seen glimpses of that version of Helena again, and he knew without a doubt that her world would be the better for it. Just as he knew, without question, that he wanted to be a part of that world.

Bartholomew took a deep breath and said, "You think you can bring her that happiness?"

"I don't know that anyone can bring such a change upon another," Daniel answered honestly. "But, by gow, *I must try.*"

The eldest boy turned to his brothers and said, "Come along now. Let's go surprise Mother at the bookshop."

Chapter 29

This back corner of the shop had always been Helena's favorite. Even after the shop had been vandalized and remodeled, Honoria had maintained the oasis-like quality of this space. The alcove was filled with loaded bookshelves that surrounded a single upholstered chair and side table. Here, if only for a few moments, the rest of the world fell away. From her seat, she reached out and traced the spines on a shelf nearby. Her eyes didn't focus on any of the words or names. She couldn't focus on anything in particular, not after the bold declarations by Gordon and Ruth Lanfield. What was she to make of them? Ruth's admission of gratitude was simply unfathomable. Out of all the pain and suffering she'd caused her family and the Lanfields and the entire village, to think that something truly, undeniably positive had resulted as well—it was a mild balm to her soul.

She didn't take much notice when the bell of the shop door rang, announcing new customers. The Needlework ladies had assured her that they had everything well in hand. So she'd absconded to this corner, knowing they'd fetch her when they needed her.

"Is Mother in the sanctuary?" When she heard Bartholomew's question, she had to smile. It was an old family joke, even before she'd truly had need for a sanctuary. But the word was all too apt, especially now, when her thoughts and emotions were in such tumult. She closed her eyes. Any minute, her garrulous sons would find their way here, and they'd all be off into the hustle and bustle of the afternoon.

"Helena." That dear voice fervently whispering her name—her mind teased her with memories she couldn't keep. She closed her eyes tighter, wanting to cling to that warm voice just a moment longer. Then she heard a masculine clearing of the throat, and her eyes flew open.

Daniel! Could he really be standing before her, cap in hand, looking so adorably vulnerable that she had to restrain herself from running to him and throwing herself into his arms?

"I missed you, Helena," he said, and her heart broke afresh. "I'm here for no other reason. It's horribly selfish of me, and I've nothing to offer you, but I need you. I need your warmth. I need your laughter. I need your reminders that there is so much more to this life than my work."

It took her some time to comprehend his rushed and loaded statements.

"You abandoned all your responsibilities to come after me?" she said, smiling up at him. "How reckless of you, darling!" She couldn't resist the delicious reversal, but she knew better. They were both older and wiser now, and Daniel would never turn his back on his responsibilities or leave his family in need.

He looked abashed. "Aye, well, to be honest, I haven't abandoned them entirely."

"Of course not! Let me see. . . . You arranged for neighbors to assist in keeping an eye on the flock? And you're planning to represent Lanfield textiles in London? And you're planning to make trips back to Marksby for lambing and shearing and whenever your brother needs extra hands?"

"Aye."

His terse responses could be maddening, but she understood—what else was there to say?

"I am long past the ripeness of youth," she said.

He studied her for a long moment and said, "It's true that you are no spring bud."

She smiled self-deprecatingly at his immediate confirmation. His hand touched her hair gently, hesitantly, soothing her ruffled feathers. Alas, she could hardly take offense when all he did was agree with her own blunt claim. She tipped her head and turned away, but he would not let her be. His hand slid down along her cheek, her jaw, brushed her chin and guided her to face him.

"Neither of us is in the dewy green stage of life. What you are is so much better than the rawness of youth. You are in full bloom, open and welcoming, bursting with color and life, for all the world to see. Yet you've been furled by grief and loss. I want to see you in all your glory."

"You are suddenly a poet. Pretty words, but they are delusional."

"Wait here. I've brought you a gift." She heard him ask someone for glasses. When he returned, he held one out to her and put the other on the table in front of her. Afternoon sun angled just so made the liquid in the glasses glow like polished amber. "Taste that."

She doubted whiskey would make this conversation any clearer, and she was surprised he would even consider trying to placate her with spirits. She took a cautious sip and the aggressiveness of the drink made her throat seize for a moment. What it lacked in complexity and depth, it more than made up for in sheer potency. She'd be bowled over if she finished this one glass.

She looked at him skeptically and said, "It's nice, but whiskey won't make me forget the loss of my youth or the impossibility of our situation, you know, not even temporarily."

"It's not meant to make you forget. Set that one aside and try the second one."

She picked up the glass he'd set on the table and sniffed at it. She could already detect subtle differences—the color was darker, the liquid flowed differently as she tilted the glass, the scent strong but somehow fuller, richer. When she sipped this one, an image flashed through her head of her father, sitting by the fireplace at the end of a long day's work, a dram of whiskey in his hand as he told stories from the day before sending her and Elizabeth to bed. No wonder the scent of this one was familiar. The intense flavor washed over her. This was quality. This whiskey had character, bold but not overwhelming. History in a glass. She relaxed back in her seat, waiting.

"This one is quite good," she said. "What's your point?"

He smiled so broadly, one of those rare full smiles that made her feel as if the sun had burst through a wall of clouds.

"It is very, very good, yes. Care to guess how old this vintage is?"

"Twenty years?"

"Older."

"Thirty?"

"Older."

She took another sip and raised a brow at him, unwilling to continue this game indefinitely.

"That one on the table is fifteen years old. Would you believe this one is fifty-two? It's true. My grandfather brought some barrels of this stuff home with him from one of his trips to Edinburgh. We're down to our last barrel. That rotgut you tasted first isn't really so bad, until you have this to compare with it."

"I see the direction of your thoughts, but this is an imperfect analogy. People do not just sit preserved in casks or barrels as time passes. We work. We wear away over time. We dry up, and our pretty petals fall away."

"What do I know of analogies? I just enjoy a fine whiskey." He winked. He actually winked.

Before she could reply, his mouth was on hers, the taste of him mixing with the whiskey. Her thoughts spun apart.

"Women aren't short-lived flowers plucked from a garden," he said, when he pulled away for air. His lips still brushed hers as he spoke. "You grow finer with age." He punctuated his words with teasing kisses. "Stronger." Another light brush of his lips. "More complex. And I want to drink you in. I want to drown in you. I love you."

She pulled him toward her, deepening their kiss, and no words were exchanged for quite some time. Still, she couldn't forget that they were in Honoria's shop, nor that her boys were somewhere nearby, possibly even in the next row. And so, too soon, she pulled away.

"I love you too, Daniel. I didn't think we'd have a future together, but with each passing day away from you, I couldn't bear the possibility of a future without you. I'm so glad you found me!"

More kisses, ardent and clumsy and needy.

This time, Daniel retreated. He released her and took a step back, as if bracing himself. "Before we go further," he began with a sweet look of chagrin, "I should tell you that I recently received word that Nancy—well, I thought all this time after never hearing from her, even for funds, I thought she'd died. And, anyway, in all this time, I never thought it would matter even if she were still alive. I never thought to have the chance to try again."

She went to him, taking his face in her hands and pushing away the dread that tried to find purchase in her heart. "What's happened?"

"I received a letter from her. She's alive."

"And does she want you—? Why did she contact you? What does she want?" Daniel loved her as he'd never loved his wife. This, she knew in her bones. Whatever Nancy wanted, they could weather it.

"She loves another and has asked me for a divorce *a mensâ et thoro*. Even that would be an expense I might not be able to afford."

"Do you still care for her? Do you want her to return as your wife?"

His glare warmed her heart. Her laconic sweetheart didn't bother to spare a word in reply.

"My dear, sweet Daniel, at our age, we have little need for formal legalities, don't you think? We've both been through the reading of banns and the signing of certificates. I believe you love me, and I don't need a piece of paper or a decree from the Church of England to confirm your commitment to me nor mine to you."

"Are you certain? I'll grant her the divorce she requests, but I still wouldn't be free to marry."

"Rest easy, love," she replied with a smile, struck by the true sense of freedom and volition between them. "There is no need for all that. Such unmarried but devoted relationships are commonplace. We have both experienced marriage in the traditional sense, and it seems to me that our lives are already complicated enough. Why add a fresh layer of difficulty on top?"

"So you would agree to be my wife in action, though not in name?" He looked and sounded stunned.

"I would! But . . ." She had to be clear. On this one point, her sons, she had to stand unequivocally. "For the sake of the boys, we would live here in London for school terms."

"That might conflict with some of our busy periods at the farm, but Gordon and I have talked about the possible benefits of having more regular presence here in London, to meet with textile manufacturers and distributors. It could be a new economic avenue for Lanfield."

"Well, you two can discuss that after dinner this evening."

"Pardon?" He looked so adorably confused that she couldn't help but laugh.

"Didn't you know? Your brother and his wife are here in London," she explained, an incredible lightness flowing through her. "They came to see me yesterday, and they're invited to dine at Elizabeth's house this evening. She sets a fine, full table, and I'm sure she wouldn't object if I brought you."

"Nay, wait a moment. Gordon and Ruth are here?"

"Yes! And they're delightful! I look forward to getting to know Ruth much better. I already suspect the other Needlework ladies would adore her."

He muttered a creative curse but grinned. "Hal, that little—he must have known his parents had already gone, and yet he said not a word to me about it! Now he's minding all at home by himself."

"He seems competent to the task, and he knows the neighbors well. I'm sure you and your brother found yourselves in such circumstances when you were his age."

"Aye, and it's true that Hal takes to responsibility well." Daniel looked both amused and stunned as he thought about these developments. "Well, it's only right that he and Ruth should be here to share a toast with our family's whiskey. I can't believe my brother has come to the big, bad city. He's always called it a cesspool, teeming with vice and corruption."

"Well, now he can see for himself that it's not all fire and brimstone." She felt suddenly hesitant, reluctant to hope, to believe her desires could be fulfilled. "So you're staying, at least for a time?"

His insistent kiss was answer enough.

"But, Daniel, what about—?"

He interrupted her question with another kiss, longer and deeper than before. Those telltale flutters began in her belly. She had to voice her thoughts before they fell right out of her head, pushed out by mind-numbing bliss.

"Wait! What about—?"

Again, a silencing kiss that left her legs shaking.

"Shh," Daniel replied. "I've learned a thing or two from you. First and foremost is this: all will be well." He punctuated the Thorton motto with delicate kisses along her jaw, kisses that melted her very bones. "'Tis true. Whatever problems or conflicts we face, they are surmountable. Whatever we have to do in order to make a life together possible, we shall do. I promise you. All will be well."

"Yes," she agreed, "we shall make it so."

Amara Royce writes historical romances that combine her passion for nineteenth-century literature and history with her addiction to happily-ever-afters. She teaches English literature and composition at a community college in Pennsylvania. When she isn't writing, she's either grading papers or reveling in her own happily-ever-after with her remarkably patient family.

www.ingramcontent.com/pod-product-compliance
Lightning Source LLC
Chambersburg PA
CBHW020444270626
47155CB00022B/1408